THE MORNING STAR

THE KATERINA TRILOGY

Volume III

THE MORNING STAR

Robin Bridges

DELACORTE PRESS

Text copyright © 2013 by Robin Bridges
Jacket photograph copyright © 2013 by Michael Frost

All rights reserved. Published in the United States by Delacorte Press, an imprint of Random House Children's Books, a division of Random House, Inc., New York.

Delacorte Press is a registered trademark and the colophon is a trademark of Random House, Inc.

Visit us on the Web! randomhouse.com/teens

Educators and librarians, for a variety of teaching tools, visit us at RHTeachersLibrarians.com

Library of Congress Cataloging-in-Publication Data
Bridges, Robin.
The morning star / Robin Bridges.
pages cm. — (The Katerina trilogy ; v. 3)
Summary: "Necromancer Katerina Alexandrovna, Duchess of Oldenburg, wages her final battle against Russia's greatest threat—Konstantin the Deathless"—Provided by publisher.
ISBN 978-0-385-74026-5 (hardback) — ISBN 978-0-375-89903-4 (ebook) —
[1. Ghosts—Fiction. 2. Supernatural—Fiction. 3. Good and evil—Fiction. 4. Courts and courtiers—Fiction. 5. Schools—Fiction. 6. Russia—History—1801–1917—Fiction.]
I. Title.
PZ7.B76194Mor 2013
[Fic]—dc23
2012046715

Printed in the United States of America

10 9 8 7 6 5 4 3 2 1

First Edition

For Shane, my world traveler.
The road goes ever on.

A NOTE ABOUT RUSSIAN NAMES AND PATRONYMICS

Russians have two official first names: a given name and a patronymic, or a name that means "the son of" or "the daughter of." Katerina Alexandrovna, for example, is the daughter of a man named Alexander. Her brother is Pyotr Alexandrovich. A female patronymic ends in "–evna" or "–ovna," while the male patronymic ends in "–vich."

It was traditional for the nobility and aristocracy to name their children after Orthodox saints, thus the abundance of Alexanders and Marias and Katerinas. For this reason, nicknames, or diminutives, came in handy to tell the Marias and the Katerinas apart. Katerinas could be called Katiya, Koshka, or Katushka. An Alexander might be known as Sasha or Sandro. A Pyotr might be called Petya or Petrusha. When addressing a person by his or her nickname, one does not add the patronym. The person would be addressed as Katerina Alexandrovna or simply Katiya.

What is this place to which I've come? There is neither water nor air here, its depth is unfathomable, it's as dark as the darkest night, and men wander about there helplessly. A man cannot live here and be satisfied, and he cannot gratify the cravings of affection.

—FROM THE EGYPTIAN BOOK OF THE DEAD
BY THE SCRIBE ANI, CHAPTER CLXXV

The Morning Star

Summer 1831, Vitebsk, Belarus

*T*he streets were full of dying soldiers and smoldering rubble. Looters scurried from house to house, dragging sacks of food and silverware they'd scavenged from the ruins of the city. Cannons fired in the distance. The Russian armies had marched on to the next city, on to the next massacre. Ignoring the scent of blood everywhere, Princess Johanna Cantacuzene searched the bodies until she found him.

Her husband, the Koldun and former king of Poland, lay dead under another soldier's decapitated body. One of the Dekebristi had been trying to protect him. The vampire princess had no tears, only cold rage that shook her entire body. She would find her husband's killer and make him and his descendants pay for his crime. "Bogatyr!" she screamed. "Will you come for me as well? I do not fear death. And neither did he." She cradled Konstantin Pavlovich's body to her. Then, seething in her hatred for the supernatural knight

3

protector of Russia who had killed his own brother, she chanted vile curses against the Romanovs.

Konstantin had given up his rights to the throne of Russia to marry Johanna, the Polish princess who was a blood drinker. His elder brother Tsar Alexander had declared him king of Poland as consolation. Konstantin had been perfectly happy with his new wife and his new kingdom. But when Alexander died, the throne of Russia went to the ambitious younger brother, Nicholas Pavlovich. Nicholas sent his armies to take Poland away from his older brother and return it to the Russian empire.

Johanna fumed. She wanted Konstantin to have not only Poland, but also to take back his rightful inheritance. She wanted him to rule all of Russia as well. But Nicholas the First had a necromancer mistress who used ancient dark magic of her own to invoke the bogatyr and defeat Konstantin and Johanna's forces. To protect her husband's life, Johanna had turned him into a blood drinker. But it would not be enough to save him.

The young tsar accused Konstantin of heresy and treason and ordered his own brother's death. The Polish people revolted against Nicholas the First and rallied behind Konstantin. But Konstantin was unable to defend them. Or himself. When the battle spilled over out of Poland into the rest of the Eastern Provinces, Konstantin Pavlovich at last confronted his brother in the muddy streets of Vitebsk.

Johanna attempted to help her husband as he flung ancient Slavic spells and incantations at the bogatyr. Her Dekebristi minions attacked the young tsar's troops mercilessly. But the young tsar's mistress had powers much stronger than those of the vampire princess. The necromancer cloaked the bogatyr with shadows and commanded the dead soldiers in the street to march against the Dekebristi. She imprisoned Johanna in the Graylands, the realm of the dead, with an ancient Egyptian spell, and Johanna was forced to watch helplessly as Konstantin fell to his brother's sword.

While trapped in the Graylands, Johanna stumbled across a very old and very angry Egyptian necromancer. She stole his spell book and made a devil's bargain that allowed her to return from the Graylands in an attempt to save Konstantin with the power of necromancy.

Princess Cantacuzene sought to bring Konstantin back to life by pouring her own blood into his mouth. But no amount of blood could restore him after his defeat at the hands of the bogatyr. Johanna had to use the blackest of black magics to bind his soul and keep it safe, using a ritual from the Egyptian's spell book and a relic she stole from her half sister, the Montenegrin queen Milena. But Johanna was not strong enough to bring her love back. After burying her husband's body in the Romanov crypt with his ancestors, she faked her own death and assumed the identity of a distant Cantacuzene cousin. She deceived the foolish Nicholas Pavlovich and gained control over the remaining blood drinkers who had not been exiled to Siberia. She hid in the heart of St. Petersburg with the stolen relic, the Talisman of Isis, slowly gathering other vampires loyal to her and waiting decades for her chance at revenge.

She waited for the day when she could restore her husband to the throne. She waited for the day when she could restore him to life.

CHAPTER ONE

August 1890, St. Petersburg, Russia

I stepped back from the dissecting table to push my hair out of my face. I'd been standing on my feet all day in the tiny, airless room, my hands digging meticulously through the entrails of cadavers. Sweat had plastered my thick cotton dress to my skin.

"Do you see the bronchiole tubes within the lungs?" Dr. Badmaev asked me, leaning over my shoulder.

"Yes," I answered. "What are these growths here?" I poked a grayish-pink mass with a dissecting needle.

"That shall be your assignment for tonight," the Tibetan doctor said. "I think we have done enough work for today, Duchess."

No one knew I was studying medicine with Dr. Badmaev, the Tibetan who treated the members of the Dark Court. I blushed with shame, remembering how I'd rejected his offer earlier in the year. And I'd finally accepted only because the tsar continued to refuse to let me leave the country to attend medical school in Zurich. He did not approve of women doctors. But it was imperative that I study medicine—now more than ever. The life of the boy I loved, Grand Duke George Alexandrovich, depended upon it.

Dr. Badmaev had proved to be a strict instructor. All the Latin and Greek I'd studied in the hopes of going to a proper medical school were useless. Studying Tibetan medicine meant reading ancient texts in Tibetan. So I had to learn from the doctor's lectures and hands-on practice. The doctor was an acquaintance of my father's and had helped me more than once before. He was very knowledgeable when it came to treating vampire bites. Unfortunately, he told me there was no way to cure the risen dead.

"Here, drink this," Dr. Badmaev said when I'd finished scrubbing my hands. He held a steaming cup of tea out toward me. "It will help purify your soul. You have been surrounded by death all day, and now you must cleanse yourself before returning to the living."

I took the tea gratefully. Badmaev knew my secrets. He knew that I was no stranger to death, and he was persistent in trying to help me understand my gift. Of course, I still did not think of necromancy as a gift. It did not save lives. It only created terrible creatures. And multitudes of problems.

The tea was smoky with a hint of lemon. "Verbena?" I guessed.

Dr. Badmaev's eyes twinkled. "Very good! And?"

"Sea buckthorn?"

"You have been studying the *Materia Medica*, haven't you?"

I smiled. He had gone to great trouble to translate a list of Tibetan herbs and their healing properties for me into Russian. I told him he should have his work published. My father would have been happy to carry this out if I asked. But Badmaev and I both knew my father would not approve of my secret studies. Even if Papa had defended my wanting to study medicine to Maman and the tsar.

Being a female student in a proper medical institution was scandalous enough. Studying Far Eastern medicine with a doctor, no matter how distinguished, who was attached to the Dark Court could only invite imperial wrath.

But I had had no choice. As long as there was a threat that the lich tsar Konstantin Pavlovich could return, I was in danger. Almost as much danger as Alexander the Third. The tsar needed me, the only necromancer in St. Petersburg, to perform the ritual that would allow him to fight the lich tsar. And the lich tsar's followers knew it. Hence, I was forbidden from leaving Russia. My dreams of studying at the University of Zurich had come to a grinding halt. And my family's palace was placed under the watch of imperial guards, the undead soldiers of the Order of St. Lazarus.

I finished my tea and went to gather my things. Dr. Badmaev stood. "Remember your meditations, Duchess. The cold light is still surrounding you."

I nodded. As a necromancer, the cold light would always surround me. It was the light of death, surrounding everyone. It grew brighter when one grew closer to death. The cold light could be manipulated by a necromancer, to either destroy or heal. Dr. Badmaev, in addition to teaching me practical Tibetan medicine, was also showing me how to shape cold light and use it in diagnosing patients. Most important of all, he was showing me how to stay sane when surrounded by so much death.

"But you can't see the cold light, can you?" I asked.

The Tibetan smiled kindly. "It is true. But while I am not a necromancer, by meditating and drinking sacred herbs, I can expand my senses and see the warm light that surrounds everyone."

"Warm light?"

"Also known as *auras* by the Europeans, I believe. A doctor's examination that only looks at the patient's physical body is not complete. Tibetan medicine examines body and soul." He put a fatherly hand on my shoulder. "We will finish our work on the lungs when you come back," he said.

"I cannot return before Wednesday," I said. "Tomorrow I'm expected to wait on the empress with Maman." The thought that I might possibly see the empress's son, George Alexandrovich, while I was there filled me with hope. George had completed his magic studies in Paris and had returned to St. Petersburg several days ago, but he had not been to Betskoi House to see me since his return. I knew a lot of his time would be taken up with imperial matters. He was now working with the Koldun to protect his father and the rest of the imperial family. I'd received several passionate letters from him during his stay in France, but what if his passion for me had cooled? Why hadn't he found the time to see me?

"The dissection table and I will be waiting," Dr. Badmaev said. "Do not forget your assignments."

"Of course not, Doctor." Hurrying through the herbal shop in front of his office, I gave a friendly wave to his housekeeper,

Masha. It was a hot August day, much too hot for me to walk all the way to our house on Millionaya Street. I purchased a ride on one of the horse-drawn trams that sped through the city, knowing I would have to hop off shortly before reaching the Field of Mars. Maman would faint if she knew I mingled with the lower classes of St. Petersburg on such a regular basis. But I liked to sit on the tram and look at the faces of people, wondering who they were and where they were traveling. I tried to ignore the tangle of cold lights swirling over and around everyone on the cramped carriage.

An old, wrinkled babushka sat next to me holding a sleeping child. The child's cold light was stronger than the woman's; the child was closer to death than she. "Has the child been ill?" I asked.

"*Da*," the woman said sadly. "He refuses to eat or drink anything. His mother died last month from the same thing."

"Has he been seen by a doctor?" I asked.

"We cannot afford the doctor," the woman answered bitterly. "We still owe him for seeing my daughter. And he did nothing for her."

"Please go and see the Tibetan doctor on Betosky Prospekt," I said. "He will be able to tell you how to save your grandson. Without charge. Tell Dr. Badmaev to please send the bill to Duchess Oldenburg."

"Bless you, dear lady," the woman said, hugging her weak grandson to her chest.

We were fast approaching the Field of Mars, close to Betskoi House, so I pulled the string for the tram to slow down. The driver did not completely stop, so I had to jump. I landed awkwardly on the dusty street, then hurried home.

A Romanov carriage waited in our driveway. My heart danced for a moment, full of hope that it was George Alexandrovich. Racing past the footmen at our door, I hurried up the staircase into Maman's parlor, hoping to see the tsar's son. Instead, I found the leader of the St. Petersburg vampires, taking tea with my mother.

"Katerina Alexandrovna," Grand Duchess Militza said, her black eyes glittering, "I've been waiting for you, my dear."

CHAPTER TWO

I curtsied politely to the grand duchess, who was now my cousin by marriage. "Your Imperial Highness," I said. I had been under the assumption that the grand duchess was still in Montenegro visiting her family.

"Elena sends you her best wishes, cousin," Militza said. "And Danilo as well."

Would I never have any peace from the crown prince and his blood-drinking family? "I believed he was still in prison," I said coldly.

Her smile was brittle. "That was merely a misunderstanding," Militza said. "He is safe in Montenegro now with our parents."

"Isn't that wonderful, Katiya?" Maman asked. "Such a dear young man."

I did not think it was wonderful that Danilo was no longer imprisoned at the Fortress of St. Peter and St. Paul. The crown prince and his faerie accomplice, Monsieur Sucre, had conspired against the members of the Order of St. John and the tsar's inner circle of mages. They had attempted a ritual to raise the lich tsar from the dead. I did not think even being a king's firstborn son would exonerate Danilo or convince our tsar to let him go free. I wondered what sort of diplomatic deal had been made.

The footman knocked on the door to tell Maman she was needed in the kitchen. "Of course," she said, standing hastily. "Please excuse me, both of you."

I had no desire to engage in further pleasantries with the blood drinker in Maman's parlor. "Why have you come, Militza?" I asked as soon as my mother was gone.

The grand duchess visibly relaxed. I'd grown used to my mother's new "gift," but as a striga, she made others around her extremely uncomfortable.

The effect she now had on other supernatural creatures was truly bizarre. When Maman entered a room, the cold light belonging to everyone else seemed to bend away from her. And the fact that strigas only drank the blood of other blood drinkers placed them at the top of the blood-drinker hierarchy. Every creature whose blood the striga tasted gave away a little bit of his or her power to her. Traditionally, the striga was the leader of a city's vampire population. And Militza was not inclined to give up her hard-won position willingly.

The grand duchess's black eyes narrowed. "I have come, actually, with a warning for you, necromancer. Konstantin is very close to returning. The wizards who seek his return also seek an artifact in Egypt. With this artifact, the lich tsar will be able to command a horde of supernatural warriors."

"And why would you tell me this?" I asked. There was no way I could ever trust the grand duchess.

"The fate of everyone you and I care for is at stake."

"You've come home just in time, Katiya!" Maman said, returning to the room before Militza could say any more. "Your cousin was about to show me the new deck of cards she found on her latest trip to Egypt!"

Militza had stiffened upon Maman's return, and her hands shook ever so slightly as she beckoned to me. "Do sit down, Katerina," the grand duchess said. "Let us discover your fortune." The grand duchess was sitting in Maman's favorite chair with a deck of tarot cards in her hand. She wore a very fashionable black walking gown that looked like it had come from Paris.

She also looked terribly warm. Militza was stubbornly trying to prove she was not afraid of St. Petersburg's new striga. Whether the striga noticed it or not.

"I have no desire to know what the cards say," I said.

"Oh, don't be silly," Maman said, pulling me toward the settee with her. "It's all great fun. And the cards are simply beautiful. Look at the artwork on the major arcana!"

I was not going to be allowed to escape the blood drinker's parlor game. I sat down next to Maman, folding my hands in my lap.

"Shall we begin?" Militza asked, shuffling her cards with the grace of an expert.

"I shall go first!" my mother said, leaning forward eagerly. Her jeweled fingers selected one of the cards from the deck in the grand duchess's outstretched hand. Turning it over, she turned toward me. "I dare not look."

15

"Maman, you know that Papa detests it when you dabble in the occult," I warned.

"But it's so very amusing," my mother said. "And your father knows it's harmless. Did the cards not save Petya from buying that lame horse last month? The cards do not lie."

"Indeed not," Militza said with a vicious smile. "You have selected the Empress card."

Maman's mouth gaped open most impolitely. "Her Imperial Majesty is coming to see me?"

I rolled my eyes, which was not a polite thing to do either. "You are going to see her at the charity luncheon tomorrow," I reminded Maman.

"Perhaps," Militza said. "Or perhaps the empress will have a request for you." She shuffled the card back into the deck and handed them to me. "Shuffle these in turn, my dear cousin. The deck needs to feel your energies to give you a proper read."

The artwork was indeed beautiful. Hand-painted drawings of swords, cups, wands, and coins with an Eastern influence. Byzantine.

I shuddered, wondering why Militza had chosen this deck. It reminded me of the cave nestled deep in the Crimea, where I'd learned how to travel to the Graylands. I handed the cards back to her.

"You must pick one, my dear," she said.

Sighing, I turned the top card over and laid it on the table. The Queen of Swords.

Militza's eyes lit up. "Secret hostility."

"Or not so secret," I said, my eyes meeting hers.

She laughed. "My dear Katerina. I am not your enemy. I believe you are in for a long journey."

"*Mon Dieu,*" Maman said, gripping my wrist. "Not Zurich? I had hoped you'd given up that foolish notion."

Militza shook her head. "The cards do not say. But the Queen of Swords is leading your Katerina to a faraway land."

I patted my mother's hand and said quietly, "The tsar will not allow me to go to Zurich, Maman. Or anywhere else, for that matter." She had nothing to worry about.

"Perhaps not Zurich, my cousin," the grand duchess said, shuffling her deck once again. "But you will soon be traveling far from home. After all," she added with a wicked smile, "the cards do not lie."

CHAPTER THREE

"Honestly, Katiya, why must you be so hostile to your cousin?" Maman fussed after Militza left.

"And why can you not see she's dangerous?" I countered. "She fears you and she is jealous of your power as the striga."

"That's ridiculous," Maman said. "I have no intention of interfering with her rule." She sighed. "Despite what the Dark and Light Court queens want."

A chill passed over my heart. Never in my life had my mother mentioned the faerie courts. Had she always known about St. Petersburg's supernatural underworld? How much had she learned since becoming one of their own?

"Has the empress asked you to take over the St. Petersburg vampires?" I asked cautiously.

Maman nodded as if we were talking of the latest opera scandal. "Of course she has. And Miechen has as well. She was positively gleeful when she heard I'd become the heir to the striga. I don't think the grand duchess likes Militza at all." She put her own deck of tarot cards back in their wooden box. "Still, it's nice when they present themselves to me, and since Militza accompanies me everywhere, they'll soon see there are no feuds between us."

"Do you have to meet all of the blood drinkers in the city?" I asked, shuddering.

"No, but they generally seek me out."

I remembered a pale young hussar and his wife who had politely approached Maman at the opera several weeks earlier. How many blood drinkers remained in St. Petersburg? How many of them would remain loyal to Militza?

"I don't see any of the upyri, of course," Maman was saying. "They generally aren't the fashionable sort." The upyri were the feral blood drinkers who lived far from the city, in the ancient forests. It was rare to see one of their kind anywhere near St. Petersburg.

Maman's calm way of handling her situation made me want to giggle—and beat my head against the wall. She had no notion of how dangerous her position was and how many dangerous creatures in the city now wanted that position. Especially Grand Duchess Militza.

"Now, the Montenegrins aren't so bad," Maman continued, fussing with the flowers in the vase on the table, "as far as blood drinkers go. The crown prince is a perfectly well-mannered gentleman. Oh, I do wish you hadn't broken off the engagement."

"M-Maman!" I sputtered. "He and his sisters kidnapped me!

They drugged me and forced me to—" I stopped. I still couldn't bring myself to tell her what I'd done in Cetinje.

My heart was pounding and my palms were sweating, partly from being so close to Maman and partly from coming dangerously close to revealing my secrets. It might have devastated her to know the truth years ago. What would she say now if she knew her daughter could raise the dead? Would she condemn me? I didn't believe she had that right anymore. She'd drunk the blood of monsters. And become one herself.

And yet I still loved her. She was the same kind and generous, if not slightly frivolous, woman I'd grown up with.

"What has Miechen said?" I asked, trying to change the subject. "About you? As the striga?"

Maman sighed. "Oh, she thinks I should make the vampires swear loyalty to her as the head of the Dark Court. Which means I would have to swear my loyalty to her as well."

I looked at her in surprise. "What about the empress?"

Maman shrugged. "Of course, she believes all the blood drinkers should be loyal only to her."

"Oh, Maman," I said. "What will you do?"

"Ignore all of them. Except Militza. I'll have to make sure she doesn't anger the empress or Miechen. Have you seen Sasha? He's been missing since Militza arrived."

I suppressed a sigh. Maman's undead cat did not like anyone but had a special hatred for blood drinkers. He still seemed to be devoted to my mother, however. Perhaps because he no longer had a cold light for the striga to affect. "He'll reappear before long," I assured my mother. "Maman," I continued tentatively. It was time to have a serious talk with her. The one I'd been dreading since I was little. "Have there been other people in our family who have had . . . special gifts? Are there any other vampires in our family?"

"Of course not!" she exclaimed.

"Dariya told me once that Grandmaman married into the Dark Court. Did Grandfather Max have fae blood, then?"

"Only a small bit, my dear. His grandmother was Empress Josephine, but I think he got his fae blood from his Bavarian ancestors."

I knew that the poor mad king of Bavaria, Ludwig the Second, was Maman's second cousin. And somehow in the tangled family tree, I was very distantly related to the Bavarian princesses Augusta and Erzsebet. The letters Augusta had written to me told me how excited they were to be in their final years at Smolni. "And there are no other unusual creatures in your family, Maman? No shape-shifters or magicians?"

Surely I couldn't be the only necromancer in Russia. My cousin Dariya had hinted that her own mother had had the dark gift, but no one knew much about the poor woman. She had died giving birth to Dariya, and Dariya's father would not speak of her, so my cousin and I could only speculate.

Maman crossed the room and sat next to me, taking both of my hands in hers. "Dearest Katiya. What you've been born with is extremely special. I know you don't like to speak of it, but I promise you, I've known since you were little. And I've been extremely proud of you for helping the tsar. You would make your grandmother and great-grandfather exceedingly proud."

The heat in the room became suffocating. My head was swimming. "You've known?" Tears threatened to leak out. "All these years, you've known?"

She pulled me close to her, the scent of her French perfume

nearly overwhelming me. "I knew when you brought Sasha back for me, dearest. I thought it was the sweetest thing. I never told your father what I suspected."

"He knows," I said, choking on a sob. "He's known that I'm a necromancer since Militza's wedding last summer at Peterhof." After a moment I added, "Petya knows as well."

Maman pulled back from me in surprise. "Well, then I suppose we have no more secrets in this family, do we?" She smiled. "And if the Dark and Light Court queens ever try to coerce you into their schemes, I promise I won't let that happen."

I wanted to laugh and cry at the same time. How could my mother protect me from the two most powerful faeries in St. Petersburg? They both feared her power, I was sure, but didn't that make her more vulnerable?

"There you are, you naughty animal!" Maman exclaimed as she picked up the raggedy cat that had slunk back into the parlor. Sasha hissed at me. He would never forgive me for what I'd done to him. And I couldn't blame the poor creature.

I sighed and stood up. I had to complete my anatomy assignment for Dr. Badmaev. Kissing Maman on the cheek, I begged her pardon and escaped from both her and the undead cat.

Anya was in my bedroom, putting away clothes. "Duchess, did you hear about my brother and his wife? They are expecting their first child soon!"

"How wonderful for them!" Anya's brother was one of the doctors at Papa's hospital and was a leading researcher for the Oldenburg Institute of Experimental Medicine. "Give them my love, Anya."

With a smile and a curtsy, she was gone, and I pulled my

notebooks out from under my bed. I needed to compare my lung tissue drawings from earlier with illustrations from the medical textbook I'd taken from Papa's library. *A Necromancer's Companion* was under my bed as well. With a shudder, I prayed I would not have to use that book anytime soon.

CHAPTER FOUR

T he next day I was seated at a small table in a large room at
Anichkov Palace, eating a delightful niçoise salad at a
charity luncheon with Princess Alix of Hesse and Grand Duchess Xenia Alexandrovna. Princess Alix was growling. It was un-
nerving to those of us who could hear her. Fortunately, only the
grand duchess and I were close enough.

"Who does she think she is?" Alix asked, stabbing her let-
tuce with a sterling silver repoussé fork that was probably older
than the palace itself. The Sèvres china service had been a
present to my great-great-great-grandmother, Katerina the
Great, from Marie Antoinette. "She is nothing but a skinny
dancer. And a witch."

Xenia patted her hand in sympathy. "She has dazzled him
with her glamour. It's nothing more."

Alix was upset because upon attending the ballet *The Pharaoh's Daughter* with her sister, she had seen the tsarevitch

24

talking with one of the dancers behind stage. Mathilde Ksches-sinskaya was a beautiful dark faerie who was bewitching all of St. Petersburg with her seductive dancing. Alix had been dismayed to see the way her Nicholas had been completely enchanted. The tsarevitch had not even seemed to notice Alix when she stepped out of her sister's theater box at the Mariinsky Theater. "The heathen," Alix growled again.

I glanced around nervously, hoping none of the empress's other guests took notice. Most people believed the Hessian princess to be soft-spoken and modest, but I knew she could be quite feral if she believed there was evil or injustice for her to battle. Even though she knew all of my dark secrets and had seen one of my undead creatures, she still counted me as a friend. She had decided that my soul was good. I was terrified of ever disappointing her.

Xenia shook her head, her dark ringlets swinging as she dug into her pheasant croquette. "Do not fear, Alix. Nicky does not feel anything for Mathilde. She is a pretty diversion, nothing more."

"And would you feel the same way if your Sandro was the one making eyes at her?" Alix asked.

Xenia frowned at both of us. "What can you do? She is protected by the Dark Court, is she not?"

"Do you truly think Miechen approves of her?" I asked. "Her husband has been seen smiling at her a little too fondly as well."

Xenia giggled. "If Uncle Vladimir acts too friendly with the girl, Aunt Miechen will see that poor Mathilde is sent to a ballet troupe in Siberia."

Alix looked thoughtful. "Could the grand duchess actually do that?" she asked. "Or the empress?"

"Mother would not deign to interfere," Xenia said. "The ballerina is a creature of the Dark Court. She is Aunt Miechen's responsibility."

As I ate my pheasant, which was unfortunately cold and dry, I was secretly glad it was not George who had caught the wicked ballerina's attention. But what would I do if I had a rival for his affections? Especially if it was someone the empress approved of? Would I have the grace and courage to stand aside and wish him every happiness he deserved? The pheasant stuck in my throat.

"Are you all right, Katiya?" Xenia asked as I tried to choke quietly behind my napkin. She waved to the liveried servant behind us. "She needs more wine."

"*Merci*," I said, noticing unhappily that the empress was now looking at our table. She did not look pleased to see her daughter sitting with a necromancer and the wolf princess of Hesse. The servant had refilled my glass and stepped back without making a sound. I took a sip of the wine and tried to push thoughts of George Alexandrovich out of my mind.

"Have they presented the awards yet?" Alix asked. "I don't think they are going to serve dessert before the awards are given out." The luncheon was to honor several aristocratic women who'd given the most time and money to charity during the previous year. My mother had received one of the awards the previous year and had promptly donated it to the Oldenburg Children's Hospital.

Xenia glanced up toward the imperial table, where her mother presided. "Not yet, I don't think. Perhaps we could sneak downstairs to the kitchens?"

"Aren't you expected to hand out an award?" I asked.

26

"*Zut alors*," Xenia said, pouting. "There's no sense in you two sitting here and suffering through the speeches as well. What if one of you pretends to be ill? Alix, you should probably take Katerina out for some air." Her faerie eyes twinkled with silver. She suddenly leaned forward with a concerned face and put a hand on my shoulder. "Oh my, you look terrible!"

I hated to make a scene, but Xenia knew Alix and I were not enjoying the pheasant. Perhaps we would find better food in the kitchens. Alix was already trying to help me stand up. She was eager to escape the empress's gaze as much as I was.

"Can you walk, Katerina Alexandrovna?" she asked with a grave face.

The shocked looks around us led me to worry that Xenia had cast a glamour over my appearance. I was too terrified to glance at the empress's table. If she saw me, she would certainly see through whatever Xenia had done. "We'll speak later," I told Xenia, and grabbed Alix's arm.

As we left the enormous white dining hall, we passed an ornate mirror that rose up from the floor to the ceiling. I did look a ghastly shade of pale. No wonder no one had tried to stop us from leaving.

We reached the grand hallway and paused. Alix looked at me again and shook her head. "You truly look awful. Perhaps you should find some water."

"I'm perfectly fine," I said, waving her concern away. "It's just Xenia's glamour. Do you wish to find the kitchens?"

"I just wanted to leave the banquet," Alix said, sitting down on a plush velvet-upholstered bench. "I should have a few minutes free before Ella realizes I'm missing."

"Maman won't notice that I'm gone," I said, sitting next to

her. "She's next to your sister." It continued to amaze me how Maman belonged to the Dark Court but walked that delicate balance to stay friendly with the empress's court as well. They were family, after all. My mother was a first cousin of the tsar.

We heard someone coming up the grand staircase. Heavy boots clicked smartly against the marble stairs. Hushed male voices carried up ahead of them. Alix glanced at me worriedly. "Your glamour is gone," she whispered.

"What does Papa say?" a familiar but tired voice asked.

"He wants to speak with you this evening, before he and Mother leave for Denmark."

The tsarevitch had reached the top of the staircase with his brother George Alexandrovich. My heart did a little dance. How long had it been since I'd seen my grand duke? Almost a month. The tsarevitch looked surprised to see Alix. And not all together pleased. "Your Highness?" he asked.

Alix stood immediately and curtsied. "Your Imperial Highness."

George smiled when he saw us. But he looked awful. His skin was pale and he had large shadows under his eyes. I stood and curtsied as well.

Nicholas Alexandrovich offered his arm to Alix. "It has been ages since I've seen you. Would you like to step into the red parlor with me and have tea?" His charming smile worked, and Alix was led away before she could refuse.

George offered his arm to me. "We could join them in the parlor. Or," he whispered as I linked my arm in his and his left hand covered mine with a tender squeeze, "we could have tea in the library?"

His touch sent a warm, happy tingle up and down my arm. "I

believe Princess Alix has something she wants to discuss with the tsarevitch," I said. "Perhaps we should give them some privacy?"

"Excellent idea," he murmured. The library was not a far walk, and he did not bother to ring for tea. The moment the door closed behind us, George's hands were around my waist, his lips on mine.

"How was Paris?" I asked when he paused for breath.

"Hot." His kisses traveled up my neck.

"I missed you," I said, my own kisses clumsily reaching his earlobe, his cheek.

"And I've missed you." His voice was husky. The familiar rush of my cold light spiraling around both of us gave me a dangerous thrill. I felt his magic rising to meet mine and relaxed just slightly. He was truly a stronger mage now, and yet I still worried I could overpower him with my cold light. Or my love.

He groaned. "Katiya," he said, slightly winded. He pulled away from me, searching my face. "Your year is almost up, Duchess."

"My year?" My thoughts came crashing back down to earth. Why couldn't he just let us enjoy the present moment?

"Remember our promise?" Last August when I tried to refuse his proposal, he'd asked me for a year to receive his parents' blessing. But a year ago, he was just beginning his Koldun studies. And I'd believed I was going to medical school.

"But nothing has changed your mother's mind," I said. If anything, I thought she disliked me even more. "Georgi, you're as pale as a ghost. Sit down." I pulled him over to one of the library chairs. Gently pushing his hair off his face, I asked, "What have you been doing to yourself?"

He was not going to be distracted with me fussing over his health. He took both of my hands in his. "I've spoken with my father. I've told him my plans."

My heart stopped in my throat. "And?"

He pulled me closer and his hands settled on my waist once again. I was very aware of the fact that I was standing between his legs as he looked up at me. "He would like to speak with you." George smiled up at me. "Don't be afraid. He does not bite."

I didn't smile back. Something in my stomach tightened nervously. What was the name of that muscle again? "When?" I asked.

"I will send a carriage for you tonight. My parents leave for their villa in Fredensborg in the morning."

"And you?"

"I must stay in St. Petersburg for the present. I have business with the Inner Circle. And the Koldun."

"Can you tell me—"

"No," he said, stopping my question with another kiss. His hands cupped my face. "There is nothing for you to worry about."

I pulled back from him. "But *you* are worried about something. You aren't healing as fast as you should." The supernatural wound he'd received dueling with Danilo must not have responded to any of the Koldun's spells. And the Koldun was recovering from his own brush with death. "I wish you would let Dr. Badmaev examine you."

"I've had my fill of doctors and wizards. I am well enough, Katiya." His hands slid up and down my arms slowly. "Leave it at that."

"You're not getting enough sleep," I said, kissing each of his eyelids. His blue eyes looked sunken and hollow. The silver sparkle was not there. He was still my beautiful boy, just more fragile. I would have to discover a cure for him on my own.

He pulled me down onto his lap sideways. "No meddling, Katiya." His lips were soft and warm against my ear. It tickled.

"You're in my head again," I said, putting a hand on his chest. George's fae abilities allowed him to hear my thoughts, but not I his. I could feel his heart pounding. *Mon Dieu*, his skin was hot.

"Your thoughts are too loud to ignore."

"What am I thinking now?" My hand crept up to his collar and my fingertips brushed against the smooth warm skin of his neck peeking out from his shirt. His lips touched my hairline. It sent nice shivers all over my scalp. "You are thinking that it is a very good thing I'm not going to Denmark with my family."

I smiled. "Yes, it could be a very good thing if I get to see you."

"I'll find a way, Katiya. I promise." He kissed me once more. "But I think you should probably get back to the luncheon."

I sighed heavily as I slid off his lap and tried to smooth my skirts. He laughed and stood up, reaching over to tuck one of my wayward curls behind my ear.

"I'm certain no one has missed you," he said, grinning. "Except probably Xenia."

I put my hand on the doorknob and stopped. "Should I go and find Alix?"

He shook his head. "You left because you were feeling ill, did you not? Now you're feeling better. You have a much healthier glow." His smile was mischievous.

I rolled my eyes and turned to go, but he grabbed my arm and pulled me back for one last kiss. "I'll see you tonight, Katiya. And we will speak with my father."

I wasn't sure if I should be frightened or excited at the prospect. I felt a little of both.

CHAPTER FIVE

That evening I was sitting down to dinner with my parents when my brother, Petya, came home. He was still dressed in his regimental uniform, having been on duty all day at the Order's headquarters. "Katiya, I am to escort you to Anichkov Palace for an audience with the tsar."

Both Papa and Maman looked shocked. I stood up quickly. "Do not be alarmed," I said, throwing my napkin onto my chair. "It is probably nothing."

"Petya, is this about the Order?" Papa asked.

"I'm not certain" was all my brother said. He was probably as mystified as my parents.

I grabbed my wrap and followed my brother into a black-and-gold-trimmed carriage. Anichkov Palace was not far from our house on Millionaya Street. As the carriage rolled through the ornate iron gates and past the wooded park surrounding the palace, my brother frowned. "What have you done now, Katiya?

I won't tell our parents, but I must know what sort of trouble you've been causing."

I gave him a nervous shrug. What did the tsar plan to say to me? Would he approve of me as a wife for his son? I didn't dare to hope. Perhaps he was ready to allow me to go to medical school in Zurich. But now that my studies were going so well with Dr. Badmaev, did I still want to leave St. Petersburg?

Petya stepped out of the carriage as it rolled to a stop at the palace entrance. He turned and offered his hand to me. I was shaking much more than I'd realized. "I won't leave you unless I'm ordered to," he said, his face stern and serious like any soldier's.

I loved my brother, even if he did always think the worst of me. "I'll be fine," I told him.

To my embarrassment, we were taken to the tsar's library. Only hours ago I'd been kissing the tsar's son in this very room. I blushed and glanced around quickly, searching for George, but the library was empty except for the tsar. He was seated behind his handsome Hepplewhite desk. "Leave us, Commander Oldenburg."

There was nothing Petya could do but click his heels and bow. With one last worried glance at me, he turned and left, closing the door behind him. I was alone with Tsar Alexander. As he stood up, the lamp on the desk cast long, menacing shadows behind him. "Katerina Alexandrovna," he said, coming around the desk and sitting on the corner. "My son and I have had a long discussion about you."

I said nothing. I was too frightened to speak. My entire future was in this man's hands.

Even if he had not been such a large man, the tsar would have been intimidating. But there was a reason he was called Sasha the Bear. He loomed over me like a Kodiak. And this was without transforming into the bogatyr, the ancient warrior hero of Russia. I hoped he had not summoned me here because he needed me to perform the ritual. If such had been the case, we would have been joined in the library by several Orthodox clergy and wizards of the Inner Circle, not to mention the empress herself.

"George tells me the two of you wish to marry."

"Yes, Your Imperial Majesty." It came out barely above a whisper.

The tsar's face finally relaxed into a smile. "My dear, nothing would make me happier. I've seen the way my son behaves around you. You've brought a light into his dark soul."

I stared at him with relief and shock. Me? Bringing George light? "I-I'd believed it was the other way around, Your Imperial Majesty," I stammered. Not that I wished to argue with the tsar.

"Nonsense. George has always been the serious one, tormented by his own demons," the tsar said. "I'm happy that he has found someone who will not let him wallow in the darkness. I've watched you grow up, Katerina, as the daughter of one of my favorite cousins. The shadows of the Dark Court haunt you, but you've always longed to stay out of their grasp. You can keep my son safe from those shadows."

"But my family," I could not help myself from saying. "Maman is attached to the Dark Court, as striga."

Tsar Alexander shook his head. "You are a princess of imperial blood, Katerina Alexandrovna, and I know you will make a fine grand duchess. However, there is one sacrifice you must be willing to make. A daughter-in-law of the tsar cannot practice medicine. So I'm afraid medical school is out of the question."

The happiness that had dared to bubble up inside me suddenly vanished. "I cannot become a doctor?" What sort of cruel joke was the tsar playing on me?

The tsar folded his arms. "You will have plenty to occupy your time raising a young family."

"And my responsibilities as your necromancer?" I asked.

His smile was grim. "We pray to God your services won't be needed any longer."

"But it's only a matter of time before Konstantin Pavlovich returns. Unless the Koldun has discovered a way to prevent it?"

The tsar frowned, and for a second I believed I had angered him. "I have faith that the Inner Circle will prevent the lich from returning, Katerina. That burden falls upon the current Koldun and will one day fall upon my son. You must only concern yourself with providing the empress and me with grandchildren." His face softened again. "But not too soon, I should think. The empress believes she is much too young to be a grandmother."

I blushed. "Your Imperial Majesty, I am only seventeen." About to turn eighteen. I did not know what else to say. The tsar was asking too much of me. Give up my childhood dream or lose the boy I loved? How could he ask me to choose?

"No hurry, my dear. No hurry. In fact, I think a long engagement might be most suitable. The empress does need time to come around. She still thinks of her sons as little children. But it's time Nicholas begins to think about marriage as well."

I kept silent. I knew neither the tsar nor his wife was fond of

Alix, so there was no point in angering him. "And Xenia as well," I offered instead.

"Xenia?" The tsar looked at me in surprise. "It will be years before she is ready to marry."

"And perhaps years before you and the empress are ready to let her marry," I said, immediately hoping I had not been too bold.

But he stood up again and retreated behind his desk, indicating that our meeting was over. No fatherly bear hug, for which I was grateful. "Katerina," he said as I curtsied and turned toward the door, "do you still have a decision to make or has it already been made?"

I stared at him, my throat dry and my heart pounding. "I . . ." But as badly as I wanted to please the tsar, I couldn't. "I have to think, Your Imperial Majesty."

He nodded. There was no way I could tell whether my answer pleased or disappointed him. Perhaps it was what he had expected.

With another hasty curtsy, I fled from his library and found my brother standing at attention outside. "Take me home, Petya," I said, sweeping past him toward the palace entrance. I did not want to see George Alexandrovich. Not yet. Had he known his father was going to ask such a thing of me?

My brother pestered me with questions the entire ride home. "It had nothing to do with the lich tsar, Petya," I said, leaning my head back and closing my eyes. "And it wasn't about the Order. I'll tell you everything tomorrow. I'm just tired."

It had been an exhausting interview. I begged him to tell our parents something, anything, so I could just go straight to bed when we got home. With a worried frown, he finally nodded.

As the carriage drew closer to Betskoi House, Petya leaned forward and put his hand on top of mine. "I just wish I knew what it was so I could make it better."

I glanced up at him. Sometimes my brother's overprotectiveness made me want to cry. "I wish you could too."

CHAPTER SIX

I spoke with my brother early the next morning. Maman was a late riser, and Papa had gone for a brisk early-morning walk. Petya was already dressed in his regimentals, ready to leave for his palace duties. "And now are you going to tell me what last night was all about?" he asked, taking a hot cup of tea from the footman's tray.

I pulled him into Papa's study. "George asked his father for permission for us to marry. The tsar agreed, but—"

"Katiya, that is wonderful news! I think George Alexandrovich is an excellent fellow!"

I shook my head. "But the tsar will only give us permission if I agree to give up my dreams of becoming a doctor."

"And you can't decide which you want more?" Petya asked. He was not condescending but concerned.

I could not hold it in any longer. The tears I'd refused to shed the previous night came bursting out as my brother pulled me into his arms. "There, there," he said, feebly patting my shoulder. "Surely you love your grand duke above all else?"

"Do I?" I asked, looking up at Petya. "What if I grow to resent my sacrifice? What if I grow to hate him?"

"Is that what you're afraid of?" he asked.

I nodded, careful not to wipe my tears on his regimentals. He pulled a handkerchief out of his pocket and gave it to me.

"Katiya, perhaps the tsar will agree to some sort of compromise. If you cannot attend medical school, perhaps he will let you open a hospital in your own name. You can spend all your free time there."

I gave my brother a slight push as I turned away. "That is exactly what Danilo proposed. But I want to make a hands-on difference. I don't want to be a silly grand duchess who simply spends money."

"But you can make a difference with money, Katiya. Never doubt that."

My back still turned to him, I blew my nose.

He sighed, exasperated with me. "I must leave now or I will be late. Are you going to tell Maman and Papa?"

I shook my head. "Not until I've made my decision. What good would it do?"

"All right," he said, squeezing my shoulder gently. "Let me know if there's anything I can do."

I waited until he left before dissolving into tears again. I had to speak with Dr. Badmaev. I wasn't expected until this afternoon for my studies, but I decided I'd rather face a table of cut-open corpses than my parents right now. I quietly slipped back to my room and grabbed my cloak. I left word with the servants that I'd gone to Dariya's for the day, hoping my cousin would not choose today to pay me a visit.

I had not seen much of Dariya since she'd traveled with Miechen's Dark Court to Biarritz over the summer. She had become more and more like her stepmother, Countess Zenaida: her head was filled with Dark Court intrigues and affairs. Dariya was intent on capturing a wealthy, titled husband. I knew what she would tell me to do if I confided in her.

I walked briskly to the nearest tram location and paid my passage to Betosky Prospekt. I was getting used to riding the rickety, cramped carriage with strangers and seeing a side of St. Petersburg I'd never seen before. Would I be able to help these people better as a wealthy grand duchess or as a research doctor? Could I ever forgive myself if I gave George up? I was so lost in my own miserable thoughts I almost missed my stop near Dr. Badmaev's clinic and herb shop. Why should the tsar force me to make such a choice? It wasn't as if George were the heir to the throne. I would never be tsarina or empress.

Brooding, I entered the doctor's shop. There were already a few patients sitting in his waiting area. I smiled at them as I hung my wrap on the coat stand. I passed through to the back of the building, where I found the Tibetan doctor drinking a cup of tea.

"Duchess! You are early! Are you so eager to dive back into the lung tissue? Did you discover the secrets of your pink growths?"

"Yes, they were tuberculin tumors," I said with a little pride. "But I came early because I am in a terrible quandary." I took the cup of tea Masha handed me. Thanking her, I sat down next to Dr. Badmaev.

"Nothing that tea can't make better, I hope?" he said, smiling.

"I'm afraid it's too terrible for tea to fix." I took a sip and told him about the tsar's ultimatum.

"The tsar is very old-fashioned. More so than his father ever was," the Tibetan said. "And this has kept you up all night, worrying?"

I laughed grimly. "Does it show?"

He smiled. "Come to the lab and we will take your mind off your problems for now. Perhaps you will be able to think clearly after concentrating on something else for a while."

I smiled back. Tumors and germs were just what I needed.

I spent the morning examining lung tissues under the micro-scope while Dr. Badmaev treated the patients out front. As I drew illustrations of the various cells, I listened to him examine his patients, asking them about their symptoms and explaining to them how to take the medicine he was prescribing.

Most of the patients were poor and ignorant and needed sim-ple, brief directions. Their illnesses could have been prevented if they had nutritious food and practiced better hygiene. One woman had put pig manure on her child's cut foot because a neighbor had suggested it. Dr. Badmaev fussed at her for listen-ing to such foolish advice. "Keep the foot clean," I heard him tell her. "Put fresh, clean dressings on it every day. And make sure the child takes this medicine every day too."

He must have seen at least twenty patients before joining me in the lab. He did not look tired at all. "And how are the lungs today?"

I could not help smiling. "I've sketched five different kinds of cells that I found within the lung tissues."

"Very good. And what herbs would one use to benefit lung

ailments?" I enjoyed the Tibetan doctor's peculiar blending of Eastern and Western medicine. I had been surprised to discover he'd received his medical diploma from the St. Petersburg Military Academy of Medicine upon arriving in Russia with his elder brother several years ago. He'd been a young boy then, leaving the monastery in the Himalayas, where he'd grown up studying Tibetan medicine, and journeying thousands of miles alone to St. Petersburg to live with his brother. The elder brother died several years ago but had been a well-known doctor respected by Tsar Alexander the Second.

"Lungwort, sea wrack, and ephedra," I said, listing the herbs I had studied the night before.

"Very good!" Dr. Badmaev beamed. "My nephew is joining me soon from the monastery. He will be studying medicine along with you."

"And he will be allowed to attend the medical academy," I said, trying to keep the sudden bitterness from my voice. Men had so many more opportunities than women. Why did the tsar have to be so stubborn?

"It is the way of the world, Duchess. But perhaps the world will change."

"I'm afraid if it does change, it will be too late for me." I stood up from the table and stretched. My back and neck were sore from remaining in the same position for so long. "And I'm afraid dissecting lung tissue has not given me a fresh perspective on my problem either. Perhaps I should be returning home."

"Not without a cup of afternoon tea," Dr. Badmaev said, ringing the bell for Masha. "Always be aware of how your environment acts upon your body. Not just the air around you, but also the people, sounds, and smells that surround you. Your body is bombarded with outside distractions constantly. Take the time to shut the rest of the world out and meditate. Focus on your cold light."

I sat in the chair he was pointing me toward and closed my eyes, breathing slowly. He was right; there were so many distractions in my life. I had to focus on what was important. It was not what I wanted most, but what was best for everyone. And what was best for George Alexandrovich would be a doctor trained in Eastern medicine. I would be of better use to him as a healer than as a wife. My cold light did give me clarity. Even if it also broke my heart. I opened my eyes and accepted the cup of tea Masha held out for me. "*Merci.*"

"You look as if you've made a decision?" Dr. Badmaev said. "Your face looks very resolved."

He was amused. But I did not mind. He was trying to lighten my mood when he knew I was making a difficult choice.

"Yes. I shall continue my lessons with you, Doctor. I will be of no use to the tsar's son without medical training."

"So you are making this decision with your head and not with your heart," Dr. Badmaev said, blowing the steam off his cup of tea.

I sighed. "My heart would break if I did not do everything in my power to save George."

"And when will you tell him your decision?"

That I hadn't decided yet. I sipped my tea and closed my eyes, wishing for more clarity. I knew George deserved to know as soon as possible. And the tsar deserved my answer in person.

"I think now is the perfect time, Duchess." It was not the doctor's but George's angry voice that made me open my eyes in alarm.

44

CHAPTER SEVEN

George Alexandrovich was standing in the doorway of Dr. Badmaev's office. He did not look happy. "Katiya, why did you not wait for me last night? Didn't my father give you his blessing?"

Dr. Badmaev stood up quickly. "Forgive me, Your Imperial Highness, but I must get back to my patients." With a quick bow to the grand duke and an encouraging smile toward me, he withdrew from the room, leaving us alone.

I stared into my teacup, refusing to meet George's eye. "How on earth did you know to find me here?" I asked him.

"The imperial guard has orders to watch your movements, Katiya. They always know where you are."

A sick feeling rose in my stomach. "So you've known about my studies with Dr. Badmaev? And the tsar knows as well?" There truly were no secrets left untouched in St. Petersburg.

He nodded as he sat down in the chair next to me. "I

understand what you're trying to do, but it won't work. My illness was caused by dueling with the crown prince at Vorontsov Palace. Blood magic wounded me. Medicine cannot help me."

"But I believe Eastern medicine can," I protested. "Dr. Badmaev is the one who cured the Koldun after I brought him back from the Graylands. Remember how awful he looked? Eastern medicine treats the spirit as well as the body. Please let the Tibetan doctor examine you."

"My parents have expressly forbidden it," he said. "Badmaev is the Dark Court's physician. Besides, the Light Court has all of St. Petersburg's finest trained physicians at hand."

"None of whom can do a thing for you," I said. "I have learned so much from Dr. Badmaev. Not enough to cure you, I know, but I'm certain that soon I'll know what to do to make you better. If the tsar will not allow the Tibetan to treat you, then allow me to help you."

"Marry me, Katiya. That is the best way for you to make me better." He took the teacup out of my hand and set it on the table. Grasping my hands in his, he looked up at me. "Make me a happy man."

He would force me to have this conversation right now. "George, if something were to happen to you and I could have prevented it by continuing my studies, I couldn't live with myself. I love you too much."

"What are you saying?" There was a flash of silver in his eyes.

"If your father will not change his mind about my becoming a doctor," I said, dragging the words out and hating myself for what I said next, "then I cannot marry you."

George's face darkened. "Katiya, the tsar does not change his mind."

"I'm sorry," I whispered, trying very hard not to cry in front of him.

He stood up so abruptly that I thought he was going to break something. Frustrated, he ran his fingers through his hair. "Why must you be so hardheaded?"

"Why must *you*?" I asked, praying he wouldn't notice the trembling in my voice. "I can't stand by and watch you waste away. Not when there's something I can do to stop it." I stood up and grabbed his arms, pulling on his sleeves. "And what if you died? What if I was tempted to bring you back for selfish reasons? I don't think I could let you go. Or what if I brought you back from the grave accidentally?" I continued as my imagination ran wild with dark thoughts. "Don't you see how horrible that would be? I would damn us both!"

He touched my cheek. "Katiya, I'd rather be damned with you than live a blessed life without you."

I held his hand in both of mine and kissed his knuckles. I did not even bother trying to stop the tears anymore. They were falling too fast. "Georgi, please don't say that. You know you don't mean it."

He looked sad. "I asked you not to give up on me last year. And I believed that you had not. Why now? When our happiness is within reach? Or was I just dreaming?" But he did not wait for me to answer. Instead, he leaned forward and kissed me on the forehead, murmuring, "Goodbye, Katiya," against my skin.

I didn't respond. I stood shaking, dazed and in shock, and watched him leave, listened to his boots echo down the wooden hallway as he left Dr. Badmaev's office. I heard the bells on the door tinkle as he opened it and walked out. Did he truly believe

I'd given up on him? On us? Why couldn't he understand that what I was doing was out of love? Had I lost him for good?

Masha returned to pick up the tea things. She hurried across the room as soon as she saw me crying. "Duchess? Are you all right? Duchess?"

I blinked slowly at her, ignoring the tears rolling down my cheeks. "Masha, what have I done?"

CHAPTER EIGHT

Masha, the poor old thing, did not know how to comfort me. I went to the washstand and dried my face. There was nothing left for me to do but dig back into my research. I spent the rest of the day finishing my studies of the respiratory system. Badmaev was pleased with my progress. He assigned me readings on the endocrine system.

I rode the tram home, not bothering to get off at the stop before the Field of Mars. Let my parents see me mingling with the commoners. Let them learn why I threw away the chance to become a grand duchess. I did not care anymore. It would not be long before the whole of St. Petersburg's aristocracy knew what a fool I was.

Maman met me on the stairs. "Katiya, where on earth have you been? Don't try to tell me you've been with Dariya, because I refuse to believe it!"

There was no point in deceiving her any longer. I took off my hat and gloves as I climbed the stairs to my room. "I've been at the Tibetan doctor's clinic."

"A doctor? Are you sick?" She followed me into my room.

"Does it matter?" My heart was broken. I felt wretched.

"Of course it does. We're to attend the ballet this evening. And you still have not told me what the tsar wanted to speak to you about last night."

I sank down onto my bed and realized right then I wanted nothing more than my mother to comfort me. "George asked me to marry him, and the tsar has given us permission," I told her, "but he said I will have to abandon my dreams of becoming a doctor. So I had to turn the grand duke down."

Maman stared at me, speechless for several seconds. There. My last secret was out.

"George?" she whispered. "George Alexandrovich?"

Had she truly not noticed the way we gravitated toward each other? Whenever I was in trouble, it seemed the tsar's son was always there to scowl at me. Or to rescue me. I began to tear up again. I was so sick of crying over him. And I missed him so much it hurt.

Maman moved toward me and wrapped me in her arms. "My sweet Katiya. My dearest. I don't pretend to understand why you have made such a decision, but if it's making you unhappy, why not change it? I'm sure the young grand duke is not happy right now either."

"I know you can't understand, Maman," I said, closing my eyes until the tears were all squeezed out.

She smoothed my hair and rocked me as if I were a baby. "Perhaps this is a spiritual test of some sort. Should we consult the tarot cards?"

"No, Maman. I think I've already failed this test. But I am not going to give up my studies now. It's too late to change my decision."

"Did you and George argue?"

I laughed bitterly. "A terrible argument."

"He will forgive you, I'm sure of it," she said, patting my hand kindly. "The ballet will cheer you up."

"Please, no, Maman," I begged. "I can't face anyone tonight. Especially if he is there."

"Nonsense," Maman said. "The tsar's sons never attend the ballet."

Which was untrue. "I'm sure they'll be there if Mathilde Kschessinska is dancing," I grumbled.

"Oh, she's not scheduled to perform, dear," Maman said. "Though I can see why every young man is fascinated with her. Such a bewitching little beauty! And the way she danced that pas de deux at her graduation! I hear she wants Petipa to revive *The Pharoah's Daughter*."

"Maman!"

"You have nothing to worry about, dearest." She peered into my face critically. "Wear your pale blue silk gown; it will bring out the blue in your eyes. Rest now for a few hours and the puffiness will go away. I'll have Anya bring up a cucumber compress."

I sighed. Maman was sure that as long as I looked presentable, everything would be back to rights. "Yes, Maman." Perhaps a nap was what I needed. And perhaps I could still convince her to let me stay home.

CHAPTER NINE

Anya's compress worked miracles on my eyes. By that evening, there was no trace of fatigue or emotional distress on my face. And Maman was right about the pale blue silk.

But she was very wrong about the ballet program. Mathilde Kschessinska did dance that night in the Mariinsky Theater. And the tsarevitch and his brother did attend, with their mother and sister, seated in the imperial box directly across from our own. George Alexandrovich very studiously avoided looking toward the Oldenburg box.

Princess Alix and her sister Grand Duchess Ella joined us after the first act. Alix looked unhappy. "What shall I do, Katerina? I am leaving for Moscow with my sister this week. Nicholas is going to forget all about me."

"I will miss you," I said, wondering when I would see my shape-changing friend again. "And I am certain that the tsarevitch will miss you as well."

"We argued at the palace the day of the luncheon," she said. "He denied that there was anything between him and the ballerina, but I don't know if I should believe him."

The ballet was about to resume, and Alix realized her sister had already left our box.

"Walk me back?" Alix pleaded. "I don't dare go alone. What if I run into Nicholas Alexandrovich?"

A glance at the imperial box told me that was highly improbable. The tsarevitch was sitting on the edge of his seat, eager for the curtains to rise again. But I knew how anxious Alix was and told Maman I would be spending the second act with Alix and Ella.

Maman, who was busy gossiping with my aunts Anastasia and Zina about the Worth gown the empress was wearing, waved me off. I told Alix to lead the way.

The upper-tier hallway was almost completely empty. Everyone had returned to their seats before the next act began. The only person in the passage was a stranger cloaked in black, with his hood pulled down over his face. He moved in front of us as we attempted to pass him.

"Duchess, it has been a lifetime since I've seen you."

I recognized the voice before he raised his head. It sent a chill slithering down my spine. "Danilo? What are you doing in St. Petersburg?" I asked as Alix gasped next to me.

"I am looking for my sister. She is in the Oldenburg box, is she not?" He did not look right. The crown prince's cold light seemed different. Brighter than before.

"The guards will arrest you if they see you." I glanced around, hoping the guards were nearby.

Alix was glaring at the crown prince. He had been one of

the wizards intent on killing her in a ritual at Vorontsov Palace. He had needed a werewolf's heart to raise Konstantin, the lich tsar, from the dead. Alix had not forgotten, nor had she forgiven him. "Perhaps we should call out for help, Katerina," she said.

Danilo was pale, but he laughed. "Of course, Your Highness. Let the guards take me away. But first allow me to speak with my sister."

"Why? What has happened to you?" I asked. I knew I should not care, but I did not know how the blood bond between us worked. If he fell sick, would I be sick as well? "Is it the lich tsar?"

Danilo looked at me with haunted eyes. "Konstantin is coming soon, Katerina. And he is looking for you, his necromancer."

"I belong to no one," I said, a little too forcefully.

Danilo's eyebrow raised a fraction. "Indeed?"

Alix tried to step in front of me. "You should die for the things you've done, blood drinker." Her voice was so low it sounded like a husky growl.

"I probably will, Your Highness, but first I must see my sister. The Dark Court must be warned about the lich tsar's plans."

"And the Light Court?" I asked.

The crown prince smiled his devilish smile. "I'll leave that to you, my dear duchess."

Alix was not happy. But she was finally convinced we should let him speak with his sister. Then we would notify the guards.

Danilo's sister, Princess Anastasia, was a veshtiza, a blood drinker who could turn into a moth, like the rest of her sisters from Montenegro. She was enjoying her first evening back out in society after giving birth to her son a month earlier. And she'd eagerly attached herself to my mother, the one blood drinker in St. Petersburg who was more powerful than her own sister, Militza.

I slipped back into the family box and whispered in Anastasia's ear, "You're needed out in the hallway. Alone." I glanced at Maman, who was enraptured by the dancing on the stage below. She did not notice my return.

Without a sound, my blood-drinking aunt followed me into the hallway. "Dani?" she whispered when she spotted her brother. "What has happened to you?"

Alix pulled at my gloved arm. "Do you think it's safe to give them a bit of privacy?"

I shook my head. "Not at all. And if the guards find him, they find him," I said. "But we should notify the Light Court of the lich tsar's threat."

"Dani, when did you return to St. Petersburg?" Anastasia asked in a hushed tone. "Does Militza know?"

He shook his head. "I'd hoped to see her here with you. I just arrived this evening. And I must return to Cetinje as soon as possible. I have discovered troubling news about the lich tsar."

"We must leave for the Nikolayevich Palace at once," Anastasia said, linking her arm in her brother's. "Militza was not feeling well enough to go out this evening."

Alix and I looked at each other warily. Was it wise for us to let the Montenegrins depart? What if the crown prince had more information than he had already disclosed to me?

I hesitated. "Your Highness, I'm afraid you cannot wander the streets outside the theater. The imperial guard is watching for you."

"Of course they are, Katerina," he said with a lazy smile. "Are you concerned for me?"

"Don't be ridiculous," Alix said. "The Light Court must be allowed to hear whatever it is you are going to tell the Dark Court."

Danilo sighed and reached up to caress my cheek. Even now, I felt the terrible pull of enchantment from him. His touch made me dizzy.

I tried to step back. "Please don't," I said.

"I came to St. Petersburg to protect you, my love," Danilo said, his words soft and sad.

I looked at him, startled. "Why?"

"He is coming for you, Katerina," Danilo whispered, his eyes haunted. "I'm afraid I won't be able to stop him." As he leaned forward and kissed me on the cheek, I was too stunned to move. "I must go," he said. "Take care, Katerina." He took his sister's arm and swiftly headed toward the stairs.

Alix blinked and looked at me. "Were we just dazzled by that blood drinker?"

I stared at the empty staircase. I could still see faint tendrils of Danilo's cold light trailing in his wake. It was like nothing I'd ever seen before. "I think so."

A roar of applause from inside the theater told us we'd missed the entire second act. The doors would be opening soon.

Alix pulled on my arm again. "Come on. I have a terrible feeling about that ballerina." She was no longer concerned with the crown prince. She led me around the upper hallway until we came to a second staircase, which led down behind the stage. The dressing rooms were full of half-dressed dancers, their faces heavily painted and garish up close. They looked at us curiously but no one bothered us. "I want to know if Nicholas is spending time with her."

"Surely he wouldn't be so foolish if he knows you are here tonight."

"I believe he's been blinded by his infatuation for her. He doesn't know I'm here."

A flurry of high-pitched voices entered the backstage area. Giddy ballerinas were flirting with a few handsome young men, and a few handsome older men as well.

"Aren't you a pretty little thing," I heard Grand Duke Vladimir saying to one of them. "If I were only twenty years younger," he added with a sigh.

Alix's eyes grew big. "Is that the Koldun? What would Grand Duchess Miechen say if she heard?"

"He wouldn't dare," I said. "The grand duchess would cut his heart out and eat it for dinner if he were unfaithful to her."

"Nicky, you brought me a present!" A melodic little voice carried from a darkened corner of the hall.

I watched Alix's face turn ghostly pale.

"I hope you like it," the tsarevitch said shyly to the faerie dancer Kschessinska. She was smiling over a tiny jewelry box. What kind of trinket had he given her?

I worried that George might be close by too. Was he also seeking comfort among the painted dancers after our fight? I didn't think I could bear to see that. I tugged on Alix's arm. "Please, let's get out of here. You don't need to see this. Maman and your sister will be looking for us."

"You're right," Alix said, turning and racing up the stairs so fast she almost left me behind. The princess's voice showed no emotion when she turned around to speak again. "I'll tell Ella and Sergei tonight about the crown prince's warning. They will send word to the tsar."

CHAPTER TEN

I was invited to the palace of Grand Duke and Duchess Sergei Alexandrovich to say farewell to the Hessian sisters before they left for their country estate outside of Moscow. Their only brother, Ernest, and their sisters, Victoria and Irene, had arrived from Hesse to accompany them on a family retreat.

Dariya and I attended the elegant French dinner at the Sergei Palace on the Moika River. It was here, on a bitterly cold winter night almost two years ago, that Count Chermenensky, the first human creature I'd ever raised from the dead, had tried to protect me from one of Princess Cantacuzene's undead creatures. I passed the glass conservatory with my cousin on our way to the dining hall. Seeing the door to the outdoor garden gave me chills, even on this unseasonably mild September night. The poor count had later been destroyed protecting me from Konstantin at Peterhof. How many more members of the

Order of St. Lazarus would meet the same fate before the lich tsar was defeated once and for all?

"Katiya, where have you been hiding yourself?" Dariya was asking. "I haven't seen you at the Vladimir Palace in ages. Your mother says you've been busy visiting the sick? Don't you ever grow tired of illness and death?"

I looked up at her, surprised. I never grew tired of studying disease processes. Death saddened me, but I was grateful for the lessons it offered. "Is that how you see me? As a ghoulish student surrounded by misery? I am not miserable."

Dariya looked at me sympathetically. "Then why are your eyes so sad? Why are you not seeking out the tsar's son?"

A sick feeling bloomed deep inside. "Is he here tonight?"

Dariya shook her head. "Why are you not where he is? Tonight he dines with his brother at his uncle Alexei's. With the ballerinas from the Mariinsky Theater."

"How do you know this?" I asked, the sick feeling in my stomach growing worse. I hoped Alix had not heard this rumor.

Dariya smiled. "Zina told me. She was furious when she found out."

"Why?"

"She and Grand Duke Alexei are fighting at the moment."

I looked at her in shock. Of course, I should have known all along. "They are having an affair? Does your father know?"

Dariya shrugged. "My father is in Biarritz with his own mistress. He left me to fend for myself against the dragon Zina a long time ago. I don't care anymore, Katiya. All that matters is that I find a wealthy prince and get a house of my own."

I wrapped my cousin in a fierce embrace. I had had no idea the marriage of her father and stepmother was so miserable. I'd grown up naïvely in a happy household, with parents who'd also grown up in happy households. I'd always assumed I'd have the same happily-ever-after. At least there was still hope for Petya.

"Gracious, Katiya! It's not quite so terrible!" Dariya said, surprised at my affection. "Oh good, it looks like we're having oysters tonight," she added, noticing the *zakuski* table. She picked up a glass of champagne and tipped it toward me. "Here's to an interesting evening."

I looked around the reception hall for Alix and noticed her speaking with Grand Duke Sergei. As much as I liked Alix and her sister, the grand duke frightened me with his cruel black eyes. I turned back and found a glass of champagne, sipping it for courage. Dariya had already slipped away to flirt with young men in the grand duke's regiment. It appeared that Prince Kotchoubey was still her favorite.

I left my half-full glass on a servant's silver tray and approached Alix. She smiled when she saw me. "Katerina Alexandrovna," she said. "I'm so happy you're here tonight."

Grand Duke Sergei Alexandrovich frowned at me, his needle-sharp eyes taking in my appearance as if he did not approve. "Duchess," he said with a crisp bow and a click of his boot heels. "I hope you are enjoying yourself this evening."

"Of course, Your Imperial Highness. You have a beautiful home."

He nodded politely. "If you will excuse me, Alix, I must find your sister."

"He wants every little thing to be perfect," Alix said. "Sometimes I think he cares more about party details than Ella does."

"It's a lovely dinner," I said, glancing around at the sparkling china and silver. Delicate orchids and roses bloomed in crystal vases everywhere.

"I dread leaving St. Petersburg," Alix said. "I feel evil creeping through the streets. And it's not just the Dark Court."

She would be overly sensitive right now. It was close to the full moon, when she and her sister roamed the streets as wolf-folk, protecting the innocent from evil creatures. I was grateful and lucky she no longer considered me one of her prey. I wondered what the grand duke thought of his wife and sister-in-law's feral activities. Rumors circulated in Moscow that he and his soldiers were the ones howling like wolves on bitter cold nights. I wondered if they joined the women in order to keep an eye on them.

Alix frowned. "Is the crown prince still in town? Has he tried to speak to you again?"

I shook my head. Whatever Danilo's plans were, I hoped they did not involve me. Since the crown prince's arrest in May, I'd asked Dr. Badmaev to teach me to block him from my mind. Danilo's ascension ritual in Cetinje had forged a powerful blood bond between us, and now I had a hard time keeping the crown prince from hearing my thoughts. The bond had linked our minds in an uncomfortably intimate way. The Tibetan had told me there was nothing that could get rid of this blood bond except death. But I had finally learned to close my mind off from him. Some of the time, at least. I suspected my efforts mostly amused the crown prince. I didn't want George to know just how strong my bond with Danilo was. Even I didn't want to know the depths of it.

We were getting ready to sit down for dinner when the footman announced the arrival of the imperial family. The empress and her eldest children had come to bid farewell to Ella and Alix. Perhaps Her Imperial Highness had cut her sons' party with the ballerinas short.

Everyone pressed forward to pay respects to the empress. George did not look surprised to see me. As soon as the crowd pushed into the grand dining room, he was at my side.

"We need to talk." His voice was low and urgent.

"About what, Your Imperial Highness?" I looked straight ahead, at the back of Grand Duchess Alexandra Iosifovna's large white hair. She was wearing her black feathers again.

He put his hand on my elbow, gently pulling me from the crowd and leading me into a small empty sitting room. "I did not want our last conversation to end the way it did."

"But you walked away first," I pointed out.

"I was upset, Katiya," he said with a sigh. "I did not want to make it worse by saying something we would both regret."

"I already regret it, Georgi." I wanted to be in his arms again so badly. "But I can't change my mind. I won't give up this chance to find a way to cure you."

He looked at me incredulously, taking my hands in his. "Even if it means giving up on a normal life for us?"

"How normal would our life be if you are dying? I don't want to lose you to whatever this wound is. And I can find a cure. I know I can."

"Katiya, my love, I admire you for your dedication, but don't you care about my feelings at all?" Looking steadily into my face, his blue eyes flashed silver. Then he frowned. "I see."

He let go of my hands and stepped back. He'd seen a glimpse

of my tangled and distressed thoughts. It did nothing to re-
assure him.

"You are afraid you might come to resent me if you give up
your education. To hell with my father, Katiya. I'll take you
away from Russia myself. Wherever you want to go: Paris, Zurich, even London, if that's what you want. They'll probably
disown me, and I'm afraid you wouldn't be a grand duchess."

"Georgi, how could you propose such a thing?" I wanted to
cry. Again. The thought of him being cut off from his family
because of me was horrifying. "Absolutely not."

He shook his head, reading my thought. "I know you're worried that I'd resent you. That is not going to happen."

"How can you be so sure?" I whispered.

He brought my hands to his lips. "Trust me, Katiya. We'll
make a new life for just the two of us."

The dinner bell sounded from down the hall. Another of
Grand Duke Sergei's perfectly regimented details. George
sighed. "We'd better go in separately. Why don't you go first?"
He pulled me close and gave me the briefest kiss on my lips.
"We'll talk again later."

I walked to the dining room in a daze. I couldn't let him
throw his life away for me. How was I supposed to make him
understand that? Or was he just calling my bluff, expecting me
to give up my medical training instead? I sat down at my table,
fury and frustration rising inside. I wished more than anything
that I had the faerie sight and could read George's thoughts, the
way he could read mine.

The delicious food, fussed over so by the Grand Duke Sergei,
tasted like sawdust. I was so miserable I could not even enjoy
the excellent dove croquette. I avoided looking at George but

noticed the empress seated with Ella and Alix. Her eyes kept traveling toward my table. I felt her gaze upon me throughout the dinner.

I ate woodenly, smiling and making polite conversation with the guests on either side of me. I nodded when the elderly countess on my right spoke of the weather, and I smiled when the young officer on my left mentioned the latest ballet. My manners were perfect and imperial. My mother would have been pleased, even if the empress was not.

CHAPTER ELEVEN

The weeks flew by, and summer turned to autumn. I continued to visit Dr. Badmaev, even though I knew the secret police followed me and reported my movements to the tsar. As long as I was not marrying his son, the tsar did not mind my unorthodox lessons.

I made progress in my studies, and soon the Tibetan doctor allowed me to examine patients in his clinic. He did not let me prescribe medicines, though, but quizzed me on my recommendations after the patient had left. My confidence grew as I learned more and more about diseases and supernatural afflictions. I could tell the difference between the bite of the upyri and that of a wolf. And I knew what would cure either one.

My grand duke left for Moscow on behalf of the Koldun to attend a meeting with the wizards in the Kremlin. He must have decided to visit with his uncle and aunt, because he remained away from St. Petersburg for some time, which suited me perfectly well. It made it easier for me to concentrate on my studies.

On a crisp October day, in the small but opulently appointed family chapel at Betskoi House, I became the godmother of Dr. Ostrev and Lyudmila's young daughter, Tamara. Papa stood as godfather, paying for the entire service and hosting the christening dinner. Lyudmila's parents were unable to journey to St. Petersburg from Kiev but sent a silver spoon as a gift for good luck. Anya stood beside me and held the white gown for her young niece. As per Orthodox tradition, the parents were not allowed to be present for the ceremony, so they waited in the red parlor with Maman. I held the squirming infant in my arms as the priest chanted prayers over her head. Her huge blue eyes blinked slowly at me, and I felt a strange tug in my heart. I hadn't been around babies much in the past few years. Young girls started classes at Smolni as young as six, but there were few at the school who were younger than twelve. My cousins were spread far and wide across Europe, so I hadn't seen many infants except the empress's and Miechen's children.

When it was time to take Tamara's gown off, the priest beckoned me to bring her forward and place her in the silver baptism font. It was the same antique bowl that both my brother and I had been baptized in years ago. I lowered the naked child into the cold water, and her pink face turned red with a heathen howl. I could see her cold light wrapped around her like a soft, hazy cocoon. Tamara Rudolfovna would have a long, healthy life, it appeared.

The priest blessed her and poured the holy water over her head. I lifted the wriggling, unhappy infant from the water and wrapped her in the clean white linen Anya held out. The white "garments of light" symbolized her new life. The priest's assistants rang bells and chanted while the priest anointed Tamara's head with holy oil.

Her howls had subsided, but her body still shook with indignant sobs. The sweet baby awakened a new feeling inside me. It had occurred to me with shock that Lyudmila was younger than I and was already a wife and mother. What kind of mother would I be?

This led to another thought: What kind of father would George be? I blushed and glanced around quickly, relieved to see that no one was paying attention to me. Everyone was watching Tamara.

Anya, standing at my side, now took the baby and dressed her in the Ostrev family's white hand-embroidered baptismal gown and the white lace cap that Lyudmila had tatted herself. Suddenly, I was conscious of an emptiness in my arms. I wanted to hold the warm, sweet-smelling bundle again.

The ceremony was soon over, and I followed Anya and Papa and the rest of the party out into the parlor, where Lyudmila scooped baby Tamara up in her arms. Maman was drying her eyes with a handkerchief and ran to embrace me. "Oh, my darling, I was just thinking how soon it will be your baby in our family chapel receiving such a blessing!"

I pulled away from her and laughed lightly. "Not for years, Maman."

"Oh, I do hope Madame Marina's prediction was wrong. The gypsy woman told me years ago I would never have grandchildren."

"Maman, either Petya or I will certainly prove Madame

Marina wrong." I squeezed her hands and left her to seek out Dariya, who was now holding the baby and smiling. She looked happy. I decided to leave her in peace as well and took a steaming cup of tea from the elaborately laid table in the dining room and walked over to the window. The late-afternoon sun was sinking, and the shadows from the houses along Millionaya Street were stretching across the Neva River. I saw people and carriages hurrying across the bridge. A shadowed figure in a long black coat caught my eye as he wandered toward the Summer Garden.

"Katerina . . . I must speak with you."

I closed my eyes and leaned my head against the glass, sighing heavily. *"What do you want, Danilo?"*

"St. Petersburg is not safe for you. You must leave immediately."

Had the lich tsar finally returned? A cold fear settled in my stomach. If Konstantin was here now, the tsar needed to know. After Alix had warned the Light Court of Danilo's visit to the ballet, St. Petersburg had been under increased security. But everyone had been holding their breath, waiting for the moment when the lich tsar made his move.

"Meet me in the park." Danilo's voice was pleading and insistent.

"No. You must leave, Your Highness." I would not be safe anywhere near the crown prince. I was no fool. I turned away from the window.

The crown prince's voice fell silent in my head, and I brought a plate of sweets to Papa, who was standing in the hallway with Tamara's father. They both looked grave.

"Thank you, dear," my father said when I handed him the

plate. "Dr. Ostrev tells me there has been an increasing number of walking dead seen in St. Petersburg."

Startled, I looked from Papa to the doctor. "Do the tsar's men know?"

Dr. Ostrev nodded. "Two more were brought to the hospital last night. Dr. Bokova is certain they were not members of the Order of St. Lazarus."

I swallowed. This meant these creatures were not under my control. Several times a month, the Koldun had me return to Vorontsov Palace to hold the Talisman of Isis and use it to issue general orders for the creatures. They could only be controlled by me, through the power of the Talisman, which was another reason why the tsar did not relish the idea of my leaving for Zurich. He wanted to keep both his personal necromancer and his personal army of undead soldiers reined in closely.

"Does this mean there is another necromancer in St. Petersburg?" I asked with a shudder. A cold dread filled my belly. There was only one other necromancer that I knew of: Princess Johanna Cantacuzene. And she was dead. Wasn't she?

Papa frowned. "There can be no other explanation, can there? You don't think they could still be your creatures, do you, Katiya?"

"*Mon Dieu*, no!" With the help of Dr. Badmaev, I had finally learned how to control my powers so that I would no longer create any more undead accidentally. I had most assuredly not raised anyone from the grave on purpose.

"I will see if the Koldun knows anything, then," my father said. "Katiya, will you tell your mother that I am headed to Vorontsov Palace?"

"Do you want me to join you?" I asked, only half hoping he

would say yes. What if George had returned to St. Petersburg? I was not ready to face him yet.

"No, my dear," Papa said, caressing my cheek and giving me a kind smile. "The Koldun can take care of this without you. If necessary, he will ask the tsar and the empress to return from Fredensborg early."

I did not bother to tell Maman why Papa was going to the palace. She would hear from Militza soon enough if any blood drinkers were involved. Maman was too busy fussing over baby Tamara to pay any attention anyway.

"Katerina, join me outside in the park."

Danilo's voice was back, and it was insistent. *"Leave me in peace,"* I thought irritably. I rubbed my temples, wishing I could steal up to my bedroom for a nap.

"Katerina, I will not leave until I speak to you."

"We are speaking, Your Highness," I thought sarcastically.

But Danilo would not be put off. *"I will stay here in the park until you come out of your house. It is imperative that I see you."*

"Why?" But he refused to answer. Tired of arguing, I flung a cloak around my shoulders and went outside to find him. I told myself I would stay within view of the guards at our front gate.

"Ah, my necromancer," Danilo said, standing as I approached him. He had been sitting on a bench surrounded by a cluster of birch trees in the Field of Mars. It was getting late in the fall, and the trees were almost completely bare. I hoped the Betskoi House guards would still be able to see me.

"I am not your necromancer," I said with a tired sigh. "Please, say what you have to say so I can return to my family."

He took my hand in a swift but elegant move before I could step back. He held my palm up, the same palm he'd drank from several months ago at Smolni. Alarmed, I tried to pull my hand away.

"Shhh," he said, caressing my hand lazily.

I was both revolted and excited at the same time.

"I am not going to take your blood here, Katerina. But I must drink soon. I am growing too weak to fight the lich tsar's pull any longer."

"What are you saying?"

His face grew serious, his eyes haunted. "Konstantin has found me, love. The bond I share with you I also share with him. He was released the night of my ascension. Now he wants to use me to get to you. I am trying to hold him back as long as I can, but I am growing weak. I must have blood. And it must be yours, my love."

"No." I pulled my hand again, and this time he let go. "How can he use you to get to me?"

Danilo's smile was malicious as his black eyes suddenly flashed green. His voice changed. "NECROMANCER, I WILL TAKE THIS BODY AND YOU WILL REPLACE MY BRIDE."

I was too terrified to move. My worst fears had been realized. The lich tsar had returned. He was standing in front of me. In Danilo's body. "You don't want me, Konstantin Pavlovich."

"I MUST HAVE A NECROMANCER. AND I WILL HAVE YOU, MY LOVE."

Was it Danilo or the lich tsar speaking? I was not Konstantin's love. "The bogatyr will stop you," I said with as much bravery as I could muster.

"Are you so very certain?" Danilo's eyes flashed again, and he appeared to be back in control. "Are you so sure the tsar and his son are willing to go through such enormous sacrifices again to protect you? The tsar would be safer if you were dead, Katerina. Summoning the bogatyr again could kill him."

I knew he was right. But I could not believe that the tsar would kill me to keep everyone safe from Konstantin. "Stay away from me, Danilo," I said, backing away from him. There were plenty of people walking around in the park, and the front gates of Betskoi House were in sight. Yet I did not want to cause a scene if I could help it. "If the imperial guard finds you, they will arrest you again."

Danilo's black eyes gleamed. "There is no prison that can hold me, Katerina. And there is nowhere you can hide that you will be safe. Run back to your family, if it makes you feel better. Just remember the lich tsar can come after them as well."

I could stay and listen no longer. My heart pounding, I turned and ran back to Betskoi House.

I made it to the front steps before I dared to look behind me. Danilo was seated once again on the bench, his hood back over his face. But I knew he was watching me. I hurried inside past the guards at the portico and slammed the front door shut, locking every bolt.

"Is something wrong, Duchess?" the footman asked.

"Do not, for any reason, allow any of the Montenegrin siblings to enter our house. Do you understand?" I was trembling and my voice was shaky.

He nodded, and the brief look of surprise was carefully concealed. "Of course, Duchess."

I hoped to slip up to my room unnoticed, but Maman caught me on the staircase.

"Katiya, where have you been? You look like you've been romping in the yard with the dogs!"

I halfheartedly smoothed my hair and sighed. "Just getting some fresh air. But it gave me a headache and now I should go to bed early."

"But we are having dinner at the Vladimir Palace tonight."

I sighed. "Please, Maman, we should stay home."

"Not attend Miechen's dinner party?" She looked at me as if I'd grown another head. "Katerina, if you are feeling poorly, I will allow you to stay home, but I wouldn't miss Miechen's dinner party for the world! Her French chef is divine!"

Not divine, but probably fae, I remembered unhappily. The grand duchess always did have a passion for the exotic.

"No one is going anywhere tonight," Papa said as the footman let him in. He took off his hat with a frown. "Except Katerina."

George Alexandrovich entered the house behind him. He did not look happy either. Nevertheless, he seemed like my knight in shining armor when he clicked his heels together and said, "Katerina Alexandrovna, you must come with me immediately."

CHAPTER TWELVE

"What has happened?" I asked, rushing back down the stairs.

Papa put a heavy hand on my shoulder and squeezed gently. "I should let the grand duke explain everything to you." He turned to my mother and asked, "Shenia, will you have Anya begin packing a trunk for Katiya?"

Maman gave a frightened little cry. "She must leave now? Where is she going?"

"I'll explain it to you in a minute, my dear. You must tell Anya to hurry. They do not have much time." He led Maman gently up the stairs with her exclaiming the whole way.

I looked at George, who was standing in the hall at the foot of the staircase. "Tell me what has happened," I demanded.

"You were right about the lich tsar. He is here, in St. Petersburg, and he's been raising a new army of the undead."

"Then I need to help your father." We would be summoning the bogatyr to fight Konstantin Pavlovich.

George shook his head. "No. The Koldun believes it is not safe for my father to go through the ritual again. There is another weapon we think might work."

"And you want to leave your father unprotected to look for this weapon?"

"He is safe, Katiya, for the time being. Both the Order of St. John and the Order of St. Lazarus are escorting him and my mother back to Gatchina tonight. The Koldun is under heavy guard as well. You are the one we are concerned about."

"Me?" I could not help thinking Danilo's words might be true. That I was a liability to the tsar as long as I was alive. Should I tell George that I'd just been standing in the Field of Mars speaking with the lich tsar?

"Without your powers, Konstantin cannot fully return to life."

"But he's a powerful sorcerer." Before he'd married the blood drinker and necromancer Princess Cantacuzene, he'd been the Koldun for his elder brother, Tsar Alexander the First.

"He is a powerful sorcerer without a physical body. He cannot perform any rituals himself."

"But he could possess someone else and use their body," I suggested.

George stared at me, and I realized neither he nor the Koldun had thought of this possibility. "He could not pick just any body to possess," George said. "It would have to be someone to whom he was closely linked. Like you." He put his hands on my shoulders and squeezed them gently. "But you will be safe, I promise.

76

I'm taking you to Gatchina tonight. The palace is built like a fortress. No one can get to you there."

"I can't go with you alone!"

"Your brother is going as a chaperone," he said with a grim smile. "And my parents will be there soon as well."

That did not make me feel any better. How could I face his parents now? I'd chosen medicine over marriage to their son. The empress might be happy that I would not become a daughter-in-law, but like the tsar, she did not believe women should become doctors.

"And Xenia will be delighted to have you. She has been lonely since her Greek cousins left."

One more thing for the empress to be displeased with. I was certain to be labeled an inappropriate influence on the grand duchess.

"And what about this weapon you're seeking?"

"It's an ancient sword, rumored to command a magical army when held by a necromancer."

"You want me to use the sword?" I asked.

George laughed. "Don't be ridiculous. We just want to keep the sword from falling into Konstantin's hands."

I was irritated by his dismissive tone. I'd never wielded a heavy sword before, but I had taken fencing with Petya when we were young. Our tutor had often told me I was the better pupil. "Fine," I said at last. If it was the tsar's will to lock me up as a prisoner, there was nothing I could do.

"You must be ready to leave immediately, Katiya. We are expected at Gatchina by nightfall."

I excused myself and returned to my room to help Anya pack.

How long did they expect me to stay? I got down on my hands and knees and pulled A *Necromancer's Companion* from under my bed. Would I have need of the book at the palace? Or should I take my medical texts to study? I decided to take both.

"Katiya?" Maman came sweeping into my room. "Dearest, Papa has told me you are going to be a houseguest of the empress at Gatchina for a few days. Have you reconsidered the grand duke's proposal?"

"No, Maman." I closed my trunk and went to embrace her. "I don't think the empress would be happy with a Dark Court daughter-in-law."

"And why not? You know very well that just because she is from the Light Court of the North does not mean all Romanovs must marry Light Court. My Romanov mother married a Dark Court husband. Twice, actually."

I smiled. It was such a simple thing to Maman. She was still dreaming about Romanov grandbabies. "I will be home as soon as I can." If the tsar ever decided to let me go.

"Whatever for? Enjoy your stay, darling. And give my warm regards to the empress."

"Of course."

Papa came to my doorway as well. "The grand duke is getting anxious, Katiya. Are you ready?"

I ran to his arms and hugged him with all my strength. "Please be careful, Papa. And look after Maman." Danilo had planted a seed of doubt in my mind. Would the tsar find some way of dispatching me in order to protect himself from Konstantin? I tried to shrug off the ridiculous suspicion but found I couldn't. Perhaps the tsar would not stoop so low, but I knew the Koldun would. He'd had no qualms about sacrificing Princess Alix when he believed it would protect the tsar. And Alix still had not forgiven him.

"Of course, my dear," Papa said. "Petya will be joining you later this evening. He is currently out on patrols with his regiment." I already knew this. The Preobrajensky Guard was out searching for more of the undead.

I took one last look around my room, making sure I'd remembered everything. I did not know if I'd be able to send for anything I'd forgotten. Papa helped me carry my trunk downstairs, despite Maman's protests that we had servants for that very purpose.

George was looking at his watch unhappily. He glanced up as we descended the staircase. "Very good," he said. "My driver can take the trunk from here."

I followed him silently to the carriage, thanking him only when he helped me inside. It would be a long drive to Gatchina, which was nearly thirty miles outside of St. Petersburg.

As we rolled out of the driveway, he leaned over and picked up my hand, pressing it to his lips. I closed my eyes. It was the same hand Danilo had claimed earlier. Why couldn't I simply choose to be a good wife to George? But I knew I would never be happy just staying at home and raising a family. Maman had her charities and her social obligations, but I wanted more than the life she had with Papa. I wanted George and I wanted my medical degree too. I wanted everything.

"Katiya, I have a plan."

I opened my eyes. George was caressing my hand with his thumb and looking extremely serious. I realized we were alone in the carriage on a dark night. The quarters suddenly seemed much smaller. "What are you saying?"

"We are not going to Gatchina. We are going to Paris. We will be married and you can attend whichever medical university you wish."

I stared at him incredulously. "Have you gone mad? What about your parents?"

"Do you think I will be happy if I continue to obey their every wish for the rest of my life? This is my life, and yours. And I want both of us to be happy. Together."

"Did you just decide this?" I asked. "I thought your parents were waiting for me at Gatchina."

"They are." He smiled. "But I began to make plans of my own last night, when the guards notified us that the crown prince had returned to St. Petersburg."

"What does this have to do with Danilo?"

George held my hands up between us, the silvery fae sparkle in his eyes flashing in the darkness. "I know he's been in contact with you. And I know you are frightened of him. He will always thirst for your blood, Katiya. The bond between you two must be severed somehow. I don't know if it's even possible while both of you are alive."

I felt chilled. "Are you saying you want the crown prince dead?"

George let out a frustrated breath. "That would make our lives simpler, wouldn't it? But no. I just do not want him anywhere around you. I'm taking you to Paris, where I can keep you safe."

I'd always wanted to see Paris. But not like this, running off in the night like a thief. And certainly not without the tsar's permission.

"We have passports," George said.

"But mine is issued under my father's name."

"Not any longer. You are listed under mine, as my wife."

Women and young girls were not allowed to leave Russia without their father's or husband's permission. I found it barbaric that even at the end of the nineteenth century, I was considered a man's property. Still, the thought of running away from all of our problems sounded so tempting.

George was stroking my hand again. "We'll be married before we reach the border. An Orthodox priest will meet us in Riga at dawn."

I leaned back and closed my eyes again. I knew my parents had a country estate near Riga. "What if our families come after us? And the imperial guard? Or even worse, Konstantin?"

"Trust me," George said, his mouth suddenly very close to my ear. My body flooded with a tingling warmth. His lips moved from my earlobe to my cheek and then down my jawline. His hands cupped my face, pulling me toward him. I kept my eyes closed and dwelled solely on the physical sensations. My fingers brushed over the medals on his coat, the golden fringe on his shoulders.

"Katiya," he murmured. "Once we're on the train, we'll have a whole night to amuse ourselves. What will we do?"

I blushed. "Sleep, I'm sure."

He laughed softly. "Duchess, I love you so."

It felt so good to hear his laugh. At that moment, I knew I would risk everything to have a life with him, just as he was risking everything for me. "I love you too," I whispered, pulling him back to me.

CHAPTER THIRTEEN

I insisted we sleep in separate berths, for I was terrified that the train would be stopped and boarded by the imperial guards or that our families would find us.

George was more concerned about the lich tsar. He insisted on sleeping in the berth below mine. I'd never slept so close to a boy before. Just knowing that he was lying beneath me, listening to his breathing all night long, filled me with fear and excitement. I was terrified and anxious for what the morning would bring. And I wondered and fantasized about our sleeping arrangements the following night.

The rocking of the train lulled me to sleep much faster than I'd expected. I dreamed of the lich tsar and his wife, Princess Cantacuzene. She was laughing at me and telling me that my time was up.

I awoke to bright sunshine and the sound of George coughing. Immediately, I pulled on my robe and slipped out of my sleeping berth. I needed to find him something to drink.

"Katiya?" His voice was weak as he emerged from his berth. "Did I wake you?"

"Of course not," I lied. "Let me ring for the porter. I'll get you a glass of water."

He reached out and touched my sleeve. "No, don't. I'll be fine in a moment. It's always like this in the mornings." He looked up at me and grinned boyishly. "I hope you can get used to it."

I couldn't help blushing, even though his breathing worried me. "How long have you had this cough?"

"Since the duel," he said grimly. He took my hands in both of his. "I am putting my faith in you, my lady doctor."

I kissed his knuckles. "I swear I will find a way to make you well."

The train's whistle blew and the engine lurched as we sped through the dark green forests of Latvia. We would soon be in Riga. "Hurry up and get dressed, Katiya. We've got a priest waiting on us."

I scrambled into the dressing closet with my baggage and paused. What should I wear today to be married in? Not the blue satin or the brown walking suit I wore to see Dr. Badmaev. And certainly not my imperial court dress, which I would have worn if I were getting married properly in St. Petersburg. I shook out the white linen dress I'd worn to the last ball I'd been to in the Crimea.

Even though it was slightly warmer here than it had been in St. Petersburg, it was still chilly, and I realized Maman would never forgive me for wearing linen in October. Even if she did forgive me for eloping. I finally decided on my soft gray blue silk gown, the one that matched the color of George's eyes. I had little difficulty putting my hair up without a maid's help. But I missed Anya all the same.

George was waiting for me in the dining car. "We do have time for a short breakfast," he said as he took a sip of coffee. "The tea is tolerable and the bread is fresh, but we will have better provisions once we reach Paris."

But I couldn't eat. I was sipping my tea impatiently when the train finally rolled into the station in Riga.

George began coughing again and stood up, patting his coat pockets. "I think I've misplaced my handkerchief."

"I'll get it for you," I said, rushing back to the sleeping car. I looked in his berth and was shocked to see drops of blood on his pillowcase. Horrified, I snatched up a clean handkerchief and returned to him. "George, you're bleeding!"

"I cough it up sometimes." He frowned. "It's nothing."

"It could be tuberculosis," I pointed out.

"Or it could be a Vladiki poison that infected me when I fought the crown prince."

I wasn't sure which option frightened me more.

We stepped off the train, arm in arm, and George hired a carriage to take us to the chapel. He squeezed my hand comfortingly. I smiled, trying to be brave. I couldn't help thinking he was making the worst mistake of his life. But if he was willing to risk so much for me, it would have been cowardly of me to back down. Together, we would face the brunt of our families' ire. After the lich tsar was defeated and George was healthy.

The young and extremely nervous black-bearded priest refused to marry us before he'd heard both of our confessions. I could not imagine what George had to confess. But I was terrified of speaking to the young man. I had brought dead people back to life. Would it be better or worse for my soul if I lied during my confession? He would surely throw us both out of the chapel if I told him all the terrible things I'd done.

I sat on a wooden bench, twisting my hands, my stomach a mass of knots while I waited for George to finish. All I could hear from the confessional were low, soft male voices. George was taking forever. *Mon Dieu*, how many sins did he have to confess? My nerves could not handle it anymore, so I stood up and stepped outside for fresh air.

I looked up at the brilliant sky on that golden autumn morning and took a deep breath. The air was crisp, and I could detect smoke from some nearby fireplace. But leaving the chapel was the worst mistake I'd ever made.

A black cloth was placed across my face with a sickeningly sweet and vaguely familiar odor. The last thing I heard as I quickly slipped out of consciousness was a voice, also sickeningly familiar: "We've found you, my love."

CHAPTER FOURTEEN

I awoke with a throbbing headache and a feeling of dread in my stomach. I was on a train. With Crown Prince Danilo. "What have you done?" I screamed at him, which made my head hurt a thousand times worse. The pain brought tears to my eyes. Or perhaps it was the fact that he'd stolen me away from my fiancé. What would George think? That I'd had a change of heart? I squeezed my eyes shut. Perhaps he could hear my thoughts and would be able to come for me.

"You belong to me now, necromancer." Danilo's voice was deadly soft, not like the lich tsar's had been earlier. And yet I still knew it was Konstantin speaking. He'd claimed Danilo's body.

"Danilo, can you still hear me?" I pleaded. "I know you must be in there. Fight him!"

The crown prince slapped me across the face with such force

I was knocked back against the wooden panel behind me. I saw stars.

I heard a young female voice laughing and opened my eyes. A girl sat across from me, not far from Danilo, dressed in the black habit of an Orthodox sister. The headdress she wore was simple and covered her hair. The girl's soft, gray eyes glittered dangerously. Was she fae or some more-dreaded creature? I'd have to be wary of her.

"Where are we?" I asked. The bright afternoon sunlight stung my eyes.

"Almost to Trieste," the crown prince said. "The chloroform kept you sleeping for almost two days. I am sure you must be hungry, Duchess. I will have them bring you a tray." He nodded at the girl, who slipped out of our cabin.

"Who is she?" I asked the crown prince.

"She is your chaperone, and that is all you need to know at the moment. When she brings you dinner, you must eat."

I shook my head, and the tiny cabin began to spin. I did not want food. I wanted a bath. And a bed. In my own home in St. Petersburg.

George. I blushed as I realized I should have been a married woman by now. Two days? Had my grand duke tried to look for me? *Trieste, Georgi,* I thought as hard as I could, hoping he could hear my thoughts from hundreds of miles away. *He's taking me to Trieste.*

I received another slap to the face as the veiled girl returned. "There is no reason for you to tell the tsar's son where you are, my love. He will not bother to come looking for you now that I have you."

"I don't believe you," I said. But deep in my heart I was frightened by Danilo's words. George would want nothing to do with me if he thought the crown prince had compromised me in any way. And since I'd been unconscious for so long, he would not have been able to hear my thoughts. My hands were bound tightly together; I had no hope of escaping, and no way to defend myself against Danilo.

No, against Konstantin, I corrected myself mentally. Danilo's greatest fear had been that the lich tsar would use their bond and possess his body. I did not know which of them was my greater enemy. The lich tsar inhabiting a powerful Vladiki's body would be unstoppable. All he needed was a necromancer bride and his return to power would be complete.

"Yes, you will become my bride, Katerina. Not the grand duke's." He was able to read my thoughts so easily. My head hurt far too much for me to focus on keeping him out.

"Why are you taking me to Trieste?" I asked. "Why not back to Montenegro?"

"All in good time, my love. I would not want you to give away our secrets to the tsar's men."

I stopped trying to hold on to consciousness as the train rocked gently. I couldn't fight the oblivion any longer.

CHAPTER FIFTEEN

When I woke again, the train was pulling into a new station. It was daytime, most likely midmorning by the position of the sun. Danilo put a fur muff over my bound hands and wrapped my coat around my shoulders. With an iron grip, he steered me off the train and toward a waiting carriage. "Do not make a sound. I don't want to mar that pretty face of yours again."

The girl in the black habit followed us silently. She would obviously not help me if I tried to escape.

My head was still throbbing. I wondered if my face was bruised from where I'd been hit. Would people notice? "Where are you taking me?" I asked.

Danilo squeezed my arm tighter, and I worried that he would actually break it. Mentally I listed the bones in the arm: ulna, radius, humerus. The hand: carpals, metacarpals. I stumbled a little as he guided me into the carriage.

I had no idea how much time had passed since the last time I'd been conscious. One day? Two? I knew we were in Trieste from the signs at the train terminal, but what was in this god-forsaken city? I smelled signs of the sea as we rode in the carriage through the streets. We approached a crowded harbor.

"Are we boarding a boat?" I asked.

Danilo smiled, but the green eyes gazing back at me were Konstantin's. "You are at the start of a long journey, Katerina," he said. "Already you are quite a ways from home."

I remembered Militza's tarot card. Had she known what was happening to her brother? And what he had planned? "Your sisters must be worried about you, Danilo," I ventured.

His eyes changed back to the crown prince's piercing black. He looked confused.

"Can you fight Konstantin?" I whispered. "Do you know where we are?"

"We're going to Egypt. He's looking for the sword." Danilo looked dazed, and scared. Of himself.

"What sword?" I asked, but before he could answer, the lich tsar was back in control. "Think about your sisters, Dani," I begged. That seemed to help him hold on and concentrate. "Militza and Anastasia are worried about you, I'm certain. They will come looking for you."

But Danilo was gone again. The lich tsar sneered at me. "They have no power over me, Duchess. Your powers are the only ones I am concerned with." His hand reached out and I flinched, but this time he was chillingly tender. He only caressed my jawline. "Soon I will show you what delightful wickedness a necromancer is born to do."

The carriage had pulled into the chaotic harbor. I was

alarmed. Egypt was thousands of miles away from St. Petersburg. Why would Konstantin take me there? Was the sword he searched for the same one George had spoken of? Surely it couldn't be a coincidence.

The harbor was teeming with people shouting in all sorts of languages. I heard threads of conversations in German, Italian, French, and even some Greek. The sea air was hot and damp, uncomfortable for a day in late autumn.

Two strange-looking men met us at the docks. They gave the crown prince three boarding passes for the steamer in front of us. With the boarding passes in one hand, Danilo gripped my arm again with his other and guided me toward the steamer. The girl in the black habit followed behind, directing a man carrying luggage whom I had not noticed earlier.

For less than a second I thought about crying out for help; Danilo had already heard my thoughts. "If you want your family to remain safe, you will stay quiet and do exactly as you're told," he warned. "These men have comrades stationed in St. Petersburg awaiting my orders. I'd hate for some sort of accident to befall the Duchess of Oldenburg. Or your proud papa."

I felt sick but remained silent. Who were these men who would follow such madness? They looked odd, not quite right. Not undead, as I had first thought, but not human either. They had no cold lights at all. What could it mean? I tried not to stumble as he pushed me up the gangplank. Danilo showed our boarding passes to the ship's purser, who welcomed us aboard.

"Allow me to show you to your cabin," a young man in a smart sailor's uniform said. He led us to a suite on one of the upper levels. It appeared we would be sailing in comfort, and perhaps for a long time.

"Why must we go to Egypt?" I demanded as Danilo pushed me into my room. "That girl is not an appropriate chaperone. I don't even know her name."

He ignored me. "You'll find your new trousseau has already been taken care of."

I noticed a trunk in the corner of the cabin. "I will not marry you, Danilo."

He smiled, and once again the crown prince's sad eyes stared back at me. "It would make your life so much easier if you stopped fighting me, my love. I will untie you as soon as the steamer puts off." He turned to go but stopped to look back at me with another grim smile. "It would not be wise of you to try and swim back to Europe."

I sank down onto my bed, my wrists raw from the tight ropes, and stared in horror at the trunk on the floor. This had to be a nightmare. I prayed to wake up, safe in St. Petersburg. *George*, I thought miserably, *please find me. Hurry.*

My cabin was cramped but elegant, and must have cost Danilo a small fortune. The bed was made with soft French linens, and there was wooden paneling on the walls. I looked out the tiny window to see the brilliant blue waters of the Mediterranean. I refused to think about what awaited me at the end of this journey.

I fell asleep on the bed waiting for Danilo to come and untie my hands. It was dark by the time he returned. The strange men were with him. "Who are you?" I asked, looking at one directly as I rubbed my newly freed wrists. He remained silent.

"They are servants of the sword, Duchess," Danilo said. "They are loyal to me, and when I possess the sword known as the Morning Star, their brothers will all be compelled to follow me. We will return to St. Petersburg in triumph and defeat Alexander Alexandrovich once and for all."

The crown prince was losing control over his body. I worried that his personality was starting to melt with the lich tsar's. Would Danilo be lost forever? There had to be a way to defeat Konstantin Pavlovich without destroying Danilo.

The Morning Star must have been the weapon of which George had spoken. A weapon to be wielded only by a necromancer. "What sort of creatures are these men?" I asked the crown prince.

"They are the Grigori. Their kind has been in hiding for thousands of years."

I'd heard of them before. George and the French wizard Papus had mentioned the Grigori when we'd been in the Crimea last year. But they had not told me who the Grigori were. "Are they blood drinkers?" I asked.

"Of course not!" Danilo said.

"But they are not alive."

"They do not die. But it is not the same as being undead." Danilo was in that strange limbo, where he was not quite himself but not quite Konstantin.

"Why must a necromancer carry their sword, then?" I asked.

"Why must a necromancer perform the ritual to summon the bogatyr?" he countered. "Both require your ability to manipulate cold light."

"But the Grigori do not have a cold light." None that I had seen, anyway.

The lich tsar's eyes gleamed in Danilo's face. "The Morning Star provides them with cold light." He stood up and looked out the tiny window at the setting sun. "You should dress for dinner.

I will return to take you to the ship's dining room at eight o'clock."

When I was left alone, I sighed and opened the trunk to examine the dresses Danilo had provided. There were expensive gowns from Paris, smart English riding suits, and flimsy nightgowns that made me blush. I decided I would sleep in my own clothes, in the gray-blue gown I had intended to wear at my wedding. My heart twisted as I slipped out of the dress and laid it on the bed. I had to believe that George Alexandrovich was searching for me. That I would be rescued soon.

I selected a pale rose gown for dinner. Its neckline was the highest of all the gowns in the wardrobe, even though it was much lower than any of my gowns at home. I carefully put away the others, praying this trip would be over soon and I would not have to wear anything else that Danilo had bought me.

CHAPTER SIXTEEN

Danilo escorted me on his arm up to the first-class deck, which held the dining room, the smoking room, and the billiards room. I heard one of the passengers in the hallway mentioning a library as well. I hoped I'd be allowed some freedom while we were on board. It was obvious I could not escape back to Russia from here.

The dining saloon for the first-class passengers on the steamer was a beautiful mahogany-paneled room with heavy velvet drapes blocking out the blazing setting sun. The plush red carpet was decorated with golden medallions. An enormous chandelier swayed gently as we passed beneath it. We had been lucky to have calm seas on the Mediterranean so far.

The oyster pie and beef Wellington were both excellent, and I enjoyed dinner despite myself. Of course, it had been days since I'd had a proper meal, and the chloroform was now completely out of my body.

Danilo signaled to the waiter to refill my glass of wine. "You look beautiful tonight, Katerina."

I was suddenly suspicious of the wine. I decided not to drink any more and sipped from my water goblet instead. Ignoring his compliment, I asked, "How long have you been planning this journey?"

"Ever since I discovered the existence of the sword."

"How did you learn of it?"

"An ancient book of Johanna's. And something Militza discovered during her honeymoon in Egypt." His voice was strange again. Not quite Danilo's, not quite Konstantin's. He was turning into a completely new personality altogether. The thought frightened me. I would have never believed such a thing possible. "Johanna had a book about the Grigori and their years of service to Vlad Dracul. The Impaler at one time wielded the Morning Star himself."

"How did he acquire it?" I asked as the waiter whisked our plates away and replaced them with berry compotes and a plate of cheeses and fruits.

"He stole it from the Ottoman pasha. Unfortunately, the Ottomans stole it back at Vlad's deathbed."

"How did the sword end up in Egypt?" I asked. The compote was heavily spiced with cinnamon and nutmeg and something else I could not place.

"It's believed to be hidden in the ruins of an ancient Coptic chapel. Or it could be hidden within the Graylands."

Coptic? I'd never been anywhere near this far from home before. The thought filled me with despair. George would never be able to find me once we reached Egypt.

Danilo drank the last of his wine and watched me. His eyes

had changed again, and now they were no longer his piercing black, nor were they the emerald green of the lich tsar's. Instead, they'd blended to a grayish hazel. The color was startling against Danilo's olive skin, and not unattractive. That was a disturbing thought that I pushed out of my mind as swiftly as I could.

"Come, I have a gift for you." He reached into his coat pocket and drew out a piece of jewelry.

"That's not necess—" I started, but then I saw what he held in his hand. "How did you get that?"

It was the Talisman of Isis. It belonged in the Vorontsov Palace with the Order of St. Lazarus. Miles away from where we were.

He smiled. "Do not concern yourself with how I obtained it. I believe it will prove extremely useful, Duchess." He stood up behind me and placed the talisman around my neck. I shivered as his cold fingers brushed against my bare skin. As a necromancer, I was the only one who could use the talisman. It allowed me to summon undead beings to my aid. But I was loathe to do so, and I prayed that it would not be necessary.

"Why do you even need me?" I asked, thankful when he began to pace the room. It made me nervous when he stood so close to me. Konstantin had once been a sorcerer, and if he was using Danilo's body, he would have no problem drawing upon all of his powers and using the Morning Star to fight the bogatyr.

"Why?" He stared at me with his strange hazel eyes. "Because I must have a necromancer for a bride, Katerina. You shall be the next empress of all the Russias. And the mother of the next heir to the throne."

A wave of nausea rolled in my stomach. "I will never marry you," I said. But I was scared and uncertain. I had no way of defending myself against him. What if he took me by force?

Danilo laughed, my thoughts crystal clear to him. "Your precious virtue is safe, Katerina. For the moment. We shall marry in St. Petersburg in front of the church patriarch and all of the Romanovs." He stopped his pacing and walked around behind me, lifting a loose curl from my shoulder. "And then, dear Katerina," he whispered in my ear, "then you will be mine."

CHAPTER SEVENTEEN

D anilo left me alone in the dining saloon, for which I was grateful. I wanted nothing more than to escape back to my cabin in peace. I spotted the two Grigori on the observation deck, speaking in hushed tones with the girl in the black habit. As much as I wished to retire to bed, I wanted to learn more about my traveling companions.

The full moon was high in the sky, lighting up the sea almost as bright as daylight. The moonlight also lent an unholy look to the pale, stone-faced men as I approached them. They were taller than any of the other men I'd seen on the boat, and they towered over the girl. "Why are you here with the crown prince?" I asked. "Why would you want to help him?"

The one on the right appeared to be the older of the two. "We serve the sword, Duchess. When the sword calls, we must obey."

The girl's smile wasn't friendly. "We must all obey the lich tsar, including you."

"But he doesn't possess the sword yet," I said. "What has convinced you to obey him now?"

She shrugged. "He has you. And you will help him find the sword soon enough."

I turned back to the strange men. "What if the one who holds the sword is wicked? Are you still forced to serve that person?"

The elder Grigori looked down at me, his face impassive. He reminded me of the members of the Order of St. Lazarus. "The sword itself is very wicked, my lady. Do you not know who first carried the Morning Star? It was Lucifer himself. With that sword, he led the angels' rebellion."

I stared at him as the meaning of his words sank in. The breeze off the water had turned chilly, and my hair was beginning to fall from its carefully arranged knot. I rubbed my arms and hugged myself. What made Konstantin believe he had the power to wield Lucifer's sword? "You are demons, then. Fallen from heaven."

"Not demons, though they are our brethren. When the Grigori fell, they were trapped on earth in physical bodies. Not mortal, but not able to leave this plane either."

"And you cannot die." What a terrible army they would make. A formidable match for my own undead soldiers. No wonder Danilo wanted the Grigori on his side.

He smiled, but the gesture did not make him appear any friendlier. "No."

His companion, the younger-looking one, said something to him in a language unfamiliar to me. Nodding, the older of the two looked back at me. "It is true. You are a necromancer and you could wield the Morning Star. But are you strong enough to command the Grigori?"

The girl laughed. "I think not."

"And who exactly are you?" I asked, whirling on her. "What has Danilo promised for your part in all of this?"

Her eyes hardened. "The crown prince has not promised anything. And what has been promised to me is not your concern." She stalked off, leaving me alone with the Grigori.

"Are you here against your will?" I asked the younger one. When he looked at his elder and they both nodded, it gave me a little courage. They probably had as much reason to hate the crown prince as I did. "So why would you allow Danilo to command you to fight the current tsar and his family?"

"We are condemned to chaos, Duchess. It is our nature," the elder Grigori said.

"You don't wish for something different?" I asked. "Don't you grow tired of the battles?"

The younger one spoke up. "We've been weary of the battles and the fighting for a thousand years already. But nothing will ever change. The sword passes from man to man, and we follow the sword."

"What if the sword was destroyed?" There had to be a way to keep the Grigori safe from the lich tsar's clutches.

The elder Grigori's face remained impassive. "The Morning Star was forged in heaven itself. It cannot be destroyed."

Their lack of emotion was unsettling. They were like wooden soldiers. I decided to return to my cabin before they tired of answering my questions. Hopefully I would be able to talk to them again before reaching Egypt.

When I got back to my cabin, I remembered that my copy of *A Necromancer's Companion* had been left behind in Riga, with George. I slumped down on the elegant iron bed, wishing I had the book with me to research the Grigori. Surely there would be information in Princess Cantacuzene's book about the creatures. Especially if they were linked to necromancers. I'd heard Danilo call them Watchers, but that implied that the Grigori stood back and did not interfere in the human lives around them. This was an inaccurate assumption, I feared.

I wondered what George had done with my things. The book was surely lost to me now, along with the medical texts Dr. Badmaev had given me. I sighed. The Tibetan doctor's clinic seemed so far away, and medicine was of no help in my predicament. Magic was what I needed. And total command over my cold light powers.

I took a last look at the moonlit waves from the porthole and wished on the one bright star I could see. I wished that I would live to see George at least one more time. It was purely selfish of me, and if I'd truly believed a wish had any chance of coming true, I should have used it to wish for the defeat of Konstantin. But I was afraid I'd need the power of every last star in the sky to accomplish that.

CHAPTER EIGHTEEN

It was three days before we put in to the rocky harbor of Alexandria. The passage through the rocks was narrow and only navigable in daylight, so the steamer had dropped anchor right outside the entrance and waited until dawn to approach. The grand viceroy's palace could be seen on a cliff high to the right of the harbor.

I could not help being a little excited about seeing Egypt. Even though I was terrified for the reason I was there. I'd always wanted to see the pyramids and the treasures of the pharaohs. I had the craziest notion of being able to purchase gifts for my family in case I made it home safely.

Then I realized I had no money. I'd had only a few rubles among my things at Riga, not enough to even buy a vial of perfume for Maman or a papyrus scroll for Papa. I sighed as I dressed in a soft light-green walking gown of linen.

Danilo knocked on my door to take me to breakfast. "We

should have something to eat before leaving the steamer. It will be a busy day for us, Duchess."

"Is the sword here in Alexandria? Why hasn't anyone stolen it before now?"

"All in good time," he said with a firm grasp of my arm. "The Grigori are waiting for us."

But the Grigori did not eat. They sat with us silently while I choked down a too-hot mug of coffee and nibbled dry toast. The girl in the black habit joined us and appeared to be enjoying some sort of sweet pastry. It smelled like cinnamon and nutmeg and looked much more appetizing than my own toast, but I did not have time to ask her where she'd gotten it. Danilo seemed to be in a hurry and was anxious for us to leave the boat.

Danilo spoke to the two Grigori in their ancient language, which later that morning I learned was Coptic. The Grigori did not seem to have any luggage with them and followed us silently as we disembarked.

It took less time than expected to move through customs. Danilo must have bribed the officials not to ask me too many questions. We joined the Grigori in a hired carriage and drove through crowded dirt streets to the Hotel Khedivial, one of the luxury-class accommodations in the city. The sounds of the city were like nothing I'd ever encountered before. The carriage fought for its space in the road with hacks, other carriages, donkeys, and women carrying earthen jugs on their heads. Half-naked children ran through the crowds, and merchants shouted out their wares. I could hear the squawking of chickens and other animals high above the din.

The hotel was very European but also exotic with its Moroccan tiled lobby. Danilo kept an iron grip on my arm, and the mysterious sister stayed close at my other side as the elder Grigori saw to us checking in. The porter, a young boy who looked no more than twelve or thirteen, appeared to take care of our luggage. He gave me a cheeky grin as he single-handedly picked up my trunk. I knew with a sad smile where the last of my rubles would be spent.

As we followed him up the stairs, I could hear the music from the hotel's restaurant. A woman was singing a haunting tune. I could not help realizing that it would be difficult not to fall in love with Egypt.

My room was a luxurious suite decorated with painted tiles and lush enormous palms. Gauzy white linens hung around my bed. "They are to protect you from mosquitoes," the young porter said. I pulled the last ruble from my pocket and handed it to him. "Will you be able to exchange this?" I asked. I had nothing else to give him for a tip.

"Of course. Madame is most generous!" he said with a polite bow.

He believed I was married. I wanted to correct him but remained silent. I shuddered as I walked to the window and looked out my balcony. I had a beautiful view of the hotel's courtyard garden below. The scents of jasmine and orange flower rose up and mingled with the lotus blossoms that sat in a crystal bowl on my dresser. It was beautiful, for a prison.

Danilo knocked briefly before walking in. The gray-eyed girl in the black habit was with him. "Katerina, I have been remiss in my introductions," he said, with one hand elegantly on his chest. "Please forgive me. This is Sister Mala, your chaperone."

I nodded as she gave me a brief but polite bow. I supposed I should have been grateful for her presence. She was saving my reputation from ruin. But I don't think she was happy with her assignment. And I did not believe she was a religious sister at all.

"It's my pleasure to serve you, Duchess." Sister Mala's eyes sparkled with malice.

The lich tsar smiled. "I want no scandal surrounding our wedding, Katerina. But rest assured, we will be married soon. And you will be crowned empress before long."

"What makes you think you are the rightful tsar?" I asked dangerously. "You gave up your claim when you married Princess Cantacuzene."

"I did not!" he said, striding toward me so violently I was afraid he was going to strike me again. Instead, he pushed past me and walked to the window. "My younger brother stole my birthright. The descendants of Nicholas Pavlovich will pay for his theft."

My imperial great-grandfather had been called many things, but never a thief. "You married a vampire, Your Highness," I said. "Russian law forbids such a marriage for the tsar."

He turned away from the window and came back to where I stood. "I am the tsar and I am the law of Russia," he said, his voice deadly calm, "and I will marry whomever I choose." He raised his cold fingertips to my chin and tilted my face toward him. "And I choose you, my lovely necromancer. I will never love another as I loved Johanna, but I must marry again and have heirs. The true Romanov dynasty must continue."

"Your Imperial Majesty," Sister Mala said. Such nerve she had treating the imposter as the true tsar. "We have heard disturbing reports of another group of Grigori in the city. We do

106

not know who they are working with, but they seek the Morning Star as well."

The lich tsar let go of me. "We must find out, then," he said to the girl. "No one must reach the Morning Star before I do."

I was left alone in the hotel room as Sister Mala swept out after him. More Grigori? How could they be serving another master?

I had not been told to stay in my room, but I heard the heavy, carved wooden door being locked from the outside. I rushed to the balcony but was disappointed to find the elder Grigori who had accompanied us standing guard below. With no way out and still wearing my clothes, I fell asleep on the bed, from boredom as much as exhaustion. I dreamed of moths fluttering outside the netting that surrounded my bed. Hundreds of the small white-winged creatures were trying to get through the netting. I knew if they reached me they would bite me and steal my blood.

It was not long before I was awakened by voices in the hall. The door unlocked and opened. It was the elder Grigori. "You must come with me," he said softly, pushing back the netting. I gasped, but there were no moths to be seen. It had only been a nightmare. "You are in danger here, Duchess."

With a swift move, he pulled me up from the bed and toward the French door leading onto the balcony. My balcony was shared with the room next to mine, so we stole quietly into the neighboring room. It was Danilo's. But Danilo and the mysterious Sister Mala were not there. We heard footsteps in the hallway—and then the sound of my door crashing open.

CHAPTER NINETEEN

The Grigori motioned for me to be silent, but it was not necessary. I was too scared to make a noise. We heard hushed voices in my room, and I strained my ears to make out the language. French?

My rescuer pulled me back from the balcony and showed me a hidden door behind the curtains. A secret staircase led down into darkness. "Follow me, Duchess," he whispered.

He did not seem to need a light to see where we were going. Blind, I placed my hands along the rough stucco walls to guide myself down the stairs. When the Grigori reached the bottom, he opened a door and the stairwell was flooded with light. I skipped down the rest of the stairs to follow him.

We were in an empty passageway lit by several small windows along the upper walls. "This is the basement of the hotel, Duchess," the Grigori explained. "It is a safe way out."

The passageway was narrow and winding, but we reached a

door that was locked from the outside. "Now what?" I asked, beginning to panic.

The Grigori did not reply but knocked once, then two more times upon the heavy wood. Nothing happened at first; then we heard the lock give way and the door swung open inward.

Sister Mala was standing outside. "Hurry!" she said. Behind her in the alley, a black carriage waited for us. She pulled me by the arm and pushed me inside. Danilo was already waiting for me. Sister Mala stayed with the Grigori as the carriage took off. I turned around in alarm, but Danilo took my hand.

"They will be fine, love. It is you and I they are after."

"Who is after us? The grand duke?" My heart began to race. Had I just escaped from George's rescue? I tried to pull free of Danilo's grasp and look back, but the crowded city traffic already blocked my view of the hotel.

Danilo shook his head grimly. "The Order of the Black Lily. They seek the Morning Star as well."

"The French mages?" Papus and Sucre had tried to raise Konstantin from the dead by sacrificing Princess Alix. "I thought they were working with you."

"Not any longer." Danilo's grip tightened around my wrist. "They have Grigori on their side as well, Katerina. If they catch us, it will be unpleasant."

"And Papus is working with the Romanovs?" Hope surged within my chest. Perhaps I was about to be rescued.

"Papus will side with whoever pays him the most. And I do not think the Romanovs are the wealthiest players on this chessboard." Danilo stared out the window, frowning as we went speeding through Alexandria.

"If there's someone else who wants the sword, why are the

French mages after us?" I asked. "Why don't they just try to find the sword before we do?"

"I'm sure they are pursuing both goals with equal determination. The Grigori are fierce, and every last one of them has been stirred by the possibility of the sword's return."

"We can't run from the French mages forever," I pointed out.

"No, but we will run toward Cairo, where the fight will be more evenly matched." He nodded toward the window. "We should be there in a few hours. More of our Grigori are there waiting for us."

"*Our* Grigori? How do you keep their loyalty, Danilo?"

His laugh was short, and tired, I thought. "That is not something you should worry your pretty little head over, my dear."

I leaned back and closed my eyes, thinking my family must be frantic about me by now. If not furious. What if they believed I'd run off on my own? Would George have traveled back to St. Petersburg and said nothing of his elopement plans? My mother must be hysterical. And what would the tsar and the empress think? I did not know if I'd ever be allowed to return to St. Petersburg.

We were passing through the outer streets of Alexandria on the desert road to Cairo. The green waters of the Nile River flowed alongside us, with large dark shapes floating lazily in the water. I shuddered, praying we would not see any crocodiles or snakes up close.

As we neared a dusty crossroads, the carriage stopped with a lurch. I slid forward and would have fallen to the floor if Danilo had not grabbed me.

"*Merci*," I said immediately, out of habit.

Danilo's face was hard. "Please allow me to do all the talking,

Katerina," he said. And before I could ask what he meant, the door on my side opened. An Ottoman, swathed in white, stood pointing a rifle at us. I raised my hands slowly and tried not to make any sudden movements.

"If you would not mind, please step out of the carriage." The Ottoman spoke in perfect, crisp English.

"Let the young girl go," Danilo said, his hands raised like mine. "She knows nothing."

The Ottoman smiled and nodded at me, his white teeth gleaming in the hot sun. "She is more important to us than you, Your Majesty. But we require that both of you join us, just the same."

Such polite manners for an armed man who was kidnapping me. Danilo could take a few lessons from him. Still, I was impressed that the crown prince tried to protect me. My hands still raised cautiously in the air, I stepped out of the carriage, with Danilo following.

Another carriage stood in front of ours, driven by two Grigori. The Ottoman gestured toward the carriage with his rifle. "If you would be so kind."

I hesitated.

"Do as they ask and you will not be in any danger," Danilo murmured. "At least, not yet."

The crown prince's voice in my head startled me. I'd not heard his thoughts since we'd arrived in Egypt. "Danilo?"

"Yes, it is me, but Konstantin is never far. We are becoming one and the same person. With powers beyond my wildest dreams."

"Can you use these powers to keep us safe?" I climbed into the carriage, afraid I would find someone inside with a rifle as well. But the carriage was empty.

I sat down with Danilo sitting next to me.

"*Only with your help, necromancer. I will need your blood and your shadow spells to defeat our meddlesome friends.*"

"Who are these men working for?" I asked.

"They are working for me," a new but familiar French voice said as the door to the other side of the carriage opened. A man in a gray linen suit and a darker gray bowler hat joined us. The mage Papus sat down across from us with a sinister smile. "As will the rest of the Grigori, when I find the Morning Star."

"You betrayed the Koldun and the Order of St. John," I said. "You betrayed the tsar."

Papus did not move a muscle, and yet I felt something cold close around my throat.

Danilo's voice was in my head again, sighing. "*That was not wise, Duchess.*"

I struggled to breathe and remain conscious, even as I saw spots in front of my eyes as the crushing feeling continued to tighten. I grasped for unseen hands, but there was nothing there.

"Leave her be," Danilo said in a bored voice. "You have proven your point. You have become very powerful since we last met."

The French mage rolled his eyes, and the pain vanished. I slumped against Danilo and tried to catch my breath. "*Hold on to your cold light, Katerina,*" the crown prince warned. "*He will steal it from you and use it against you again if you let your guard down.*"

"How can he do such a thing?" I murmured. Papus was not a necromancer. My head was pounding and I just wanted to lie down and sleep. But I concentrated and pulled my cold light as close to me as possible. The white tendrils floating around me began to curl inward.

. "Dear, dear," said Papus. "We cannot have you in suspense, Duchess. But all will be revealed to you soon. For now, sleep."

With the slightest movement of his fingers, I fell into a black oblivion. But not before I felt a tug as Danilo grasped my hand.

CHAPTER TWENTY

I nstead of sleeping, I found myself in the Graylands, the realm of pure cold light. Danilo stood beside me, his cold light so bright it hurt to look at him. "What are we doing here?" I asked.

"We are bound, Duchess. I did not want you getting lost."

"How did you know I was going here?"

"This is where Papus sent you. He intended to follow you himself. Papus can only travel these lands with the aid of a necromancer or by using a Grigori portal." Danilo gave me a wicked grin. "But alas, he could not follow you since I held your hand instead."

I pulled my hand out of his grasp. "How do we get back?" I'd used the Throne of Constantinople the last time I'd been in the Graylands. But the throne had been destroyed by the tsar's men. On my insistence. This place was dangerous.

"We will leave when I say it is time to leave," Danilo said, the raspy voice of Konstantin breaking through. "We have a sword to find."

"I thought we would find the sword in Cairo." I'd half expected to be participating in a necromancy-laced ritual in a dark and dusty pyramid. Instead, I'd been kidnapped, again, and dragged here.

"Or perhaps it is hidden here after all," Danilo said. "I know for a fact there are clues to the sword in the Graylands. Only those who walk with cold light can see them." Konstantin had spent decades trapped in the Graylands, waiting for Princess Cantacuzene to return him to life. He'd had plenty of time to explore this place. "Follow me, Duchess." He walked into the bluish-white mist and disappeared.

Having no other way to leave the Graylands than with him, I too plunged into the mist. Danilo was not far ahead of me. Through the swirls of mist, I could just see the top of his black hair. He called back to me frequently but would not slow down. He knew exactly where he was going in this limbo place.

After what seemed like an hour, he finally stopped. "Here," Danilo said as I caught up with him. He waved his hands and suddenly an arched golden door appeared. He opened it slowly. There was no mist inside the small room, only a basket of papyrus scrolls and a dark-skinned, elderly man in Egyptian dress. He looked up at Danilo, his black eyes filled with hatred.

"Why do you return?" the man said with a scowl. "Have you not tormented me enough, Konstantin Pavlovich?"

Danilo pulled me forward. "I bring you a gift, Ankh-al-Sekhem. Another necromancer. You will be able to share her cold light."

"What?" I asked, dragging myself away from Danilo in alarm.

"All those years I spent waiting for Johanna were not wasted. I learned how to manipulate cold light." The green eyes of the lich tsar glittered as he stared at me. "I learned how to become the most powerful necromancer ever. And yet I could not raise anyone from the dead on my own. Not in this realm where the dead already walk. Their cold lights illuminate the mist. I needed flesh to make my rituals work. I needed a body of my own." He placed his hand on his chest. "I needed a beating heart.

"The knowledge I gained came at a great cost. I studied with the Egyptians and also with the Greek necromancers. I promised a tithe to Ankh-al-Sekhem, the oldest and most powerful necromancer of the ancient world," he went on, nodding toward the Egyptian, seated on a plain pallet on the floor. "I promised that I would return his greatest treasure to him, the Talisman of Isis. But I need the Morning Star before I will do so."

"What does that have to do with me?" I asked. Ankh-al-Sekhem did not look as if he believed Danilo was here to fulfill his promise.

"This Egyptian's apprentice stole the Morning Star from his pharaoh's tomb. He hid it somewhere and was killed by the Grigori before he had a chance to use it or to reveal where he'd hidden it. But his master knows where the apprentice is buried and how we can make his spirit talk to us."

"Give me the talisman, necromancer," the elderly man said, "and I will tell you everything."

"Do you still think us fools, old man?" Danilo sneered. "Tell us where to find your apprentice and then we shall bring you the talisman."

"What can he do with the Talisman of Isis here?" I asked,

116

alarmed. I felt the amulet underneath my clothes, warm against my skin. I prayed the Egyptian necromancer could not sense its presence.

"Nothing," Ankh-al-Sekhem said. "I desire it merely for sentimental reasons."

I didn't trust him, and I knew Danilo did not either. Ankh-al-Sekhem was dangerous, even if he looked frail huddled on the floor.

"What are in these scrolls?" I asked.

"Knowledge, Duchess," he said, grinning a brilliant smile. "Which you are forever seeking. What price would you pay for this knowledge?"

I hesitated. There was only one thing I wanted to know: how to cure George from the magical wound the crown prince had given him. But I did not want Danilo to know he'd hurt the tsar's son so badly. "What price do you ask?"

"Enough of this," Danilo said. "We are not here for dirty scrolls. I have already read every one of these parchments of paper. There is nothing worth sacrificing your cold light over, Duchess."

"Is that even possible?" I asked. "How can a necromancer use the cold light of another?"

"They cannot steal your cold light. It must be given freely. To receive another's light makes the recipient much stronger." Danilo put his hand on the small of my back. It was not a comforting gesture. It felt possessive. I shuddered with revulsion. I would never give my cold light to anyone willingly.

"We must have the sword, Ankh-al-Sekhem," the crown prince said. "Once it's in our possession, you will have all the cold light you desire. And the Talisman of Isis."

"Perhaps I should come with you," the ancient necromancer said as he rose to his feet.

"You must be mad," Danilo said, laughing. "You have been dead for thousands of years."

"She is very powerful," the Egyptian said, nodding toward me, a sly grin on his face. "Powerful enough to bring me back."

"But you would be a monster," I said, horrified at the idea.

"Duchess, I am a monster now." His grin was terrible. "Go to the temple pyramid in the desert where I am buried. Go and call me back. Or you will never get your precious sword."

"No." It was Konstantin's cold, hard voice speaking through Danilo again. "You are a foolish man for thinking we would fall for your tricks. Tell us where your apprentice is buried, and we shall invoke his spirit. Once he tells us where the sword is, I will return to give you the talisman."

"Perhaps I will keep your pretty necromancer here with me until you do?"

The crown prince rolled his eyes. "You know I would not allow that."

I tried to hide my relief.

Ankh-al-Sekhem sighed heavily, as if he had known all along he would not get what he wanted. "The apprentice's tomb lies outside of Cairo, near the pyramid of my lord Ramses. You can use the Graylands to reach it. Use this scarab to show you the way." He held a small black stone carved in the shape of a beetle. He whispered words over it, so low that neither Danilo nor I could make them out. Suddenly the stone scarab spread out wings and took flight. "You must make haste," the necromancer said, cackling. "It won't slow down for you."

I did not want Konstantin to have the sword. Could I keep it from him by preventing the return of the Egyptian? Could I prevent the French mages from finding the sword as well? Such a dangerous weapon did not belong in anyone's hands. I did not trust the Grigori. And I could not trust Danilo, for it would not be long before the lich tsar had complete control of the crown prince.

"Let's go," Danilo said, his hand on my arm. "Remember to keep your cold light reined in, Katerina."

"The more time you spend in the Graylands, the more you become like us," Ankh-al-Sekhem warned. "Do not tarry long here, Duchess."

"Do not worry about us, old man," Danilo said. "We will return soon and you will have your talisman."

We followed the scarab out of the necromancer's room and back into the thick mist. The clouds mingled with the tendrils of the crown prince's cold light, as well as my own. It grew harder for me to keep my light pulled in close. I tried to wrap it tighter around me like a cloak. "Ankh-al-Sekhem said it was dangerous to spend so much time in the Graylands," I said to the lich tsar. "But you were here for decades."

"Yes. But I was already dead, Duchess. You have only walked the Graylands as one of the living."

"So it does not affect you? What about the crown prince's body?"

"We are strong, your Danilo and I. Together we will be the most powerful tsar ever."

"Why do you even want to be tsar?" I asked. I could not imagine someone desiring such a burden.

"I am a Romanov," Konstantin said stubbornly. "I was destined to rule from my birth. My grandmother dreamed of reconquering Byzantium and setting me upon the throne."

"But she never intended for you to rule Russia."

"I was the second son. She never expected my brother to die without an heir."

"Nor did she expect you to marry a blood drinker or become a lich."

He turned to me sharply and growled, "I would be nothing without Johanna!"

"You could have been tsar," I said pointedly. And if he had, then my great-grandfather Nicholas would never have ruled. Nor would his son, Alexander the Second, or his grandson, Alexander the Third. "But you chose love over a crown."

His arm shot out and his fist closed around my throat. "I chose the power of blood over the power of a crown. Do not think that I am weak or swayed by petty emotions. Yes, I loved Johanna. But I loved her because of the power she gave me. It was a pity I underestimated my younger brother."

I stood very still, and he released his grip on me. He began walking again through the mist. I struggled to keep up with him. "Are you saying you would not have loved Johanna if she had not been a necromancer?" I asked.

He did not bother to slow down as he talked. We had to hurry or the enchanted scarab would leave us behind. "When I was just a boy, I thought I loved my first wife, the Saxe-Coburg princess. She was the beautiful girl Grandmother had picked to be my bride. I was infatuated with her. And she . . . she was infatuated with my elder brother."

"But Alexander was married to Elizabeth Alexievna," I said.

As far as I knew, she'd been completely human and one of the most beautiful empresses who ever lived in St. Petersburg. She was also one of the youngest empresses, and the most naïve.

"Theirs was an unhappy marriage," Konstantin said. "Just as mine was. Grandmother had picked the right brides for the wrong brothers."

I could not believe I was having this conversation with the lich tsar. He sounded so vulnerable. So normal. "Do you mean to say that you and Elizabeth Alexievna . . . ?"

"No." The scarab had finally stopped and fell to the floor, lifeless again in front of us. "But she knew I cared for her. That was before I met Johanna." He picked up the scarab stone and whispered something in Egyptian. A golden door appeared in front of us. He pushed it open. "Follow me."

We entered a dimly lit room, which smelled of hot, dry air. And death.

CHAPTER TWENTY-ONE

W e were inside a tomb. "Is this Cairo?" I asked. The mist had disappeared completely. We had left the Graylands behind. I had a horrible headache from the transition. Or perhaps it was from the heat.

"We are several miles outside of Cairo, actually. This should be the temple of Ankh-al-Sekhem's apprentice. He served as a high priest under Ramses the Second and died in the Tenth Dynasty."

"This is his tomb?" I glanced around at the brilliant gold-leafed paintings on the walls. Lit torches cast unholy shadows across them. An alabaster sarcophagus stood in the center of the temple. Hieroglyphics decorated all four sides, no doubt a curse upon whoever disturbed the apprentice's grave.

I could not help shuddering. The crown prince drew a small knife from a scabbard inside his jacket. "Katerina, your assistance is required."

I realized what he intended to do. "No. I will not let you take my blood."

"Relax, Duchess. I do hope it will not come to that." He laughed as he used the blade to break the wax seal on the sarcophagus. "You must help me lift the lid."

"Must we open it?" I asked.

"Where else do you think the apprentice hid the sword? It is buried with him. I'm sure of it."

Relieved he did not intend to resurrect the Egyptian, I helped him shove the heavy lid to the side. I took a torch from the wall and held it over the open sarcophagus, giving Danilo light to examine the body inside. The heat from the flames was oppressive in the tiny space.

The apprentice's mummified body had been wrapped in linen that had long since dried in the arid desert climate. No gold ornaments adorned his body. The only thing of value buried with the unfortunate man was a scroll that was clasped in his calcified hand. The fingers broke off as Danilo pried the scroll out. He unrolled it and held it up to the light, his face first triumphant, then clouded with disappointment. "It is not here." He threw the scroll to the floor and turned back to the tomb. He reached in and pulled at the linens. "The sword must be in here with him."

"What does the scroll say?" I asked.

"It is rubbish. A prayer to the gods." He pulled great frayed lengths of linen out of the sarcophagus. He was destroying the mummy. If the Egyptian authorities discovered us, we could be arrested. "What has he done with it?" Danilo shouted. "It must be in here!"

Thick black smoke began to pour out around the sarcophagus.

The dim light the torch gave us was not enough to help see through the smoke. I was too frightened to move.

"Stupid Egyptian," Danilo snarled. "Does he think he can frighten us with his tricks? Katerina, it's merely levers and chemicals. A way to frighten off grave robbers. Pay no attention to it. Bring the light closer."

I stepped toward his voice, finding him leaning over the sarcophagus. "Shine the light in here," he said.

I held the torch over his head. There was nothing left of the mummy of Ankh-al-Sekhem's apprentice except a pile of shredded linen at the bottom of the alabaster tomb. "There is no sword, Danilo."

"Damn!" He banged the side of the sarcophagus with his palms and stared into the dark tomb for several moments before finally speaking. "Well, there's only one other thing to do, then." He drew out his blade again. "I will need your hand, Katerina."

"Absolutely not."

His sharp teeth gleamed as he smiled. "I'm afraid you have no say in the matter." He grabbed my wrist and twisted it, wrenching my palm up. With a quick slice, he opened my palm, the blood rushing to fill the cut. My hand throbbed in pain.

Danilo closed his eyes as he raised my hand to his lips. "The strength of Isis, the heart of Isis, the power of Isis is mine," he said.

As he drank my blood, I felt dizzy, and the room began to spin. The talisman around my neck grew warm.

A horrible moan, low and deep, rose out of the sarcophagus and grew into a screech. All of the black smoke in the room gathered in the center, creating a whirlwind. The smoke was being drawn back into the sarcophagus.

"What are you doing?" I cried as I pulled my hand out of Danilo's grasp. "We must get out of here!"

"No!" the crown prince shouted. He glared at the smoke. "Apprentice! Show yourself!"

Out of the black smoke, the ancient Egyptian rose. No longer wrapped in the burial linens, he was little more than a shrunken corpse. There were no eyes in the sockets in his face, only black holes. But I could still recognize him. Ankh-al-Sekhem had tricked us. This had been his tomb. Not that of his apprentice.

The smoke turned into a swarm of insects, black moths and scarabs. I tried to shield my face with my arm.

"Konstantin Pavlovich." The undead Egyptian's voice was hoarse. "I will have my revenge upon you at last!" He reached for me with a cold, clawlike hand.

I stumbled backward in fright. "Danilo! Do something!"

"He should be under your control, Katerina! Use the talisman! Make him return inside the sarcophagus!"

But the Egyptian was not under my control. I had not raised him from the dead. He had used ancient black magic and my blood to return from the Graylands.

Ankh-al-Sekhem's laughter was raspy. "You are both powerful, but not that powerful. The prayer your vain crown prince recited brought me back. It needed only your blood to add to the magic and set off the spell." He climbed out of his sarcophagus, surprising me with his sudden agility. "And now, at last, I can seek my revenge upon you, Konstantin Pavlovich!"

The crown prince pulled me out of the way just in time and

ran to the next chamber, a room crowded with stacked piles of sarcophagi. The chamber opened up onto a long hall lined with more mummies. I didn't know where to run. We were surrounded by the dead.

"You cannot escape me!" the Egyptian wheezed.

We had nowhere left to run.

"Katerina, we must work together if we are to defeat him," Danilo said. "Give me your hand!"

"No! There must be some other way!" I shouted. *"Sheult Anubis!"* I raised my hands and drew a cloak of shadows around us. It was the only spell I knew as a necromancer.

But as soon as the shadows began to gather, Ankh-al-Sekhem waved the bony fingers on the hand he had left. "Clever, young duchess. But not clever enough." His magic caused the shadows to scatter.

I had nothing left with which to protect us. Except the Talisman of Isis. I held it to my bleeding hand and closed my eyes. "The blood of Isis, the strength of Isis, the power of Isis is mine," I whispered. My hand burned and it took everything I had to hold on to the talisman.

"Katerina, what are you doing?" Danilo shouted. He held his knife out, as if he could defend us against Ankh-al-Sekhem with it. But the Egyptian necromancer smiled as the blade flew out of Danilo's hand and skittered across the stone floor.

I felt a low, rumbling vibration as the temple shook. Most of the moths and scarabs had scattered, although there were a few with broken wings fluttering helplessly at my feet. With my incantation, the dead insects became my servants. They heralded the arrival of Danilo's and my new allies, the mummies that had been buried in the temple with Ankh-al-Sekhem.

Hissing and moaning, the mummies shuffled into the burial chamber. Most of them had been sacrificed ritually to accompany the necromancer in his death. They were ready to reap their vengeance upon Ankh-al-Sekhem.

As dozens of scrabbling dried mummies clawed their way toward us, I tried to stay calm. I had to keep them under my control or we'd be dead. "Defend us!" I shouted to my new minions.

The ancient necromancer was able to deflect those first attacks, but the mummies continued to come after him. Danilo laughed. "Very clever, Katerina. Now we must go while he is distracted." He pulled me by the arm down the long hallway. We saw light at the end and hoped it was a doorway to the outside.

"You will never learn where the Morning Star is hidden!" Ankh-al-Sekhem yelled after us.

As soon as we made it into the fresh air, Danilo pushed the stone door shut and sealed Ankh-al-Sekhem inside his tomb, along with the angry undead mummies. We could no longer hear his screams.

I sank down into the sand, clutching the talisman to me. My breathing was ragged and uneven. Why had I helped Konstantin instead of the Egyptian? Wasn't one evil necromancer just as bad as the other?

CHAPTER TWENTY-TWO

Danilo was laughing like a madman. "I didn't know what else to do," I began. "I—"

He stopped laughing and helped me up, pulling me into a ferocious embrace. He spun me around until I was dizzy. "You . . . you were brilliant!"

"But the sword . . ."

"We will still find it, Katerina. And without Ankh-al-Sekhem's meddling." He placed me gently back on my own two feet. Danilo's face grew serious. "You will make a wonderful tsarina, my love."

I pulled out of his arms, uncomfortable that I'd noticed how muscular they were. "I never wanted to be tsarina. All I ever wanted was to be a doctor."

Danilo laughed again. "Such a small imagination you have. Do you not realize you could conjure up all the ancient teachers of medicine—Hippocrates, Galen, even da Vinci—and have them at your command?"

"How ridiculous! I don't want to study ancient medicine. I need to know the latest in research. I need to study at a real medical university!"

In an instant, the friendliness was gone from Danilo's face. The lich tsar had returned and was in complete control of the crown prince. He grabbed my arm painfully. "You need to remember that you are my betrothed, Katerina. You will act accordingly."

More angry now than afraid, I decided to push back. "You have to be strong, Danilo," I shouted. "You cannot let Konstantin win." I searched his face and held my breath. His eyes were still a murky hazel as the two people battled within the same body. Finally, the crown prince's eyes resumed their normal black.

He nodded toward the road. "We need to get out of here. The Grigori could arrive at any minute."

In all of the excitement of being attacked by an evil mummy, I'd forgotten about the Grigori. "If they don't have the sword, how can Papus and the Order of the Black Lily command the Grigori to chase after us?"

He rolled his eyes. "The same way I have persuaded the Grigori to be loyal to me. The promise of freedom."

"And they believed you?" I asked. "What will they do when they discover you lied to them?"

Danilo shrugged, but I was no longer sure if it was the crown prince or the lich tsar I was looking at. "By then I will possess the sword and they will have no choice but to obey. There is no way to free them. The sword is not of this world and cannot be destroyed. Nor can the Grigori touch it."

I could not believe the Grigori would be so naïve. I foresaw only more trouble and misfortune ahead once we found this cursed sword. I looked up and down the dirt road, wishing desperately for a hat to keep the sun out of my eyes. There was nothing for miles in either direction but shimmering mirages. "Which way are we to go?" I asked.

"This way," Danilo said as he headed toward a temple complex. We wandered through the necropolis, Danilo muttering to himself as the hot wind swept stinging sands around us.

"Is there another necromancer we are to meet today?" I asked. I was tired and famished. I had lost track of the days since I'd been abducted and was not even sure of the last time I'd had a decent night's sleep. The adventure had become one strange and endless nightmare.

"No more necromancers today," Danilo said with a mirthless laugh. The crown prince stopped in front of a battered statue of a sphinx. This was not the famous monster at Giza but a much smaller version. I'd always loved the two sphinxes that adorned the waterfront of the Imperial Academy of Arts in St. Petersburg. The teachers at Smolni enjoyed taking students to the Academy and telling us the story of how the sphinxes had been brought from Egypt to Russia in the seventeen hundreds.

This sphinx was human-sized. She sat like a cat on her back haunches, her head held high regally like a queen. Her right front paw was missing. She appeared to be guarding a very plain stone building.

I watched Danilo as he approached the statue quietly. He

went down on one knee, with his right hand over his heart. "My lady," he whispered. "I have come to you seeking wisdom."

The stone creature's eyes opened. "You are a strange one. More of a puzzle than I," she said.

The sphinx had come to life. I could scarcely believe my eyes. Or indeed, my ears. The voice was young and feminine, slow and deliberate. There was no cold light surrounding her, but my own cold light seemed to shy away from her. As for Danilo, his brilliant cold light strands clung to him, as if in fear of her. How very odd.

Danilo smiled. "I am a riddle as well, my lady. Answer my question and I will answer yours."

"You seek the Morning Star."

"Yes."

"You believe I can help you." The sphinx's voice gave me chills.

"Yes, my lady."

"And you will answer my question when I have answered yours."

Danilo did not move. "Where will I find the Morning Star?"

The sphinx blinked. "Past the seven gates of heaven, the Morning Star lies, betwixt the steadfast darkness and the unfailing light."

"I seek the sword known as the Morning Star," Danilo clarified, doing his best to sound patient and humble, but I could sense his irritation.

"And I have given you the key to find your sword," the sphinx repeated. "Now you must answer my question. What sort of creature are you?"

"But you have not answered mine!" Danilo shouted.

"He is a lich!" I said quickly. I had no desire to see what an angry sphinx could do to us. "A blood drinker who has possessed another's body. They share one body, my lady."

Danilo glared at me.

"Most curious," the sphinx said. "But you did not ask me a question. And I did not ask one of you."

"I beg your pardon, my lady." I felt compelled to kneel down on the hard-packed sand.

This seemed to appease the sphinx. "But you have given me the answer that I sought. And so I shall give you an answer that you seek. That answer is yes."

I had no idea what question she was answering. But her yes gave me a faint sliver of hope. "Yes" meant possibility. It meant I might survive my journey with Danilo. That I might see George again, if the sphinx could indeed see the future. What other questions did I have except for ones regarding my future? "Thank you, my lady."

Danilo stood up. "This has been a waste of time. Let's go." He jerked me up by the arm.

"How are we going to get back to Cairo?" I asked him.

"Follow the Morning Star," the sphinx growled. And her stone eyes closed at last.

Danilo cursed under his breath. "She delights in making men mad."

"Tell me more about the sphinx," I said, curiosity getting the better of me. "Was she ever a mortal woman?"

"Yes." Danilo was walking quickly back toward the road. He took a pocket watch out of his vest and consulted it with a frown.

"So who was she? When did she live?" I stumbled over some rocks as I tried to keep up with him.

"Later, Duchess. We must hurry."

I glanced at the road in despair. "We cannot walk all the way back to Cairo. It must be miles from here."

"It is."

"And across the river."

"True."

But the road was already touching civilization, and we began to pass beggars and children and stray dogs. I'd given away all of my coins in Alexandria, but Danilo shrugged off the cries of the villagers without a second glance. I stopped when I saw a young wisp of a mother with a screaming and dirty infant in her lap. "Does the baby need medicine?" I asked.

The woman stared at me blankly, not understanding French or English. I tried Greek as well. Finally I sighed and placed my pearl earrings in her hand, closing her fingers around them. "For the baby," I said.

She grabbed my hand and kissed it, chattering in a language I did not recognize.

Danilo turned around to see what I'd done and rolled his eyes. "Forget the beggars, Katerina. We must hurry."

Traveling north along the road, we soon came to the recognizable Giza Plateau. The electric tramline began here, taking tourists from the most famous of the Egyptian pyramids back to the comfort of Cairo. A former royal lodge, the Mena House Hotel sat near the tram station. This luxury hotel was run by a wealthy English couple who'd done little to alter the royal furnishings and décor but included every convenience a sophisticated traveler could possibly desire.

Danilo sighed as the hotel came into view. "About bloody time."

"Do you think the Grigori know where we are?" I asked.

"At this point, Duchess, I honestly do not care. We are checking in and I am taking a hot bath. I suggest you do the same."

CHAPTER TWENTY-THREE

Sister Mala and the Grigori who'd rescued me in Alexandria were waiting for us in the lobby. Sister Mala accompanied me to my room, exclaiming sarcastically the whole way how much she enjoyed my company and hoped I was pleased with her service. "I'll have the servants send up hot water for you, Duchess."

I glared at her but did not mention what a poor chaperone she made. I had no idea if she even would have been able to travel in the Graylands with me and the lich tsar. "I don't suppose I have fresh clothes here, do I?" I asked.

"We were unable to bring the trunks with us. However, I will find something suitable for you," Sister Mala said. "The crown prince will expect you downstairs in the dining room properly dressed."

"Not tonight," I begged. "I want nothing more than a bath and a good night's rest."

She shrugged. "If the crown prince will allow it" was all she would say.

Fortunately, the crown prince was merciful. By the time I'd finished scrubbing several layers of desert sand off my skin in the bathtub, Sister Mala had returned with a beautiful blue gown, comparable to the latest Paris fashions, with matching blue kid slippers and soft kid gloves. She also brought a gossamer nightgown and robe.

"The crown prince hopes you have a pleasant night's rest and requests your presence in the morning at breakfast. He begs that you at least take some tea and bread before retiring to-night."

I sighed. "Tell him he has my gratitude. I will have just a little tea, if you would be so kind as to send for it."

Her eyes were cold as she nodded. "Of course, Duchess."

As soon as she left, I slipped into the nightgown and robe before she could return. The ensemble was close to indecent. Maman would be horrified to see me wearing such a gown. A lump formed in my throat as I thought of her and Papa. They had probably given up looking for me, Petya as well. Maman had either taken to her bed with hysterics or set off for Biarritz to escape the scandal of a runaway daughter. I only hoped the tsar's men did not harass my family thinking they knew where I was.

Sister Mala returned with a sharp knock. She entered, followed by a servant with a tea tray. "Put it down over there," she said. As soon as the servant had left, Sister Mala sat in one of the chairs.

"Are you joining me for tea?" I asked, clutching my robe. I wished I had a long black habit, as she did.

"We are good friends, you and I," she said, her words startling me. "We have been traveling companions for a while now. The crown prince would not want any scandal to arise that could taint your betrothal."

I understood her perfectly. She would lie to anyone who asked whether I'd been out of her sight.

"He and I are not betrothed. We have not been betrothed for over a year."

Sister Mala shook her head as she poured out two cups of hot tea. "How silly of you not to remember, Duchess. You and the crown prince are to be married in St. Petersburg next month. It has been a long-standing secret engagement. But as soon as Konstantin becomes the tsar, he will want to be married as soon as possible."

She handed me one of the teacups and smiled. "He is certain you will be just as anxious as he is."

"Why should I be?" I hesitated before drinking the tea. I did not trust Sister Mala one bit.

"Are you not excited about becoming tsarina? It's a fairy tale come true!"

"Not my fairy tale. And I don't believe he will become tsar. The Romanovs will stop him."

"The Romanovs and their foolish bogatyr?" Sister Mala laughed. "The Romanovs are weak, especially the current tsar. He can do nothing without his precious necromancer. And now his necromancer has changed her loyalty to the true tsar. Konstantin."

There was something familiar in the girl's laugh. And a familiar faint fae sparkle in her eyes. I could have sworn I'd known her before the trip to Egypt. "Which court do you belong to, Sister Mala?" I asked. "Dark Court or Light?"

Her eyes flashed in anger, and I saw my guess had not been wrong. "There are those of fae blood who do not belong to either court, Duchess." She drew herself up, sitting regally in her chair as if she were a queen. "There are wild fae as well, and we are more dangerous than any court creature you'll ever meet."

"Truly?" I murmured. "Then why do you follow the crown prince?"

She stood up. "I follow the true tsar, Konstantin Pavlovich! His lady, Princess Cantacuzene, saved my mother's life." As she crossed the room in graceful strides, she seemed almost to float. "My mother was a wild fae, hunted by one of the Dark Court princes."

"Princes?" The Grand Duchess Miechen had several boys, but none of them were older than me. To have been hunting Mala's mother . . .

"It was not the Grand Duchess Miechen's court at the time," she said, as if reading my mind. "Almost twenty years ago, the Dark Court was ruled by a French faerie. My mother was a Polish noblewoman who attended Princess Cantacuzene. She was attacked by one of the French princes and left to fend for herself and her unborn child. Princess Cantacuzene took me at my mother's pleading and brought me to a Polish family of dancers in St. Petersburg."

I sat up, finally recognizing the gray eyes. "You are Mathilde Kschessinskaya, the ballerina Nicholas has been obsessed with!"

She smiled as she pulled her head covering off. Black curls fell down around her shoulders. "He will always love me, Duchess. And I will be there to comfort him, of course, when his father loses the throne."

"He is the true heir! And you don't love him at all, do you?"

"He is nothing but a handsome young fool. Konstantin Pavlovich is the true tsar. It is at his command that I keep the young tsarevitch occupied. Along with many other grand dukes."

"Danilo told you to flirt with Nicholas?" I was astonished. It seemed to me Danilo would have wanted George's attention diverted. Perhaps it was truly Konstantin's logic dictating the crown prince's behavior.

"He is no longer your precious Danilo," Mala snapped. Then her face melted back into the icy smile. "But if it makes you happy to pretend, Duchess, what can it hurt? It is still the crown prince's lips that will be kissing you and the crown prince's arms that will hold you in the night, when you become Konstantin's bride."

I stood up and walked to my bed, protected from insects and other nasty creatures by a thin gauze canopy. I pushed the curtains aside and turned to Mala. "I think I would like to retire now, if you do not mind."

She laughed and rang for the servant to pick up the tea tray. "Sweet dreams, Duchess."

She followed the servant out, leaving me to sink down on my bed in misery. My only comfort was knowing that she was here in Egypt and not mesmerizing the tsarevitch. I curled up under my covers, hoping at least that Princess Alix and Nicholas were happy now.

CHAPTER TWENTY-FOUR

When I went down to the dining room for breakfast the next morning, I was wearing the blue walking gown that Mala had brought me. Danilo rose from his seat to kiss my hand. "*Enchanté*, Katerina. I trust you slept well?"

"Not a single dream," I said, sitting in the chair he held out for me. I had been worried my night would be full of nightmares of mummies and blood drinkers and evil fae ballerinas. Instead, I'd had a blissful night of dreamless sleep. I wondered if Mala had put something in my tea after all.

And now I was ravenously hungry. A waiter appeared at my elbow, pouring hot coffee into a cup.

"I've already ordered for us," Danilo said, settling back into his own chair. "They make the most wonderful crepes here."

"This isn't your first time in Egypt, then," I said, thankful for the strong Turkish coffee.

"I came with Militza and her husband on their honeymoon."

"How cozy."

He laughed. "Militza only knew that I was searching for Ankh-al-Sekhem. She did not know why."

"Because she did not know of Konstantin's hold on you."

He set his coffee down and looked up at me. This morning, it was truly the combined crown prince and lich tsar, whose oddly colored green eyes stared back at me. "That might have been a mistake, but now it makes no difference," he said. "If she wishes to keep her hold on the St. Petersburg vampires, she must support me as tsar."

Then Danilo did not yet know about my mother. The fact that the new striga was actually more powerful than his sister might make my mother appear to be a threat to him as well. I would keep her secret as long as I could to protect her. "Did you speak to Militza that night after the ballet?"

He nodded as the waiter brought our breakfast dishes. The food smelled heavenly and slightly spicy. There was cinnamon in the crepes filling. "Militza told me I needed to see you, Katerina. That as a necromancer, you could help me exorcise Konstantin. But it was already too late. We've become one entity. And I've found it not displeasing."

"Militza thought I could help you?" I was shocked. The grand duchess was greatly overestimating my abilities.

"She told me you were the only one with powers close to those of our mother's. Or Princess Cantacuzene's. She did not realize I'd already found Ankh-al-Sekhem in the Graylands."

Of course Danilo knew the ancient Egyptian was far more powerful than I. But we had defeated him, hadn't we? Danilo and I together. It made me feel strange to realize we had been on the same side. We were definitely not on the same side now.

Mala and the elder Grigori approached our table, and Danilo invited them to join us. Mala leaned close to whisper something in Danilo's ear. It was not happy news for him. With a scowl he told her, "Take care of it."

The elder Grigori bowed and followed Mala toward the hotel lobby.

"What has happened?" I asked the crown prince.

"It is nothing. Another band of Grigori has arrived in Cairo. Along with a few of the French wizards. Mala is going to see to it that they are distracted."

"Do you trust her?"

"Of course. Why wouldn't I?"

"Her loyalties lie with Konstantin because of Princess Cantacuzene, who was your mother's half sister and mortal enemy. How does Mala feel about your mother?"

"We do not discuss my mother." Danilo frowned. "Mala has sworn on her life to protect me. I will not doubt her."

"Of course," I said. But I remained wary of her. And it was not because I worried about the crown prince. I worried about the stability of Russia.

Danilo sipped his coffee silently while I finished eating. As the waiter cleared our plates away, I asked the crown prince when we would be returning to St. Petersburg.

"Patience, my dear Katerina. We still have business here in Cairo."

"What sort of business?"

His hand came down on the table suddenly and violently. "We still have not found the sword!"

I jumped, once again startled by the sudden change in his personality. "Is there anyone else who can tell us where it is?" I asked calmly. We would receive no more help from Ankh-al-Sekhem. And the sphinx's advice had been too cryptic.

A commotion in the hallway drew our attention. Danilo stood up and reached for my arm. "We must go quickly."

I stared at him, hesitating. As cruel as Papus had been in the carriage, I could not believe he was working with George and the Koldun. Still, I couldn't help praying for a rescue.

"Quickly!" Danilo repeated as he herded me out of the dining room and into the courtyard. There was a spiral staircase leading to the second-floor balcony. He dragged me up the stairs and into the music room. It was not even midmorning yet, but a trio of Egyptian musicians already sat playing haunting folk songs. The air was smoky from pipes and incense, making it hard to see.

Mala was here as well, dressed in a shockingly low-cut bloodred gown, her long black hair hanging in wild curls. Silver hoops dangled from her ears, and a belt of delicate silver bells hugged her hips. She wore silver on both wrists and one ankle as well. I gasped as I noticed her bare feet turning prettily in time with the music. Her arms were graceful and thin as she wove them upward in circles. She was swaying her hips to the exotic music, moving in a hypnotic rhythm like a cobra.

She had a captive audience. A group of travelers stood just inside the doorway, staring in silent admiration. Several other men sat at tables around the room, all eyes on Mala, the wicked faerie dancer.

Danilo pulled me back behind a large potted palm tree before the travelers could spot us. He stood very close behind me, his lips inches from my ear as he whispered, "Do not make a sound, Duchess."

I began to feel the old hypnotic pull of the Vladiki prince as his lips barely touched my skin. I could not give in to him. I reminded myself that what I felt for him was not real. I tried to pull away, but he merely laughed.

Finally he let me go. "I think it is safe for us to go back downstairs and find a carriage. We have business in the city this morning."

"What is Mala doing?" I asked as he dragged me away. I'd seen no signs of the Grigori, and no mages that I recognized. "Won't she be cold in such a scandalous dress?"

Danilo laughed softly. "Do not worry about her, my dear. But I live for the day I see you dressed like that for me."

"That will never happen," I said, blushing fiercely. I hated to admit it to myself, but her dancing did look far more fun than any polonaise.

Danilo laughed again. I blushed even more as I realized he was listening to my thoughts.

He found us a carriage and seemed to relax as we left the hotel. I stared out the window, taking an interest in the loud and colorful streets of Cairo. "Where are we going?" I asked.

"To the museum. They have several artifacts on display that have been recovered from the pyramids over the years."

"Would the sword be in a museum?" I asked, hoping it would not be that simple.

"No. But the emerald scroll attributed to Ankh-al-Sekhem is in a display case there."

"And you read hieroglyphics?"

Danilo nodded. "It is one of the many languages I have learned over the years."

"How extraordinary. Will you be needing my services in the

144

museum?" I asked sarcastically. I was wearing the Talisman of Isis beneath my gown, just in case.

He shook his head. "No, Katerina. Please do not resurrect any mummies while we are at the museum. However, I do not intend to let you out of my sight as long as there is danger in Cairo. And we will not leave before I find the sword."

The Egyptian Museum was located on a street near the river, past the marketplace and several European hotels and bars. Past places that admitted only men and where girls danced wearing almost nothing at all. Mala had not looked ashamed to have all those men staring at her. She seemed to thrive on the attention. Perhaps it fed her fae powers somehow.

Danilo held out his hand for me as we pulled up in front of the museum. "Stay close, Duchess."

The museum was flanked by two small sphinx statues. I shuddered as we walked between them, but neither one seemed to notice us. Perhaps not all sphinxes spoke; I'd never heard the ones in St. Petersburg utter a word. They'd been brought to the Academy of Arts years ago, bought by Tsar Nicholas from the French to decorate the Neva riverfront.

Danilo took my arm in his as we strolled through the front doors of the museum. "I think the exhibit we want is on the second floor," he said. We walked up the enormous white staircase, and at the first landing, I glanced back down at the marble lobby, onto a very large column covered in hieroglyphics. Large statues of cats and ibises stood guard around the stone column.

When we reached the top landing, Danilo swore under his breath. I spotted two of his Grigori rushing over to us. "They've already been here, Your Majesty," the elder one said.

"Did they find the tablet?"

"They looked at it, but they did not take it."

"Hurry!" Danilo said, his grip on my arm tightening. We rushed toward the Writings Room. The tablet that Danilo sought was in a glass case in the center of the room. He let go of me and put both of his hands on the case, peering down at the tablet.

"Perhaps they didn't know how to read the hieroglyphics," I said. I truly wished that Danilo were not so talented in languages either. A sword as dangerous as the Morning Star needed to stay lost. It did not belong in anyone's hands.

"It does not matter," Danilo said. "The tablet mentions nothing. Only the same seven gates of heaven spoken of by the sphinx. More meaningless text about the star that rises in the morning sky."

"What if it's not meaningless?" I couldn't help asking. "What if they're not talking about Venus?"

"'Past the seven gates of heaven, the Morning Star lies,'" Danilo said, repeating the sphinx's words. "What else could the sphinx have meant? Unless . . ." He turned around and glared at the Grigori. "The gates are part of a mage's highest initiation, are they not?"

"The seventh gate can be opened only by those who have completed the most extensive training in ceremonial magic," the elder Grigori said. "Mages who have successfully mastered all the secret rituals of the Emerald Tablet."

"The mages of the highest degree," Danilo said, frowning. "No one in the Order of the Black Lily is that talented, save Papus himself."

"But you were a member of the Black Lily," I said. "How far in your training did you progress?" And how far had George progressed when he studied with them? I did not dare ask Danilo.

"Not far enough. It takes decades of studying to be able to complete such a ritual." The crown prince pounded both fists on the wall. The shelves nearest him rattled but thankfully did not fall. He swore under his breath in six different languages.

I felt a slight wave of relief flood through me. If Danilo had not been a member of the Order long enough to be initiated, he would not be able to retrieve the sword.

Papus had been the one to rescue me the first time I found myself in the Graylands. He'd told me he called on the powers of higher beings to help him travel back and forth between the worlds of the living and the dead. I realized now it had been the Grigori who helped him.

Still, even though he'd rescued me once, he was a dangerous magician. He had betrayed George when George was studying magic in Paris. Papus had lured George into the Order of the Black Lily in order to gain access to the Koldun. With Danilo's help, the French magicians tried to raise Konstantin Pavlovich from the dead. And Papus had just tried to kill me here in Cairo.

"Why did Papus ally himself with you to begin with?" I asked the crown prince. "What would he have had to gain by Konstantin's return?"

"Money, of course," Danilo said. "I promised him the riches of the Romanovs when I became tsar. But after my arrest, the traitor ran to the Koldun and his brother and begged for forgiveness." The crown prince scowled. "He will regret this one day."

"We will find the French mage and his associates for you," the elder Grigori said. With a bow, he turned and departed.

A sliver of hope rose in my chest. Could Papus be working with George and the Koldun now? What if George was here in Egypt?

"Katerina, there is something else of interest on this tablet," Danilo said to me, beckoning me to look closer.

He pointed to the stone lying beneath the glass. "This is the history of the sword up until the time Ankh-al-Sekhem wrote this. The first human to wield the sword was a pharaoh princess: Meresankh, a daughter of Menes. She united Upper and Lower Egypt with the Grigori's help."

"A daughter?"

"A Queen of Swords." Danilo shook his head. "How ridiculous! Still, she must have been a powerful necromancer for the sword to succumb to her. And for the Grigori to follow her."

A Queen of Swords. I shuddered as I remembered the superstitious Pushkin tale. And Maman's tarot deck.

"If the sword can only be carried by a necromancer," I asked, "then why would it be hidden where only a magician can find it?"

"It is bitterly ironic, yes?" He had not anticipated this, I realized. "To force the magician to work with the necromancer. We must make Papus see reason."

I worried then for George and the French mage. They could not let the lich tsar find Papus. Konstantin would force the mage to escort him past the seven gates and retrieve the sword.

"Shall we go, Duchess?" Danilo asked. "I believe there is some beautiful jewelry downstairs that belonged to the wife of Ramses the Second." But he really wasn't asking me. He led me off to the floor below and showed me the elegant necklaces and earrings made of faience and gold that were thousands of years old. The museum was lucky to have these priceless artifacts in their possession. Most of the tombs found had long been robbed of their riches by adventurers wishing to sell the artifacts on the black market. Egyptian antiquities were a lucrative trade. I'd seen many suspicious but beautiful pieces not only in the Vladimir Palace, but also in the Winter Palace itself.

We paused in front of a golden statue of a fierce-looking lion-headed goddess. "That is Sekhmet," Danilo said quietly. "Both a deity of war and of medicine."

I stared at the statue in wonder and had a pagan urge to ask the goddess for her blessing. But before I could commit such blasphemy, the crown prince was pulling me toward another jewelry collection.

I wondered how the Cantacuzene family had gotten a hold of the Talisman of Isis. I suspected it was an artifact that should have been under a glass case in a museum as well. I examined the beautiful ruby bracelets and sapphire earrings and lapis necklaces in the case. Dariya would have been beside herself to see these jewels. She would have enjoyed vacationing in such an exotic place as this.

But I was not here on vacation. I'd been abducted by an insane lich tsar who believed I was going to be his tsarina. And I had to keep him from finding the sword that could destroy the whole world.

CHAPTER TWENTY-FIVE

We passed through the marketplace on our way to the hotel. The bazaar was a dazzling chaos of colors and sounds and scents. Merchants ran up to us, shoving silks and foods and perfumes, while children pulled on our clothing, begging for coins. Haunting songs from the minarets called the faithful to prayer at intervals throughout the day. I watched the shopkeepers stop and prostrate themselves on their rugs and face west to pray.

Danilo ignored them. "This way," he said, leading me toward the stalls of the spice market, where one could buy frankincense and myrrh, cinnamon, and the precious attar of roses. Wax candles hung by their wicks from one stall, and an old woman sat in the shadows in front of a tray of glass vials. Some were filled with narcotic drugs: opium and morphine. Danilo pulled me onward, until we came to a young man with frankincense resin.

Danilo took a handkerchief out of his pocket and used it to pick up a piece of the resin. "Dragon's blood?" he asked.

"Yes," the young man said. "From the southernmost part of Arabia."

"Do you have myrrh as well?"

"Of course, my lord."

"I'll need some of each."

I noticed that Danilo seemed reluctant to touch the frankincense, which the empress had used as an antidote to the hemlock poisoning caused by Danilo's veshtiza sister at Smolni. Militza, too, had used frankincense to poison her veshtiza aunt, Princess Cantacuzene. Did the resin affect him as well? "What do you need these herbs for?" I asked innocently as Danilo completed his purchases.

"They are key to the ritual outlined in the papyrus. These are the fragrances that helped souls cross back over to the land of the living."

"Whose soul are you planning to aid?" I asked warily. I wanted no part of this.

But Danilo merely laughed. "Come, Duchess, no need for you to fret. Let me buy you some food at the other end of the market. Let us enjoy this beautiful weather."

I looked up at the clear blue sky and took in the dizzying pandemonium swirling around me. Above the sounds of barking dogs and shouting shopkeepers, amid the dusty streets crowded with carts and donkeys and people, it was indeed a beautiful day. Danilo bought two pieces of warm flatbread sold by a shy girl who did not look to be older than eight or nine. She took the coins from him greedily and scampered back to her mother's bakery stall. The bread was delicious and soft.

151

The crown prince tried to buy me several trinkets as we walked back toward the entrance of the marketplace. Red silk slippers, silver bracelets, statuettes of ivory and alabaster were all offered to us by loud men and women. I admired the woolen blankets and rugs from Tunis and the damask silks of Arabia. But I would not let Danilo buy me anything expensive, as I had no way of repaying him.

I did stop, however, when I saw the bookseller's stall. Here, stacks and stacks of books and clumsily sewn together folios were being sold by an elderly man in a red fez. I tugged on Danilo's coat sleeve. "May I take a look?" I asked.

"Of course," he said politely. "Let me know if you find anything you like."

Wedged between two piles of Arabic poetry were a few old medical journals. Many were written in Arabic, but one was from England and another from France. They were not too terribly out of date, both written in the past ten years.

At the bottom of the pile, I found a leather-bound reprint of an ancient Greek text about the Alexandrian physician Herophilos. "How much for this?" I asked the shopkeeper, sliding the faded brown book out from beneath the others.

The elderly man happily bargained with Danilo for several minutes in Arabic before Danilo finally handed him a paper bill. "The book is yours, Duchess."

"Was it very costly?" I asked.

"Don't be ridiculous. We must rejoin the others."

I placed my hand on the crown prince's arm. "*Merci*, Danilo."

He took my hand and kissed it. "It is nothing. I am happy to find something here that pleases you."

Mala and the elder Grigori met us at the front gates of the

bazaar. "Did you acquire what you needed, Your Majesty?" Mala asked with a formal bow.

"Yes. Now it is time to prepare Katerina for the ritual."

"Ritual?" I asked. "What are you talking about?"

Mala took me gently by the arm and pulled me away from the crown prince. "You will not be harmed, Duchess." In a lower voice she added, "The necromancer who performs the ritual must be ceremonially pure. She must not have eaten the flesh of any animal, and she must not have consorted with men."

"What does that mean?" I asked.

"It means that His Majesty needs you to remain a virgin until after the ritual," she answered, her eyes sparkling with mischief. "But after that, he will wish to marry you as soon as possible."

CHAPTER TWENTY-SIX

That evening, the elder Grigori escorted me to my room, waiting patiently outside while I washed up and changed into a clean gown for dinner. I decided to wear the blue dress again and found Danilo and Mala waiting for me in the dining room.

They stopped talking as soon as they saw me. Whatever they'd been discussing had surely not been pleasant, as neither looked happy.

"We will make plans to board the boat in the morning," Danilo said. "It is safer than the carriage, I believe. Especially with our own steamer."

"You've found Papus, then," I said.

"No," Mala said, frustrated. "I've told His Imperial Majesty that he should not believe the sphinx's cryptic words. But he feels we are very close on the French mage's tail." She turned to Danilo. "The Order of the Black Lily is dangerous. They could be luring you into a trap."

Danilo laughed. "My dear dancer, your concern is touching. But we are leaving in the morning nevertheless."

"Papus and his band of Grigori were seen leaving Cairo this morning," Mala told me. "Our Grigori believe they have found the resting place of the sword. And I worry that they will reach it before we do."

"Does Papus know any necromancers he would take with him past the seven gates?" I asked. I hoped Papus had joined forces with George and the Koldun for real this time. But what if he was still pursuing his own ambitions? What if he was working with another necromancer?

Konstantin stared into his wineglass, his eyes glowing green, his face bitter. "The French mage betrayed me. He turned to the Pretender's side when the ritual at Vorontsov Palace went wrong and he escaped like a coward. He will pay for his betrayal. But I must complete tomorrow's ritual first. Then we shall be able to deal with Papus."

Mala nodded obediently. "The Grigori will speak with their brothers in Armana, then. They will prepare everything for the ritual." She waited until the waiters served our plates before telling me, "The Grigori are able to talk to one another mentally across thousands of miles. Not deep, meaningful conversations, of course, but they are able to relay simple messages. Short commands and such."

If only I could convince the Grigori with us to betray Konstantin and send a message to those working with Papus. And George. But I had no idea how to gain their loyalty. And I still was not sure about Papus.

I was about to remark on the fact that my plate consisted entirely of rice and vegetables, without a main course of meat, but the mention of the Grigori's special abilities reminded me of something that had puzzled me earlier. "If we can enter the Graylands in one location and leave them in another, why can we not just travel through the Graylands to get home to Russia? Or to wherever it is we need to go for this ritual?"

Danilo laughed. "It is much more dangerous to travel through the Graylands than it is to travel through our world, Katerina. It can take years off one's life or drive one insane. Mortals cannot spend long stretches of time in the Graylands."

I sank back in my chair. "I see." Even as a necromancer, I was still mortal. Unlike Danilo. Or Mala, the wild fae. And yet Danilo had still dragged me to that place in order to escape Papus.

I barely tasted dinner. Danilo was preoccupied with his dark thoughts and Mala did not seem eager to engage in conversation either. The elder Grigori appeared and spoke into Danilo's ear.

Danilo sat straight up. "We're leaving," he announced. "Immediately."

I stood up. "Fine. I wasn't very hungry anyway."

"We're leaving the hotel, Katerina. You have five minutes to gather your belongings from your room."

"Five minutes!" I exclaimed.

Mala grabbed my arm. "Hurry, Duchess."

But they weren't even my belongings. Danilo had bought everything that was in my trunk. I didn't care whether I ever saw that wardrobe again. "I'm ready now," I said.

Danilo and Mala were not, however. Reluctantly, I followed Mala back to her room, where she threw her things into a small suitcase. She was cursing in Polish in a low voice.

"Why did our plans change so quickly?" I asked.

She muttered something under her breath, and I caught a whisper of the Romanov name.

"Are they here?" I asked. Had George come for me after all? My heart began to pound.

"Who? You are being silly for not taking your things, Duchess. It will be a long time before you will see fancy dresses again."

"First tell me why we must leave so quickly." I would stall as long as possible if it meant helping George and Papus stop Konstantin.

"The Grigori who sided with the French mages were seen traveling south. They know where we are headed, it seems. But Konstantin Pavlovich does not wish to face them before he's completed his ritual. We are in danger here. Now you must go get your things."

"Why do you remain loyal to Danilo?" I asked her. "Because of your loyalty to Princess Cantacuzene? The Montenegrins killed Johanna. Konstantin may mourn her death, but the crown prince does not."

Anger flashed in her eyes. She looked as if she wanted to strike me, but her hands remained clenched at her sides. "I will remain loyal to Konstantin, for one day he'll be able to bring the princess back to me."

I looked at her in shock. George had cut off the blood drinker's head after Militza had poisoned her. There was no way Princess Cantacuzene could return. Not even the lich tsar was that powerful, was he?

"Now," Mala said, pushing me down the hallway to my room, "no more stalling. The crown prince's Grigori will not allow you to interfere with his plans. You have five minutes to gather your things."

Reluctantly, I hurried next door and hastily packed as much as I could from the wardrobe Danilo had provided. Once I was safe in St. Petersburg, I would burn every last one of these dresses.

My five minutes were up before I could finish. One of the Grigori came to carry our baggage. Danilo entered my room behind him. "Are you ready? Very good. We must go quickly."

"Why?" I demanded. "If the grand duke is coming, you cannot stop him. He will find me, Danilo."

I received a slap to my face before I knew what was happening. It was Konstantin's harsh laugh I heard. "Forget about your precious grand duke. He already knows we've been together for the past week and he assumes we have eloped. He will never marry you now, Katerina."

Tears leaked from the corners of my eyes, as much from the pain of being struck as from utter despair. He was right. There was no way George would ever believe I had not been compromised. Mala was not a sufficient chaperone. I would not have trusted Petya's dog with the faerie dancer.

"Please hurry, Your Majesty," Mala hissed. She was standing in the hallway, dressed once again in her black habit and head covering. No one would recognize her as the tempting belly dancer from yesterday.

"Come along, Katerina," Danilo said, clutching my arm so tightly that he bruised my skin.

We descended the staircase flanked by several Grigori. They did not appear to be armed, but I could tell they were prepared to defend Danilo to the death.

We made it through the hotel's lobby and into the waiting carriage outside without incident. Mala sat across from Danilo and me, glancing out the window repeatedly as we raced to the dock at the river, where a chartered steamer was waiting. But surely traveling by rail would be faster? How far south did Danilo plan to take us?

The moonlight glimmered across the dark waves on the wide river. I was a little sad to be leaving such a beautiful city.

"Step quickly, Katerina," Danilo said as he rushed me up the gangplank. I stumbled, but two ship porters standing at the entry were quick to offer their assistance. Danilo brushed them aside and gently pushed me onto the steamer. "Your room is this way, Katerina."

He took me directly to a small cabin on the upper level and promptly locked me in.

CHAPTER TWENTY-SEVEN

I awoke in a tiny room, not remembering at first where I was. And then it all came back to me. I'd given in to the tears and cried myself to sleep. Now my head ached and my eyes were puffy. The ship rolled gently, and glancing at the window, I could see the lights from the waterfront passing by slowly. The sky was just beginning to lighten. We'd left Cairo. I had no idea where we were.

I washed my face in the tiny basin in my cabin and tried to make my hair presentable. I finally gave up and twisted it into a topknot. I was shocked to find my door unlocked.

In the early-morning sun, I could see that the steamer we were on was just a small cruiser, with only a few cabins and one large common room on the main deck. In the common room, I found Danilo and Mala. They were arguing over a piece of papyrus in Mala's hand.

"They won't know what they're looking for," Mala was saying. "I'm sure it will be safe."

Danilo tore the papyrus out of her hand. "It won't matter if the tomb has already been desecrated."

"What tomb?" I asked. "Where are we headed?"

Mala turned away and went to stare out the window and sulk.

Danilo pulled a chair out for me, gesturing for me to sit. "Abydos."

"Isn't that south of Cairo?"

"Quite a distance south, actually." Danilo sat in the chair opposite me and stirred his coffee. "I had a private steamer chartered to get us there as fast as possible. I'm afraid we have no time for sightseeing at Sakkara or Armana. And I've had to persuade the captain to travel through the night as well to get us there in record time."

"I don't understand. What is in Abydos? I thought we were returning to St. Petersburg."

Mala laughed and turned to face me. "We must go to the temple in Abydos for Konstantin's ritual. Once it is completed, Papus will have no choice but to help us."

"The ritual you spoke of in the bazaar?" I had an uneasy feeling about ancient Egyptian rituals, and I hated that Mala knew more about the crown prince's plans than I did.

Danilo smiled. "I don't believe it will be anything you have not done before."

A chill slid down the back of my neck. I did not want to take part in anything Danilo was planning. Konstantin was a powerful necromancer in his own right. "You have no need

161

of me, Danilo. You know perfectly well you are capable of handling this on your own."

He leaned forward and tucked a loose strand of my hair behind my ear. His voice was soft but deadly. "Oh no, Duchess. The necromancer who recites this ritual must be pure. Something, alas, that is too late for me."

Revulsion washed over me. I felt cold and clammy. And slightly nauseated. I had no desire to think about Danilo's . . . impurity. What if he and Mala had . . . ? No, I did not want to think about it.

"I still have a part to play," he continued. "This ritual will require every ounce of power the two of us possess. It requires a small sacrifice."

"You would never kill me." But I did not believe my own words.

His smile showed his sharp, tiny fangs. "I wouldn't say never, Katerina. But no, not at this time." He glanced from me to Mala enigmatically, his eyes flashing from black to green and back to the strange hazel color that told me the two men were fighting for control of Danilo's body again. I feared it was only a matter of time before Danilo would surrender completely to the lich tsar.

Then the crown prince's mood changed as he sat back and dumped three heaping spoonfuls of sugar into his coffee. With a much more pleasant smile, he said, "Have you never heard of the Temple of Osiris at Abydos?"

I shook my head. "Is it near Luxor and the Valley of the Kings?" A few years ago, I'd read about a Russian explorer who had traveled all the way down the Nile to Luxor. His discoveries had been the talk of all the Dark Court balls that season.

"Close, but on the opposite side of the Nile. Abydos was the site where the pharaoh Seti built his pyramids. He also built a beautiful temple to the god Osiris."

"The god who was brought back from the dead by Isis," I said, remembering my Egyptian mythology. A *Necromancer's Companion* would have come in handy if I'd had it with me.

Danilo nodded. "The temple at Abydos is allegedly where Osiris was brought back to life. And where his greatest treasures were interred. This site is one of the most recently discovered, so it has not been completely excavated. Nor has it been plundered by grave robbers."

"Isn't that what you intend to do if you find the sword?" I asked. I wondered if we could be arrested for disturbing a historical site. I wondered if it would be foolish to alert the authorities to Danilo's plans.

"The Morning Star is not an Egyptian artifact, Katerina. It is not of this world."

"Which means it does not belong to you any more than it does to anyone else."

His hazel eyes narrowed as he glared at me. "And what would you have us do with it?"

"Find some way to destroy it," I said. "Or give it back to the Grigori. Such a dangerous weapon should not be placed in anyone's hands."

"Impossible." He laughed, but it was a cruel and cold laugh. "You are so naïve." He took my hand and smoothed over my skin with his fingertips. "I wish sometimes that I were as innocent as you, Katerina."

I'd never felt less innocent than at that moment. His touch made my stomach squirm. I was revolted. I jerked my hand back from him. "How long will it take us to reach Abydos?"

"By pressing forward without stops along the way, we should reach Abydos by tomorrow afternoon," the crown prince said.

One of the Grigori brought us breakfast, a few pieces of flatbread and dates. Danilo did not even allow me a cup of coffee or tea. "You are fasting in preparation for the ritual. Only light foods and water for now. And after tonight, only water until the ritual is complete."

The flatbread and dates were delicious, but I feared that I would be weak by the time the ritual occurred. Somehow, I would have to keep my wits about me.

Danilo and Mala, I noticed, were eating light meals as well. Mala nibbled on her fruit and Danilo only picked at his bread. I wondered if he was actually nervous about the ritual. As much as I hated and feared the lich tsar, I had come to feel sorry for the crown prince. I didn't think he'd ever planned on any of this to happen when we conducted his ascension ritual in Cetinje. Being possessed had in fact been one of his greatest fears.

I wondered if there was a way of defeating Konstantin without harming Danilo. I had no wish to marry him, but it did not mean I hoped this would all end badly for him. If I had to kill the crown prince in order to kill Konstantin, could I do it?

A chill crept over my skin. Danilo glanced over at me and frowned. I put my napkin on the table. My appetite was gone.

"Before we reach Abydos, I must tell you a little about Egyptian magic," the crown prince said. "You've used it each time you call upon the shadows to hide you."

"The *Sheult* spell was in *A Necromancer's Companion*."

"That book was taken from some of the writings of Ankh-al-

Sekhem, as well as those of ancient Arabic and Greek necromancers. A French sorcerer compiled the book in the late sixteen hundreds."

It was strange to think I had the bitter old Egyptian mummy to thank for the *Sheult* spell. It had protected me many times.

"The Egyptians knew about one's cold light. They called it the *ka*," Danilo continued. "Or the body double."

"I thought the ka was the soul they built their pyramids for." I'd not read much about Egyptology, but I'd overheard a few conversations between tourists and tour guides while we were in the museum in Cairo.

"According to the Ani Papyrus, the soul contains several parts, and the cold light, or the ka, is merely one part. Most of the rituals in the papyrus aid the deceased in restoring all the parts of the soul together so it may rise again."

I frowned. "Danilo, everyone did not return from the dead in ancient Egypt. One does not see streets populated with walking corpses."

He shook his head. "That is because they remain in the necropolis. In the cities of the dead. And only royalty was given the rites of resurrection, Katerina. Not everyone could be brought back."

The slaves and the merchants and the soldiers and the rest of the pharaoh's people had to be content with their short, hard lives, while the pharaoh cheated death and lived on in his beautiful, gilded pyramid. It did not seem fair. "When did you have time to read so much?" I asked. "Surely you did not glean all of that information from that fragment of the papyrus."

"Of course not. I read Johanna's *Companion* many, many

years before it fell into your hands, my dear." He nodded to the younger Grigori, who came forth with something wrapped in an old black cloth. The Grigori presented his bundle to me.

With a bewildered "Thank you," I took the bundle and unwrapped the black silk. The fabric was fragile, and I was afraid it would crumble in my hands. "Where did you get this?" I asked, astounded. It was *A Necromancer's Companion*. But it was not my copy. This one was written in French.

"It is a pity you did not bring your own book, Katerina," Danilo said lazily. "Fortunately, the Grigori were able to find a replacement."

"You are most gracious," I said to the Grigori, whose face betrayed no emotion. I carefully wrapped the silk around the book again and placed the seemingly innocent bundle in my lap. It had been responsible for the fate of possibly thousands of Egyptians. "Has it ever occurred to you how much our tsar is like the ancient pharaohs?"

"They rule by divine right," Danilo said with a shrug. "It is the will of the gods."

"But the people had no voice," I said. "They lived and died at the whim of the pharaoh."

"Who is the voice of God." Danilo's eyes narrowed.

Mala's voice broke in on our conversation. "Your education has been filling your head with revolutionary ideas, hasn't it?"

"Of course not! But it does pain me to see people who believe the tsar does not care about them."

"Why should he care about them?" Danilo said, leaning forward. "They pay their taxes and fight in the tsar's armies, and in return, the tsar protects them from foreign attacks."

"Do you think that's all a tsar is responsible for?" I asked.

"Tsar Pavel never prepared you for ruling Russia. Your father never wanted you to be tsar." I knew I was risking Konstantin's anger again. But I had to get Danilo to see how dangerous the lich tsar was. He would not be a good tsar. He would not listen to the people.

Danilo's hands pounded the table in anger. "It was not his choice! Grandmother wanted me to rule Byzantium! Nicholas tried to recapture Constantinople and failed. But now that my brother is dead, I will rule both Byzantium and all of the Russias! The two kingdoms will be united under my power."

Mala stood up from the table and went to kneel at Danilo's side. "You will make a wise and powerful tsar, Your Imperial Majesty," she told him. Her faerie eyes shimmered and it seemed to calm him.

The Grigori standing nearby said nothing. The two men revealed no emotion, nor did they seem fazed by the lich tsar's anger. They believed he would carry the Morning Star. And they would follow whoever carried the sword.

"The Ottomans are too powerful for Russia to wage war against right now," I said. "Even Empress Katerina realized this before she died. Capturing Byzantium was nothing but an old woman's dream."

Danilo glared at me. "You do not deserve to carry her name, Duchess." He stood, pushing Mala to the side as he reached out and grabbed my arm. "It is time for you to retire to your cabin and meditate for the coming ritual."

His fingers dug into my arm and he dragged me out of the dining room back out to the cramped deck. With a rough shove, he pushed me into my cabin. "You will be allowed out when we arrive at Abydos," he said, locking the door behind me.

I stumbled toward my bed. I had no idea how to prepare myself for the ritual, other than worrying about it and working myself up into hysterics. That was not something I cared to do, so instead, I opened up the French edition of A *Necromancer's Companion* the Grigori had given me and searched for information on the ka. Was it really one's cold light? That would explain why a necromancer could manipulate that light, and shadows as well.

I flipped past the pages of incantations to Osiris that prevented the deceased from forgetting his name and past an incantation that allowed the deceased to take any physical form he wished, from a lion to a hawk. I flipped past the drawings of ornate inscriptions on ceremonial daggers and pictures of enchanted scarabs that were to be placed on the deceased's breast.

And finally, I came to a chapter that mentioned the Morning Star.

CHAPTER TWENTY-EIGHT

According to the *Companion*, the Morning Star could only be carried by one who could walk both the worlds of the living and the dead. A necromancer who knew the secrets of the ka and the shadows. One who knew how to coax the ka back to the land of the living.

I was still reading the book when Mala knocked and opened my door well before dawn. "Duchess, these are your clothes for the ritual." She handed me a white linen robe. I was surprised she did not have a golden headdress for me as well.

"Am I to appear as Cleopatra?" I asked, taking the robe and tossing it onto the bed.

"You are to dress as a proper Egyptian priestess." She stopped at the door and turned around with a vicious smile. "A proper *virgin* Egyptian priestess."

I wanted to roll my eyes at her. "How close are we to Abydos?" I asked, but she'd already closed the door behind her. I peeked out the tiny window and could see palm trees lining the dark green river. I had no idea where we were.

I ignored the priestess robe on my bed and was going to continue reading about old Egyptian gods when I spotted the medical text I'd found in Cairo. I opened it up instead. I was amazed at how far I'd come in my Greek lessons. I only had a little trouble reading some of the ancient Greek words.

The physician Galen wrote mostly of the organs of apes and pigs that he had dissected. The Roman Empire forbade human dissection, so he made do with animals whose anatomies were similar to our own. I soon grew tired of reading about intestines and lung tissue. I fell asleep dreaming about a pig that wore the headdress of a pharaoh.

A sudden lurch of the boat awakened me. My head bumped up against the wall. Rubbing the sore spot tenderly, I crawled out of bed and tried my door, but it was still locked. I could hear footsteps and shouting above as people scrambled up to the deck.

It was not long before someone came to check on me. The elder Grigori opened the door. "Are you unhurt, Duchess?" he asked.

"I'm fine. What has happened?"

"The boat has run aground on a sandbar. The captain is refusing to continue to sail in the dark."

"I take it the crown prince is not happy."

"They are arguing right now. It is perhaps better if you remain in your cabin."

I sighed. "No, perhaps I can calm him down." The crown prince's temper was nowhere near as volatile as the lich tsar's. I hoped between me and Mala we'd be able to make him see reason. I followed the Grigori up the steps to the deck.

Danilo was shouting at the captain, who looked frightened but who refused to send his crewmen down to the sandbar until daylight. It was too risky.

"Your Majesty, the Nile is full of crocodiles and other hungry creatures," Mala said, most rationally. "The men will be of no use to us if they get eaten."

But the crown prince would not listen. "We have no time to be cautious! Send your men down to make their repairs. I will guarantee their safety."

"How can you make such a promise?" the captain asked.

"I shall cast a spell of protection around them. They will be safe as long as they stay within the light."

The crew looked at the crown prince warily but finally agreed to climb down to the sandbar. A generous-sized bag of golden coins helped persuade them. One of the younger Grigori accompanied them as well.

The lich tsar's green eyes flashed as Danilo spoke an incantation in ancient Egyptian. Mala stood next to me, gazing at him in silent adoration. Her worship of the lich tsar was unsettling. I understood her gratitude toward Princess Cantacuzene, but that did not mean she was obligated to follow Konstantin blindly. Unless, of course, she was starting to have romantic feelings for the crown prince as well. She certainly seemed to have forgotten all about the tsarevitch.

The lich tsar's spell was empowered with a drop of Danilo's blood. He pricked a finger with his penknife and held it out over the river. It was only a single drop, but it was enough to create a magical barrier around the sandbar.

It was also enough to attract a very large crocodile that had been dozing nearby. A dark shape just under the water approached the sandbar. It couldn't come any closer because of Danilo's spell, so it hovered in the dark muddy waters and waited.

The men did not notice the reptile as they hurried to dig the boat free. Danilo sent two more of the Grigori to help push the boat back into the water. Their inhuman strength was invaluable, and they were able to free the boat in no time at all.

But as the Grigori pushed the boat, the crew moved beyond Danilo's circle of protection. Suddenly, there was a great splash followed by a piercing cry. I saw one of the ship's men disappear into the river. My stomach turned.

The rest of the men scampered to board the boat while the Grigori searched the water for the man who'd gone under. But there was nothing left of him to save. The waters turned bloody, and the man's red cap floated up to the surface.

Mala reached for my hand silently, and I squeezed it. The captain removed his own fez and wept. Danilo said something to him quietly, but it did not sound like words of comfort.

"You are a monster, my lord!" the captain said. "What kind of evil have you brought down upon us all?" Ignoring the rest of us, he returned to the wheelhouse to continue our journey.

The Grigori climbed back onto the ship empty-handed and silent.

Mala joined Danilo, who stood at the rail, gazing down into the river. "All great leaders make great sacrifices," she said to him. "It will be worth it in the end, Your Imperial Majesty."

Danilo said nothing to her, and at last she walked away to return to her own cabin, glaring at me as she passed.

I turned to go as well, but the crown prince finally spoke. "They will say this is a bad omen."

I walked over to him by the railing. The sky was beginning to grow lighter. It would be dawn soon. "Perhaps it is."

He gave me a dark look. "You have never been superstitious, my dear Katerina," he said. "You are far too intelligent for that."

I wished I had the strength and the courage to push the crown prince overboard. That would be a certain way to solve our problems. But the Grigori hovered nearby and I did not think they would let me harm their master.

And I had to believe there was a way to destroy the lich tsar without harming the crown prince. "And are you superstitious?" I asked.

"I come from Montenegro, a country steeped in superstitions." With that, he left me alone at the rail wondering what he planned to do next.

I remained outside to watch the sunrise, and the Grigori let me be. I guessed they were certain I would not make any attempt to swim for the shore now. I made the sign of the cross over my heart for the man we had just lost. I prayed for his soul and then said another prayer for my own.

CHAPTER TWENTY-NINE

We reached the dock of Belianeh later that afternoon. The excavated temples of Abydos lay several miles inland and unfortunately were only accessible by pack animal. We were met at the rail station by a herd of various-sized donkeys and young boys willing to be our guides into the desert.

Danilo haggled with them and finally agreed upon animals for each of us, another one for carrying supplies, and two boys as our guides. The boys were anxious to set out and anxious that we return to town before sunset. I wondered how long the ritual was supposed to last.

We left our trunks aboard the boat, for there were no inns in the small village. Mala insisted that I bring the linen priestess robe in my bag. The Talisman of Isis was still around my neck, tucked beneath my traveling dress. The lightweight wool skirt just barely covered my ankles when I climbed onto my donkey, a sweet-natured creature named Amin. The young guide told me the animal's name meant "trustworthy." The guide's name was Tumani, and as we rode along he sang songs that apparently had naughty lyrics, because the other boy, who seemed a little older, yelled at him to be quiet, that his song was not suitable for a lady's ears.

Amin's fur was soft between his ears. He plodded along with the others in single file as we passed through fields of wheat in the fertile area between the river and the desert. We passed a few smaller villages that dotted the landscape built up above the floodplain upon dirt mounds. Dirty children ran up to us begging for coins or sweets. I had neither, but I saw Mala pass out a few silver pieces to the youngest ones. I wished I had something to give them.

The ruins of Abydos sat where the green fields met the desert. The trip had taken almost two hours by donkey ride. I was hot and thirsty. Tumani and the other boy offered water to each of us before taking care of the animals.

Mala and I fell in behind Danilo, the Grigori following us as we approached the Temple of Osiris. Legend stated that the ancient god himself was buried here. That this was where the goddess Isis had carried him. The wind was stronger here than down by the river, and my hair was coming loose from its pins. Mala had no such problem, as her hair was hidden beneath her black headdress. We both stumbled, though, as the excavated path leading to the temple was not cleared as often as the ones in the more popular sites at Giza and Luxor.

The site was not vacant, however. Excavation was going on at the far side of the temple complex, with men directing a group of boys to carry dirt and rubbish from one of the temple ruins. A pack of tourists was exploring one of the smaller tombs nearby. Their guides sat waiting with their donkeys in the shade of a palm tree.

"What if they try to visit the temple during the ritual?" I asked Mala.

"The Grigori will stand guard and not let anyone inside," she replied. "The crown prince has planned for everything."

The Temple of Osiris had actually been rebuilt on the same site several times over a period of three to four thousand years. Not much remained of the Great Temple, save for the main hall and its enormous columns. The stone columns were covered in hieroglyphics that told of Egyptian history. Curses, long-forgotten curses, were inscribed to ward off grave robbers. But most of the treasures in these tombs had been plundered before the first French explorers found Abydos in the eighteenth century. A few valuable pieces had survived and were now safe in museums. Other artifacts, such as the Talisman of Isis, remained in private hands. Princess Cantacuzene had stolen the talisman from the Montenegrin queen. I wondered how long the relic had been in the Montenegrin royal family.

Not much remained of the forecourt leading to the temple except for a few carvings and the stairs, which led to the upper court. The outer hall had carvings of Egyptian gods and the pharaohs bearing them gifts. Giant columns stood in the inner hall and were decorated with even more carvings of gods and hieroglyphics. Behind the inner hall, several small sanctuaries had been excavated. In the last one stood the altar of Osiris.

Mala and I found a small alcove near the altar where she helped me change into the linen robe. It was sleeveless with a beautiful beaded collar of lapis and jasper. Thankfully, she did not notice the Talisman of Isis I was wearing underneath. She brushed my hair and left it down. I had lost most of the pins to hold it up anyway. She stood back to look at me and shook her head. "You do not look Egyptian by any stretch of the imagination, but you do look beautiful. His Imperial Majesty will be pleased."

I blushed. I felt naked in the linen robe, even with my modern underthings still on beneath. My bare arms and feet were exposed in a shocking manner. Mala had not allowed me to replace my boots and stockings and had consented to my keeping the camisole and petticoats only after I begged her.

The afternoon had grown late, and the sun was beginning to set far to the west. I began to smell a heavy perfume in the air. Danilo had lit the frankincense at the altar.

Mala nodded. "It is time."

Danilo had said this ritual would somehow aid us in finding the Morning Star and would ready him to face Papus. But I could not help thinking that any ritual requiring such elaborate preparations must be for something much darker than merely seeking a lost object. Or merely for seeking protection from a foe. Disturbing ancient gods was not something even a lich tsar would undertake lightly, I would hope.

The sanctuary holding the altar of Osiris was a small square chamber supported by four enormous columns. Each column had carvings of Osiris and Isis and hieroglyphics begging for the deities' intercessions. The room was dark except for the two gas lanterns Danilo had lit. A tiny skylight high above us let in fresh air but little light, as the sun was sinking fast. I worried for our two young guides waiting by the animals outside.

Mala turned to leave the sacred chamber, but Danilo stopped her. "Your assistance is needed as well, my dear," he told her. As his gaze flickered over me briefly, I caught disapproval or possibly even disappointment in his eyes. *Now what have I done?* I wondered.

Mala looked surprised but pleased. She took the place he indicated behind the altar, opposite him. He motioned for me to stand to the left of the altar. I saw a carved panel on the wall behind me that looked as if a doorway had been sealed. The paint on the figures could still be seen, the dark brown of the people's skin and the blue and reds of their clothing. Two jackals stood guard patiently behind them. The guides had said that Seti's successor, Ramses the Second, had blocked off several doorways in the temple following Seti's death. I wondered what had been behind the panel.

The fragrance of the incense was making me dizzy, and I remembered it had been hours since I'd had any food and days since I'd had anything substantial. All I'd been given on the caravan out to the temples had been water. I stood in my ceremonial robe, barefoot on a dusty stone floor, dreaming about a nice roast game hen or a lamb steak.

The lich tsar had translated the ritual in his neat handwriting from the ancient Egyptian into Russian. He rubbed a sweet-smelling oil on my forehead, then handed me the new scrolls. "Begin reading, Katerina. The ritual will explain what must be done."

I took a deep breath. Perhaps we would not be raising anyone from the dead, for once, since there was no tomb here. This room was the alleged burial place of the god Osiris, but the sarcophagus had long since been removed. Still, I could feel the power in the space. The air was charged with magic. I hoped the talisman would protect me from any evil that we might conjure.

"Hurry up!" Mala said, eager to see the ritual completed.

Danilo merely smiled but used his thumb to rub the oil on Mala's forehead as well as his own.

I glanced down at the scroll and began.

CHAPTER THIRTY

"'Hail, Power of Heaven, opener of the way for those who have before,'" I read. "'We have brought you cakes and ale and joints of meat. Hear the pleas of the departed.'"

Danilo placed a small red stone on the altar. It was carved in the shape of a scarab beetle.

I felt my cold light rise as I continued to read. The hair stood on the back of my neck as the energy in the room rose higher and higher.

"'Hail, Power of Heaven, who rises in the east and sets in the west. Restore the beloved into this vessel before you.'"

The red scarab on the altar began to move. It looked as if something were inside it, trying to get out. Mala's eyes grew big with fear. I wasn't sure if she'd ever witnessed a formal ritual before. Unfortunately, I was becoming an expert at them. Did Danilo expect something or someone to be drawn into the scarab, or were we coaxing something out? Perhaps we would see a ghostly presence above the altar. I read on.

"'Hail, Power of Heaven, who art exalted above the stars, I have come to you in a purified state. Restore the beloved into the vessel before you.'" It seemed strange to me to use the term "beloved." I wondered if there was something wrong with Danilo's translation. But I saw a sliver of cold light rising up out of the scarab.

Danilo smiled triumphantly. Without warning, he reached forward and grabbed Mala, twisting her as he dragged her across the altar. There was a golden flash as his other hand came up to her heart.

Mala screamed. And then she was silenced and became still. Her blood dripped onto the altar, bathing the scarab. As Danilo's dagger fell to the floor with a clatter, he gently laid Mala's body across the stone altar. He placed the bloodied scarab on her chest.

"Continue!" he shouted to me.

"What have you done?" I said, not believing what had just happened.

"We needed a vessel for the spirit. Mala seemed the perfect choice. She will make an attractive vessel, don't you think?"

"A vessel for whose spirit?"

He picked the dagger back up and pointed it at me. "There is no time to explain. Continue the ritual or you will die with the dancer."

My throat was dry, and my hands were shaking. I could not believe he had killed Mala in such a cold manner. All for a sword. Danilo grabbed me, the bloodied knife shoved up against my heart. But it was the lich tsar's cold eyes staring at me. "Do not think you are safe, my dear. If you refuse to read the ritual, I will kill you and hunt you down in the Graylands and kill you again."

The cold light rising up from the scarab hung in the air like a silver thread. It was waiting for me. Just like Danilo. I could feel my own cold light rising up inside as well. It was surging forward dangerously. If I did not complete the ritual, what would happen to my own light? I felt as if I were losing control. "'Hail, Power of Heaven, who journeys beyond time and space, restore the beloved into this vessel.'"

The silver thread of cold light began to move toward Mala's mouth. It glided through the air like a serpent. It made my skin crawl with revulsion. The cold light of this person was stealing Mala's body. I could not see Mala's cold light. Where had it gone? I wondered if I could travel to the Graylands after the ritual and find her. This was a horrible way to die.

As the cold light of the beloved slid into Mala's mouth, her corpse seemed to take a deep breath. And she opened her eyes.

With a sickening feeling, I realized who the beloved was.

She sat up with a wicked, gleaming smile. Blood was still drying on the front of her black gown, but it did not seem to affect her. The lich tsar picked up her hand and kissed it. "I have longed for this day, Johanna."

"As have I," she said. Then Princess Cantacuzene turned to me. "I have wanted to kill this young necromancer for a long time."

"Why?" I whispered. The evil vampire had been a sort of mentor to me, helping me discover my dark powers. She'd given me her copy of A *Necromancer's Companion*. And she'd tried to protect me from the Montenegrins.

Or had she? "You planned all of this long ago, didn't you?" I said, backing away from the altar. "You made sure that Danilo used the Talisman of Isis for his ascension. You wanted Konstantin to have a powerful sorcerer's body to possess."

"And I would have picked your body to return in, if you hadn't been protected." She reached over and tore my linen gown, revealing the Talisman of Isis. "Fortunately, Konstantin had a second plan waiting in the wings."

I glanced at the lich tsar, whose eyes were shining a bright green now. I had no idea if any part of Danilo still existed in there. "You had her soul hidden in the scarab all this time?" I asked him. "I thought vampires did not have souls."

"There's much that you do not know, silly girl. Most of us do have souls, and I performed the ritual myself when I realized what Militza had done to me," Princess Cantacuzene said. "I would have returned to my own body if you and the tsar's son had not destroyed it."

It made me sick to think of that day. George had to cut her head off when she'd killed my friend Dr. Kruglevski. "When I find the Morning Star, I will sever your head again," I said, my voice deadly calm.

Her cruel laugh echoed in the tiny crypt.

I looked from her to the crown prince, still attempting to piece everything together. "How did Danilo even know the scarab existed?"

"Mala has kept the scarab safe with her all this time," Princess Cantacuzene said. She stretched out her arms and examined her hands—Mala's hands—as if she were trying on a new pair of gloves. "She sought out the crown prince when she saw signs of Konstantin's return. She has always been faithful to me."

"And this is how you repay her!" I exclaimed.

"The greatest gift," the princess said with a smile, "is immortality."

"Where is her soul now?" I demanded. If it was the last thing I did, I would make sure Mala's soul was at peace. Even if it damned my own soul in the process.

"Do you wish to join her?" Princess Cantacuzene's sharp fangs looked odd in Mala's mouth. "That is part of this new plan, isn't it, my love?" She held out her hand, and Danilo placed the bloody dagger in it. As graceful as a cat, the princess drew herself up and slid down from the bloody altar.

I glanced around, trying to fight the panic that was fluttering in my chest. There was nowhere for me to run. The tiny chamber had only the one door, guarded by the Grigori.

The Grigori. "You can carry the Morning Star. Both you and Konstantin can walk the lands of the living as well as the lands of the dead." My heart filled with dread. She was the Queen of Swords.

"Yes. And soon we will find Papus, and then we will retrieve the sword. My Konstantin will carry it back to St. Petersburg. He will lead the Grigori to battle against the bogatyr and his precious Light Court queen. And I will be empress, Katerina. You, my dear, have missed your opportunity."

I ducked around one of the columns as she leapt at me. I dodged the lich tsar and grabbed the handle of the door. I whispered the *Sheult* spell under my breath, but I only managed to draw a few wisps of darkness around me. I was too scared to concentrate.

The Grigori would no doubt chase me, but at least I had a chance outside of the tiny sanctuary. I tore open the door and my body collided with someone standing in the inner hall of the temple. Hands grabbed me by the arms. I screamed.

"Katiya?" The familiar face looking down at me in shock was the most beautiful face in the world.

CHAPTER THIRTY-ONE

"George!" I pushed him back so I could close the door to the sanctuary. But it was too late. Konstantin and Johanna rushed out after me, stopping as they saw a band of Grigori and the tsar's two sons, sabers drawn. Papus stood behind them, a pistol in one hand and a spell book in the other. He gave me a cheeky salute with the pistol. I scowled at him.

The Grigori who'd been guarding the door were nowhere to be seen. I did not know if George and the others had frightened them off or if they'd fought. I hadn't heard any sort of scuffle in the hall from inside the sanctuary, but then again, I'd been quite distracted.

I wanted nothing more than to fall into George's arms and cover him with kisses. But the lich tsar and his newly risen consort had to be stopped. And I was afraid ordinary weapons were not going to be enough.

"*Sheult Anubis!*" I shouted, this time not manipulating my

own shadows but those of George and Nicholas. They momentarily vanished from sight.

"You can't protect them, Duchess," Konstantin shouted. He had fed off Mala's blood and now his powers as a lich tsar were stronger than before. He threw the dagger and it cut straight through the shadows, scattering them into oblivion. My heart stopped in my throat. The dagger missed hitting anyone, but now George and Nicholas were no longer hidden.

Johanna had not fed, so she was still weak from her journey back to the land of the living. Mala's body had spilled a lot of blood, and then the lich tsar had drunk from her as well. Johanna would need more blood soon. It had been far too long since her soul had been locked away.

I tried to stay between her and the Romanov brothers. At least, I thought gratefully, she did not carry the Morning Star right now. I had to keep her and Konstantin away from Papus. Since both had returned from the land of the dead, there was nothing to prevent them from traveling across the Graylands. And if they entered the Graylands, there was no way we could return to St. Petersburg in time to stop them from attacking the tsar.

Konstantin was drawing a magic circle around himself and Johanna while she fought off the Grigori. The creatures did not have blood, so she could not feed from them. She would have to attack me or George or Nicholas. Or Papus, who was standing behind a pillar, shouting out spells and trying to shoot the lich tsar. Princess Cantacuzene decided to try for the tsarevitch.

"Nicky, why are you trying to hurt me?" she asked, batting her eyes. She pulled back her head covering and shook her black curls loose.

"Mathilde?" The tsarevitch was confused for only a moment, but she used it to her advantage.

Johanna pushed him back against one of the columns, her fangs and claws out to attack.

George rushed at her with his saber. "Katerina, why is the ballerina from the Mariinsky Theater trying to eat my brother?"

"Because Princess Cantacuzene came back from the dead and has taken over her body," I shouted over the fighting. The Grigori kept coming at Konstantin but were unable to get past his magical defenses. He was chanting something, but I could not make out what it was over the rest of the noise in the room. George reached Nicholas and the two of them circled the princess. She was backed into the circle with Konstantin.

"No, wait!" I yelled, but as soon as her feet entered his sacred circle, the lich tsar grabbed her arm and the two of them disappeared in a blinding flash of cold light.

"*Merde!*" I said. There was no way of telling where they had gone. "We've lost them. But they will be back. I'm sure of it. They need Papus to reach the Morning Star. He's the only mage initiated who can access the seventh gate in the Graylands."

George helped his brother up from the ground, where he'd been knocked in the fighting. He brushed the dust off of his jacket and loosened the top buttons so he could breathe easily. "Now, Katerina, start at the beginning."

Papus took the Grigori and went into the altar sanctuary to look around. Bewildered, Nicholas followed them.

I took a deep breath. But before I could start, George interrupted me again.

"No, wait." He walked over to me calmly, took me up in his

arms, and kissed me. Passionately. "Do you have any idea how crazy I've been looking for you?" he murmured. "I never should have taken you out of Russia. I'm so sorry, Katiya."

I put my fingers on his lips, my forehead touching his. "It's not your fault, I promise. He would have found me in St. Petersburg just as easily."

"Danilo wouldn't dare be seen in the city. He would just be arrested again."

"He's not really Danilo anymore. Konstantin was bonded to him through the ascension ritual, and slowly, the lich tsar has taken over."

"Did he hurt you?" George's blue eyes searched my face anxiously. "I don't care who he really is. I promise I will kill him if he touched you."

I shook my head. "He needed me . . . untouched for the ritual. But he kept saying we were going to be married. I think he was going to use my body to bring back Princess Cantacuzene. But the Talisman of Isis protected me somehow. So he ended up sacrificing Mala instead."

George didn't let go of me. His kisses were possessive. "The ballerina? How did she get involved in all of this?"

"She was a loyal servant of the princess. Years ago, Johanna saved her mother's life. Mala was a wild fae. She did not belong to either of the Petersburg courts."

"And did she flirt with my brother at the princess's command?"

I shook my head again. "At Danilo's. Or Konstantin's. She was supposed to be dangling after both of you."

George's short laugh made my heart dance a mazurka. "She never had a chance with me," he said, his lips traveling up the side of my jaw. "Especially when you run around dressed like this. I take it this is the rage of Egyptian fashion?"

I laughed, despite the tears running down my face. I'd forgotten all about the ridiculous priestess costume I was wearing. "I don't know what Mala did with my clothes. I had boots and stockings when we arrived at Abydos."

He swept me up in his arms with one more heart-stopping kiss. "I'm sure we'll find them somewhere."

"Georgi?" The tsarevitch returned from inside the sanctuary with the scroll in his hand. There was blood smeared on it. "I think you should take a look at this."

George did not put me down but leaned closer to see the paper his brother held out.

"That's the spell he made me read," I said. "He told me he needed to speak with the spirit of the one who had carried the sword last. I had no idea that person would be Princess Cantacuzene. Or that he would kill Mala."

I realized I was shaking. George stroked my bare arm comfortingly.

"This is from the Book of the Dead," he said.

I nodded. "We found the fragment of papyrus in the caves at Giza. After we fought off Ankh-al-Sekhem."

"Who is—" Nicholas started to ask.

"The Ankh-al-Sekhem who lived three thousand years ago?" Papus interrupted, joining us again.

I nodded in wonder, amazed that he recognized the name. "Konstantin was trying to get information out of him."

George's face clouded. "Papus and I tried to speak with Ankh-al-Sekhem in the Graylands. But we were unable to find him."

Only because I'd accidentally helped the Egyptian return to life. But I did not think George needed to hear about my adventures with the crown prince in Cairo. "You went to the Graylands? It's too dangerous!" I said. "Especially with your illness."

George shook his head, dismissing my concern. "It needed to be done. Even if it was unsuccessful. You say only Papus can access the sword?"

I nodded. "'Past the seven gates of heaven, the Morning Star lies, betwixt the steadfast darkness and the unfailing light.' That is what the sphinx in Cairo told us."

"The seven gates of Isis," Papus said, rubbing his chin. "Of course. But I am not the only mage initiated in the highest degree of the Egyptian mysteries."

I looked at the Frenchman in alarm. "Danilo said you were the only one he knew of. How can we trust you? You tried to kill me in Cairo."

Papus shook his head gravely. "My apologies, Duchess. You were never in danger from me. We wanted the crown prince to believe we were working separately. It was for your protection. But it's true that I am not the only qualified mage for the ritual. The grand duke finished his initiation last month."

George finally put me back down but kept a protective arm around my waist. "What is required of me?" he asked. "I'd been led to believe only a necromancer could carry the Morning Star."

Papus looked at me. "If you are correct about the sphinx's riddle, it sounds as if there must be both a mage and a necromancer to retrieve the sword."

"I thought it took years of study in order to be initiated past the seven gates," I said. "George, how did you push through so quickly?"

"Russia is in danger. My father is in danger," he said, his blue eyes boring into mine as he squeezed my hand. "*You* are in danger. I needed to finish my studies and return to St. Petersburg as swiftly as possible."

Papus looked guilty. "I told him it was foolish, but he was stubborn, Duchess. Even when his health seemed at the brink of collapse, he refused to quit."

I gave a little cry and looked from the Frenchman to the grand duke. "What have you done to yourself?" I demanded. If he was truly as powerful as Papus now, what was the cost to his health?

"We know where to find the seven gates, Your Imperial Highness," Papus said.

I looked behind him and noticed the Grigori had regathered. They seemed tense. And excited.

I was grateful that George had found me. But I also hated that he and Papus had been searching for me instead of the Morning Star. I did not want him distracted from what was important. Stopping Konstantin and protecting the tsar was most imperative.

"Let me go to the Graylands with Papus, then," I said. "He can get me through the seven gates and I will bring back the sword."

"Fine. I'm going with you." George spotted the bundle containing my clothes and picked them up for me.

"You can't," I said. "It's too dangerous."

"Too dangerous for you to travel without me, Katiya." He

pulled me close to him once more. "I can't lose you again. I am not letting go of you until we are husband and wife."

A hot flush crept over my skin. "You still want to marry me? No one will believe that Danilo did not compromise me. Even if Mala was with us, pretending to be my chaperone."

"I don't give a damn about that. Unless you've changed your mind about us?" he said, his faerie blue eyes shimmering with silver specks. He was trying to read my thoughts.

I stood on my tiptoes to kiss him. "Never." I would never stop loving my grand duke.

"Then we should be married now," he said. "Before we leave Egypt."

I held out the folds of my theatrical gown. I was wearing white already, but the hem was stained with Mala's blood. "This can't be a good omen," I said.

George was not superstitious. "You look beautiful," he reassured me.

"But we should stop the lich tsar and Princess Cantacuzene first," I said. "They will come after Papus. He's in danger."

The French mage only smiled at this and shook his head.

George took my hand and raised it to his lips. "Marry me first, Katiya. Papus and the sword are both safe from Konstantin, I swear to you."

There was a Coptic monastery between the ruins of Abydos and the riverside town of Belianeh, where a much nicer priest than the one in Riga listened to our confessions. He looked at my odd dress curiously but thankfully did not notice my bare feet. George showed him the papers he'd brought from St. Petersburg: copies of both of our baptism records and the letter the priest in St. Petersburg had written, stating that we were both of legal age and unmarried to anyone else.

Brother Ananias looked younger than his fellow priests, but his beard was still peppered with gray. He was dressed in a simple black cassock with a black turban covering his head. His dark brown eyes were kind as he gestured for me to sit with him in the empty, quiet kitchen. "I can see that your heart is troubled, Duchess. And you have the Grigori with you. Are you in danger?"

He knew about the Watchers, I realized with a start. Could he know about the other creatures that walked among us? Since the monastery was built just outside the ruins of an ancient pagan temple, I wondered how often the priests had encountered mages searching for lost knowledge. Did he know of the blood drinkers and the fae as well? "Have you encountered any members of the Order of the Black Lily?" I asked tentatively.

"You are safe here, Duchess," he said, smiling. "No creature can harm you within the walls of our sanctuary. Now, tell me what burdens your soul."

I breathed a sigh of relief and before I could stop myself, everything tumbled out. I'd been holding it all in for so long. My terrible gift, the undead creatures I'd made, and the lies I'd told to hide my secret from my loved ones. And worst of all, the terrible things that Danilo had made me do in the ancient crypt. I'd been an accomplice to a murder. I confessed it all to the Coptic monk.

Brother Ananias frowned when I finished telling him about

Konstantin's plot. "For the Grigori to be divided and fighting against each other is not right. They chafe under the bonds of the Morning Star."

"I've been told the sword cannot be destroyed," I said. "Is that true? Would destroying the Morning Star free the Grigori?"

"It would free them from the bindings of the sword," Brother Ananias said thoughtfully, "and they would no longer have to serve the bearer of the sword, but it would not end their curse. Because of their rebellion, they can never return to heaven. But without the sword urging them to fight, they would remain only as Watchers and would no longer be compelled to interfere in our petty human battles.

"I'm afraid, however," he continued, "that a sword forged in Heaven is indeed impossible to destroy. Besides, you need to carry the sword and lead the Grigori if you wish to defeat Konstantin."

"It's the sword of Lucifer," I said. "I don't want to stain my soul any more if I can help it. If we can prevent Konstantin from using the sword, won't that be enough?"

Brother Ananias took my hands in his. The skin on his palms and fingers was rough, and I imagined him working in the monastery gardens, patiently tending the roses that grew in this harsh land. "I do not feel you have to worry about your soul, Katerina Alexandrovna. The ancient Egyptians believed when a person died, his or her heart was weighed against a feather. The heart that was judged pure would not weigh more than the feather. I do not believe there is any malice in your heart, Duchess. I am certain it is pure."

"But I have brought the dead back to life and disturbed their rest," I said in protest. I could not possibly be forgiven for these things, could I? "I belong to the Dark Court."

"God dwells in both the thick darkness and the unfailing light," Brother Ananias said. His words were eerily close to those of the sphinx. It made the hair stand up on the back of my neck. "Your gift was given to you by God, and no one can fathom what God has planned for him or her. Not even you, necromancer."

My heart did feel lighter after our talk. Even if I knew there was still darkness ahead. Brother Ananias made the sign of the cross over me and together we recited the Lord's Prayer. I left the kitchen with a new sense of hope, and George gave my hand a gentle squeeze as he passed me on his way to confess to the monk. He did not take nearly as long this time as he had with the priest in Riga.

Following the Coptic tradition, George and I entered the simple chapel together, holding hands. I carried a small bouquet of Nile lilies and damask roses, picked for me by one of the men in the monastery's sunken garden. The scent was heavenly.

Nicholas Alexandrovich was happy to stand up for his brother. Amin, my donkey, and the little boy from the village waited outside the monastery with the Grigori. Papus stood quietly in the shadows in the back of the sanctuary. I knew he was anxious to find the sword. I was too, and I was worried about facing Konstantin and Johanna again. But George stood beside me with a reassuring smile. Everything was going to be all right in the end. Or so we hoped.

Our ceremony was much simpler than it would have been if we'd been married in St. Petersburg. I remembered Grand Duchess Militza's wedding to my cousin. She'd worn a silver gown embroidered with pearls and the jewel-encrusted Romanov nuptial crown with a veil of lace. The ceremony had taken place in the great Orthodox chapel at Peterhof Palace. It had lasted for hours as we stood in the crowded chapel in the summer, made even hotter by banks of burning candles.

Brother Ananias chanted the litany in a beautiful bass voice as the other monks lit incense and chanted the responses. Everything became a blur after that. It had been days since I'd had a proper meal, and the exhaustion I felt from escaping Konstantin and Johanna earlier that morning had finally caught up with me.

I remember repeating the words that the priest asked me to. I remember him blessing two golden rings, and I remember the smoky fog from the incense. I remember the embroidered capes they draped on both George's and my shoulders. I remember the simple crowns placed on each of our heads, to symbolize our roles as the king and queen of our newly created household.

George held my hand and placed the golden ring upon my finger. I remember feeling nothing but happiness when George kissed me as his wife. "I will love you always, Katiya," he whispered. At last, I felt a sense of peace.

We took the train back north, which was slightly faster than the trip by boat. The railroad line began at Assiut, several miles north of Abydos, so we used the hired steamer to bridge the gap. The dragoman was not sorry that Danilo was absent from our party. He accepted the extra gold offered by the tsarevitch, and within an hour we were boarding the train. I'd changed back into my blue traveling dress. I'd never been so happy to wear stockings and shoes in my life. George ordered the Grigori to see to my trunk.

"That is not necessary," I said. "There's nothing in there that I want to keep. Except this," I said, picking up the French copy of *A Necromancer's Companion*. "And this," I added, stuffing the medical book from the bazaar into a small suitcase Nicholas had purchased for me. I would repay the tsarevitch for the luggage and repay Danilo for the book. I did not want to have a reason to feel obligated to anyone.

At my request, the Grigori took the trunk to the local orphanage where the nuns would distribute the clothing among the poor. Everything except for the almost-indecent negligee, of course, and even that I hoped could be torn apart and made into infant's clothing or a child's dress. But now I would be faced with a similar dilemma. I did not want to feel obligated to George for buying new clothes for me, even if we were now husband and wife. I could not get over how pleased I was with how that sounded.

"The bride should be able to provide her own trousseau," I said, feeling ridiculous. George could not stop grinning. We made a ridiculous couple. And it made me grin too.

"Think of it as a wedding present," his brother Nicholas suggested with a kind smile. He seemed happy to help us get married, even if he knew the trouble we would face when we reached St. Petersburg. I only hoped he would not share in our punishment.

We stayed in the dining car all night as the train rolled north in the darkness. Neither of us suggested moving to the sleeping car. As Nicholas and Papus discussed the merits of Polish and French ballerinas at their own table, I fell asleep against George's strong shoulder, hardly able to believe that we were together again after everything. My hand clasped in his, I dreamed of a future we might have after all.

CHAPTER THIRTY-TWO

We reached Cairo by sunrise. At some point, George had wrapped a blanket around both of us. I awoke to his gentle kisses up and down the side of my face. "Good morning," he murmured. "We're coming into the station, Katiya. It's time to get up."

The Graylands awaited us. As did the Morning Star, hidden beyond the seven gates. I groaned and reluctantly stood and stretched. We did not stay on the train for breakfast. Instead, we took the electric tram through the city and headed east across the river, toward the necropolis. The Grigori loyal to Papus sat silently in the seats behind us. Nicholas and Papus were seated in front of us, also silent, each one wrapped up in his own thoughts.

The great pyramids of Giza rose up out of the desert. I had a sinking feeling in my stomach as we drew closer to the ancient tombs. George seemed to sense this and took my hand in his.

It had been decided that Papus would not go to the seven gates after all. He would accompany Nicholas back to Russia. Papus would use the Grigori portals and escort the tsarevitch through the Graylands swiftly so they could reach St. Petersburg before us—hopefully before Konstantin arrived. George wished his brother could travel the Graylands with us, but we both knew it was impossible.

"But it would be safer for the two of you if Papus and I went along to retrieve the sword," the tsarevitch argued one last time. "We would make a formidable team."

George shook his head. "Out of the question. You are the heir. Go with Papus straight to St. Petersburg. And don't worry about us." He squeezed my hand affectionately. "Katiya and I will be fine. We'll meet up with you as soon as possible. It should not take us long."

George embraced his brother as we stood at one of the temple walls near the sphinx. The two Grigori stood at attention, awaiting Papus's instructions. "Give Mother Dear and Xenia my love," George told Nicholas. "I hate that you will face Papa's wrath before I do."

Nicholas smiled and shook his head. "There will be plenty of wrath to go around when you get back. Take care of yourself, Brother."

"You too, Nicky." George stepped back and wrapped his arm around my waist.

"Be careful, Your Imperial Highness," I said. I dreaded the return to St. Petersburg. The tsar may have given his blessing for our engagement, but only at a price I was not willing to pay. The empress would be furious with us for eloping and depriving her of a wedding to orchestrate. I hoped her anger would not last. It would not be long before she would have Nicholas's wedding and Xenia's to plan. And many years in the future, the weddings of Olga and Mikhail.

Papus murmured an incantation in a language I could not understand. A doorway appeared in the side of the temple, between the two Grigori. With a polite tip of his hat, the French mage stepped through the doorway with Nicholas following him.

"Are we to use the same portal?" I asked George. The doorway remained open, but I could not see past its threshold.

"No, we will use a portal you create," he said. "That way I can save my energy for the seven gates." Before our eyes, the doorway between the Grigori faded. George motioned for me to follow him and we walked around to the main entrance of the temple.

I paused to look at him anxiously. Had he lost more weight since we'd been in Riga? "Are you certain it's safe for you to go?" I asked.

He answered with a reassuring kiss on my forehead. "Stop worrying about me. We're wasting time."

This area had been excavated decades earlier and then abandoned, as there had been nothing worthy of stealing within. A few carvings along the walls looked as if someone had tried to chip into the granite and remove the carvings. Images of pharaohs and other men wearing crowns lined the narrow entrance hall. And at the end of the hallway I saw a carving that alarmed me. A figure in a robe held his hands out as rays of light spiraled up around his body.

"The sun?" I asked.

"No, the cold light. The ka," George said. He told me to put my hands on the figure and push. I gasped in surprise when the carving turned into a door and opened. George took a dripping candle from its handle on the wall and followed me inside.

The opening did not lead to another chamber but directly into the Graylands.

"Are you certain it's safe for you to be here?" I asked. I clasped George's arm, feeling his solid warmth for reassurance. His heart still beat. He still drew breath.

"I am to be the next Koldun, Katiya. I walk many of the same paths you walk. But it is a much greater price that I pay. Come, we must hurry to the seven gates. Before Konstantin finds us."

Not letting go of my hand, he led me through the swirls of fog for what seemed like forever. How could anyone tell where they were going in this strange place? How could you hope to find anyone in such fog?

George began to hum a tune that sounded similar to the chanting of the monks at Abydos. I struggled to keep up with him, and finally we arrived at a wide river. "Is this the Nile?" I asked.

"No, it's the river of the dead." He took two coins from his pocket and set them down on the dock.

It wasn't long before a boat arrived, directed by a jackal-headed man. I stood closer to George as the man retrieved the coins from the dock. He held a hand up and beckoned to both of us. George supported my arm as I took a step into the small barge.

No sooner had we both arranged ourselves in the boat than the man pushed off from the dock and the boat floated down the dark river. "Where are we going?" I whispered.

"Into the heart of the underworld," George replied. "Beyond

the seven gates." His face was grim. "Don't worry. We'll make it to the sword soon, love."

I reached over and threaded my fingers in his. "How did you learn so much about the Morning Star?" I asked. "From the Order of the Black Lily?"

He nodded. "We also found an old manuscript in Moscow that described it. It took Papus and me several months to find the ritual that would reveal its hiding place."

I shivered as we floated through the mist. The motion of the boat was making me sleepy, and I leaned my head against George's shoulder.

"Don't fall asleep, Katiya." He shook me gently. "That is one of the worst things you can do in the Graylands. Focus on your cold light."

It was like sleepwalking on a boat. I started to see visions of girls in white ball gowns dancing the mazurka with dashing young Cossacks dressed in red. I saw crocodile shapes swimming in the water. I saw skinny wolves trotting warily alongside the riverbank, tracking us. I did not know if I was dreaming or if these visions were real. I tried to focus on my cold light and hoped that George knew where we were headed.

We came at last to a stone landing, and the boat pulled up close enough to let us out. George went first, then held my hand and helped me. He led me up the stone steps to a great hallway lined with enormous golden doors. We hurried through the hall, not stopping at any of the doors.

"Katerina, you realize that once you hold the sword, we will have to destroy Konstantin and Johanna once and for all. It's the only way to end the threat against my father."

"How, though? Death did not stop them before."

"Only a necromancer can grant the second death that the pharaohs were so terrified of in ancient Egypt. Only you can prevent them from ever returning to the land of the living. The words you'll have to recite should be in your *Necromancer's Companion*."

He had insisted I bring the ancient book with me. I opened it and began flipping through the pages. I knew I'd seen a spell that mentioned the second death.

"And what of Danilo and Mala?" I asked. For certainly their souls were still here in the Graylands. "What if we could bring them back instead of Konstantin and Johanna?"

He picked up my hand tenderly. "Katiya, you know that for us to be absolutely safe, the crown prince and the ballerina must not return. I'm sorry."

"But Mala did not ask to be sacrificed for Princess Cantacuzene," I said. "She did not deserve to die like that. And if Konstantin and his princess are gone, there's nothing to cause Danilo to act against the tsar."

George shook his head. "There will always be that wound on Danilo's soul. The cold lights of Konstantin and Danilo are so tightly woven together now that I don't believe you can ever separate them. Johanna has not been in Mala's body long, and Mala's soul is here somewhere in the Graylands, but we can't risk any ties between the two women either."

"I must defeat Konstantin here in the Graylands, then?" I asked. I'd found the ritual of the second death in *A Necromancer's Companion*. I had a feeling it would not be a pleasant task. Nor would it be easy.

George looked over my shoulder at the open spell book in my hands. "The second death is also mentioned in the Ani Papyrus, the Book of the Dead. You will need to use the sword."

A hooded figure stepped out of the dark mist.

"There is no one else, my Queen of Swords." It was Grand Duchess Militza, the vampire sovereign of St. Petersburg.

"What are you doing here?" I asked as George moved to stand protectively between us.

Militza smiled. "It is easy to travel the ways of the Graylands when one is the daughter of a necromancer, Duchess. My mother sent me to look for you. You are the only one who can help my brother."

I'd almost forgotten that Queen Milena, Johanna's sister, was also a necromancer. One more person who must never hold the Morning Star. I clutched George's hand in alarm.

George shook his head. "Absolutely not. Katerina is not putting herself in danger to save that bastard."

Militza's eyes flashed bloodred. "Katerina is not the cold-hearted killer you want her to be, George Alexandrovich. She knows it would be wrong to take the lives of two people who have no control over the dark forces inside them. I do not think Katerina is willing to live with the consequences of such actions." Militza smiled. "The Koldun wishes that Mala be spared as well. Even if Miechen does not."

"Does the Dark Court know all that has happened in Egypt?" I asked, astonished.

Militza nodded. "The Grigori have been excellent messengers. And now Nicholas and the French mage have returned and given their detailed report." She looked from one of us to the other. "Both the Light and Dark Courts have been watching the situation. We have decided to work together to defeat the threat of Konstantin."

"Then surely both courts realize Danilo is too dangerous to be allowed to live," George said.

Militza's face was white as stone. "Both courts agree it would be easiest to allow his soul to share the second death with the lich tsar. But there is another way. I will not give up on my brother until every option has been examined."

"You believe there is a way to separate his soul from Konstantin's?" I asked. "Is it safe?"

The blood-drinking grand duchess laughed. "Why should you expect anything in the land of the dead to be easy, Katerina?" she asked. "Or safe?" She looked at me with piercing eyes. "Doing the right thing is sometimes very difficult. And very painful."

"Are you saying that saving the blood-drinking crown prince is the right thing?" George asked. I knew he did not share Militza's opinion.

"The Dark and Light Courts have agreed to work together to save Russia from the lich tsar and his soldiers. This includes the faerie courts, the blood drinkers, the Order of St. Lazarus, and the Order of St. John and all of its sorcerers. The wolf-folk have also pledged to help. As long as you carry the sword, Katerina, we will have the Grigori on our side too."

I glanced at George nervously. We had no reason to trust Militza. "Do you have proof of the Dark and Light Courts' cooperation?" I asked.

She nodded and waved her hand across the grayish mist. The clouds parted to reveal a scene in a large looking glass hanging at the end of the hall. There, in the mirror, I saw the tsar and the empress kissing the cheeks of the dark faerie Miechen and her husband, Grand Duke Vladimir, the Koldun. At Miechen's side, my mother knelt before the tsar.

Militza nodded grimly. "You have your proof. Everyone is committed to see this through, Duchess. We're all in danger if Konstantin defeats our tsar."

I looked closer at the edges of the picture and saw a silver-white wolf and a much larger black one standing at attention beside Grand Duchess Ella. Ella was gently scratching behind the ears of the black wolf.

My brother and father stood at attention, both in smart dress uniform, in the tightly disciplined formation of members of the Order. They would be joining the battlefield as well.

I turned to Militza. "Isn't there a way I can prevent the battle?" I asked her. "If I kill Konstantin with the sword and give him the second death, then no one would have to go to war."

"I doubt you'll be able to just walk up to the lich tsar and expect him to allow you to kill him," George said.

Militza's tiny, razor-sharp fangs showed when she smiled this time. "It is too late to avoid battle now, Duchess. We are going to war, whether we want to or not."

"I know why you do not wish to go to war, Militza," a sickeningly familiar voice said as two figures approached us out of the mist. George took a step closer to me. It was Mala's body, but it was Princess Cantacuzene's voice that dripped venom. "You will lose the support of the St. Petersburg vampires once I return."

Militza hissed. But she did not attack either the princess or the lich tsar. "Konstantin Pavlovich, you will pay for what you have done to my brother," she threatened.

The lich tsar laughed. "It was your mother's ambition, as well as your own, that destroyed your brother. You should have known that stealing the Talisman of Isis would demand a heavy price."

I still wore the talisman around my neck, hidden by a high-collared jacket. I did not know what good it would be to me, unless I needed to command an army of corpses. Unfortunately there was no such army around.

George gave my hand a comforting squeeze. Murmuring a few words, he raised a small protective circle around Militza and the two of us. The invisible walls went up before Princess Cantacuzene could reach out for the grand duchess.

The vampire princess scowled and countered George's spell with one of her own. Immediately the cold light glowing around George grew bright and tightened around him. He faltered, and I could feel the protection of the circle shrinking.

"George!" I cried, feeling helpless. I did not know how to counteract the princess's spell. Then, with one uttered word, Konstantin added his power to Johanna's and George's cold light exploded in a burst of shimmering dust. George looked at me before he fell to the floor.

"No!" I whispered, sliding to my knees beside him. His eyes were closed. His cold light was completely gone. "George? Don't leave me. Please, don't leave me," I begged. I touched his cheek gently and sent up a prayer of thanks when I felt him draw a ragged breath.

With the circle of protection collapsed, Militza and Johanna were now attacking each other, claws out and fangs bared. Konstantin was trying to help distract Militza.

"George?" I whispered. "Don't try to speak. I'm going to get you out of here."

He finally opened his eyes. He reached up and cupped my face with his hand, wiping the tears off my cheek with his thumb. "Don't waste your strength on me. You must find the sword. I love you, Duchess."

I heard an enormous rushing sound in my ears. My cold light was spiraling out of control. I tried using it to hold on to George, but there was nothing for my tendrils of light to latch on to.

"No! I won't let you go," I said, squeezing his hand. The air was being sucked out of my lungs. He was breaking my heart. And I was on the edge of hysterics.

His grip on my hand was slipping. "One more thing, Katiya. Tell Papus he must become the Koldun when Nicholas is tsar."

"Are you certain?" I still did not trust the Frenchman.

He nodded. "I'm certain. Promise me, Katiya."

I couldn't do anything to save him. I was not a doctor, and I was definitely not a strong enough necromancer to counter whatever Konstantin and Johanna had done to George. I finally gave in to the tears that were boiling inside. *"Je te promets,"* I whispered.

He smiled weakly, mumbling something that might have been a last endearment or a Koldun spell. All of a sudden, George Alexandrovich disappeared from in front of me.

I screamed from both shock and fright. In a heartbeat I was back on my feet, searching the area. George had simply vanished. What had just happened?

The two vampires shoved me as they fought as two wildcats. I was astounded. I'd seen Militza transform into a moth before, but never had I seen either woman shift into such large and dangerous creatures. There were torn patches of fur and blood on the floor around me. I stumbled around them in a daze, trying to find my husband. "George?" I pleaded, choking on my tears. "Where are you?"

Konstantin laughed and raised his hand to cast a similar spell on Militza.

She stopped fighting almost immediately and transformed back into her human form. "Dani?" she shouted imploringly. "Dani, I know you're still inside that body. You wouldn't hurt your own sister, would you?"

Her cries gave me enough time to cast a shadow around the two of us. I heard Princess Cantacuzene howl in frustration.

The grand duchess had tears mixed with the blood on her cheek. "Come quickly," she told me. "As long as they do not have the sword, we still have a chance."

In the back of my head, a dull thought slithered up to the surface. *What does it matter? George is dead. I should be dead as well.* But the tsar and the empress were still in danger. I had to keep going even if only to return to St. Petersburg and tell them of their son's death.

CHAPTER THIRTY-THREE

Militza led me all the way down to the end of the large stone hallway. One corridor veered to the left. A massive door blocked off the right hall. The grand duchess said, "This way," and headed down the left corridor without stopping to see if I was close behind.

I wanted to glance over my shoulder and look for Konstantin and Johanna, but I was afraid of what I would see.

I hurried to catch up with Militza. Her tears had dried and there was a hard bitterness to her face. She was worried for her brother, but now was clearly not the time to mourn him. Or to mourn George. We had to save the tsar. For all of our sakes.

"We cannot pass the seven gates without an initiated mage," I said, following her down another corridor. "How can we reach the sword now?"

"You will have to enter on your own. We can only pray your

heart is pure enough, Katerina. Although I suspect you will have little trouble."

"But I am not a mage!" I said.

Militza sighed, exasperated. "Listen very carefully, because we are running out of time. Papus told us there was a chance that a necromancer who was sinless could withstand the trial of the seven gates on her own and retrieve the Morning Star. He did not want Konstantin to discover this. Obviously, Johanna cannot claim any sort of innocence." Militza took my hands and squeezed them tightly. Her fingers were cold as ice. "You are the only one, Katerina. You must believe in yourself."

My mouth dry and my heart pounding, I nodded slowly.

"Here," Militza said as we came to the end of the hallway. She waved a hand across a golden door on our right. The door opened and we slipped inside quietly. "Can you ward the door so they cannot get in?"

I shook my head, terrified. I felt useless.

"It makes no difference," Militza said. She beckoned me deeper into the room, which was a long, narrow chamber not unlike those in the pyramids. But there were no hieroglyphics on these stone walls. Only seven pairs of torches that gave off a strange light. A cold light. It baffled me.

"Those lights are actually guardians of the sword, Katerina," Militza explained as she saw my confusion. "Some Grigori gave up their physical forms in exchange for a spirit and eternal service to the Morning Star. When the sword is placed in the right person's hands, they will be allowed to join their brothers in the land of the living."

"What if it's placed in the wrong person's hands?" I asked.

Militza's smile was cold as she gazed at the lights. "Then they will execute that person. Are you ready?" I stared at the inner sanctuary at the end of the narrow chamber. A statue of a man stood in the tiny room, holding a sword horizontally in his outstretched hands. The sword did not glow, but I could feel my own cold light drawn toward it.

"Do I need to say something? Something to unlock the sword?" I asked.

Militza shook her head. "If we had a mage here, he would know the words to recite at each of the gates. But you are the necromancer who walks among both worlds and can bend cold light to your will. Hopefully that will be enough."

Shaking, I entered the narrow chamber and approached the first pair of torches. Closing my eyes, I took a step so I was standing between them. The cold light flickered, but nothing else happened. Cold sweat dripped down my back as I took another step forward. Still, there was nothing.

"You're wasting time, Duchess!" Militza hissed.

My heart pounding in my ears, I continued. Perhaps I was hallucinating, but I could have sworn I heard voices whispering as I passed each pair of lights. The voices were too low to understand. Whether the guardians of the gates were blessing me or cursing me, I could not tell.

Finally, as I reached the last pair of torches and passed between them, I felt cold, invisible hands pulling me back. I shrieked, both from fear and from frustration. I could see the statue holding the sword, just out of my reach.

"Don't give up," Militza called from behind me.

I took a deep breath and closed my eyes, willing my fear away. The invisible hands let go of me and I was able to step forward again. I was finally in the inner chamber, standing in front of the statue.

With a trembling hand, I reached out to take the sword. The hilt was beautiful, a heavy silver piece with winged creatures engraved along the sides. Two large stones were embedded in the hilt, both a brilliant dark black. It reminded me of the onyx in the Talisman of Isis. I bore the talisman and lived. I hoped I would fare the same with the sword.

As I took the sword, the tiny room flooded with cold light. "Those are your guardians!" Militza shouted. "Command them to do your bidding!"

"I command the guardians of the Morning Star to follow me," I said shakily. The sword was not as heavy as I'd expected it to be. The lights flew about the room in a spiral; then in a burst, they entered the sword. I felt a strong vibration and almost dropped the weapon. Behind me I heard Militza cry as she was knocked down by the force of the lights whirling around the room.

Militza slowly stood up. "Now, Katerina. We must hurry back to St. Petersburg."

As I rushed back down the narrow chamber toward her, the outer door crashed open. The guardian lights rushed to converge upon the invaders. I heard Princess Cantacuzene's cry as Konstantin tried to cast a spell. Militza grabbed my arm. "Use the sword. It is what you were born to do."

I nodded, my mouth dry and my heart pounding. A roar of cold wind had risen up inside the chamber. There was a small tempest whirling around us that kept Konstantin and the princess from reaching us.

I could end everything here and now if I killed Konstantin in the land of the dead. I hated that Militza would have to watch me attack her brother's body, but deep down she knew it had to be done. I would have to cut the lich tsar's head off and say the ritual of the second death. This would damn the lich tsar to oblivion. And probably Danilo as well.

Princess Cantacuzene was trying to fight the sword's guardians with her shadows. Her cold light had begun to grow strong again and she was drawing on its power. I closed my eyes and uttered the words of the second death as I lunged toward her.

Militza was standing behind me, fangs out to aid if she could. "Take her head!" she shouted, and the guardian lights seemed to wrap around her in my defense as well.

Princess Cantacuzene screamed when she realized she was trapped. There was no other spell that could help her now. I begged God in heaven to forgive me for what I was about to do and swung the sword at her neck, praying that the blade was sharp and my aim true.

My prayers were answered. Johanna's head fell from her shoulders onto the floor. I was amazed to see there was no blood. I remembered the first time I'd seen her die, in a different body, in a pool of blood at a St. Petersburg hospital where she'd killed Dr. Kruglevski. As Konstantin roared in fury, I hoped that the doctor's soul was at peace. I hoped Mala's soul would now be at peace as well.

"No sun shall rise over your grave. No birds will sing for you," I said wearily. "Nothing but eternal rest awaits you, Johanna Cantacuzene." The sword suddenly seemed much heavier.

Konstantin's face was contorted in cold rage. "I will kill you, necromancer, and there will be nothing peaceful about it."

I leveled the Morning Star at him. I was too numb to be

afraid of my own death anymore. "Come and join your bride, Konstantin Pavlovich," I shouted.

The guardian lights swirled around him as if to hold him for me as they had the princess.

"No," Konstantin said softly, with a demonic, half-crazed smile. "Not this time."

I rushed toward him then, but before I could lift the sword, the lich tsar disappeared.

Suddenly the wind died down and the lights returned to their posts along the side walls. Only Militza and I were left in the room.

She stood next to me like a statue, not showing any signs of fatigue. In fact, she looked very regal. "Katerina, are you ready to return to St. Petersburg? We must use your magic to get there quickly. There is no other way."

I nodded, ignoring the hollow feeling inside. In St. Petersburg I knew I would have to face George's death all over again. And I would have to face his parents.

Militza turned toward me. "I am truly sorry, Katerina, that you did not marry my brother last summer. Perhaps you would have been able to help him hold on to his humanity."

"But would I have been able to hold on to my own?" I asked.

Militza said nothing at first. Her black eyes were moist but I saw no tears. "I am about to show you the secret to journeying through the Graylands. It is extremely draining, but we must hurry if we are to find Konstantin."

I nodded but secretly I felt defeated. I was already drained. I did not know how much energy I had left. Yet as long as Konstantin remained a danger to Russia, I had to keep going. I followed the grand duchess back out into the great hall, where she approached the enormous mirror we'd seen earlier. With a wave of her hand, the scene at the Gatchina Palace appeared again.

It was the most easily defended of the imperial palaces. The safest place for the tsar to be at this moment. Unfortunately, Konstantin knew the defenses of Gatchina well.

"You must take my hand, Duchess." Militza did not wait for me to respond but instead clasped her cold fingers around mine. "This might hurt a bit."

She took a step toward the mirror and pushed me through. My cold light did not like this method of traveling through space and time. Tendrils of light seemed to catch in the Graylands, dragging me back slowly while Militza prodded me forward. "Don't slow down," she said. "You must keep going."

I kept trying to forge ahead, toward the palace. Toward my family. But the weight of my cold light was heavy. Militza was firm. "It wants to remain in the land of the dead, Katerina. This is where the cold light naturally belongs. But you must convince it otherwise. Keep moving!"

My cold light wanted to stay in the Graylands because that was where George was. I was sure he was still there somewhere. If only I'd been faster. If only I'd not been rude to Dr. Badmaev and had accepted his generous offer to teach me sooner. How much time had I wasted remaining at Smolni when I could have been studying with the Tibetan?

Mentally, I tried to pull my cold light as close to me as possible, and I willed myself to move forward. Now even Militza was surprised at how I was pulling her the rest of the way through the passage.

We landed on the ground in the snow-covered gardens of Gatchina. I wanted to cry. There had not been snow before I left St. Petersburg. How long had I been gone? Members of the Order of St. Lazarus and the Order of St. John met us before we could stand up. The Grigori arrived as well, followed by Papus. "She bears the Morning Star!" one of them said. A hundred waxen-faced Grigori went down on bended knee before me. Papus nodded his head in respect as well.

Murmurs passed through the other soldiers, and I saw them part as one of the officers pushed his way to the front.

"Katiya! Thank God!" It was Petya. He swept me up in a suffocating embrace. "You have no idea how glad I am to see you, brat!"

I closed my eyes and clung to him tightly. He smelled like tobacco and horses. Over his shoulder I could see Prince Kotchoubey, Dariya's friend, standing behind him. He wore the same smart uniform as my brother and clicked his heels with a gallant bow to me. Another brave soldier who would fight for the tsar.

"Katerina Alexandrovna," a familiar and uncertain voice addressed me. It was the tsarevitch. "Where is George?"

CHAPTER THIRTY-FOUR

"We need to get her inside to see the tsar," Militza said, pulling me away from my brother and the tsarevitch.

"Of course," Petya said, clearing the way for us among the crowd of soldiers. The Grigori were still down on bended knees.

"Please, get up," I told them.

"Tell them to stand down," Petya whispered.

"Stand down," I said, hoping I did not sound ridiculous.

My brother smiled. "You command an army just as well as our great-great-great-grandmother Katerina did."

I blushed. I hoped I would make my ancestors proud today.

Nicholas hurried to catch up with us as we made our way to the palace. "Where is Georgi?" he asked again. "Did he stay behind in Cairo? Father will be furious!"

"Katerina will tell the entire imperial family when we get inside," Militza said crisply.

For once, I was grateful for the veshtiza's bossiness. I did not want to tell my sad story more than once.

The grand doors at the front entrance opened and I entered the palace, followed by Petya, Nicholas, and Militza. Members of the Order of St. Lazarus stood guard at the door. I smiled shyly at them, even though I knew the undead soldiers would not smile back.

Nicholas led us up the grand staircase to the Gathering Hall, which was lined with guards from the Preobrajensky Regiment. The tsar and the empress waited for us in the hall, along with Grand Duchess Miechen and her husband, the Koldun, Grand Duke Vladimir, and the rest of the Inner Circle of the Order of St. John.

"It would be an asset if we had the striga here as well today," Militza whispered in my ear. "Unfortunately, the effect she has on even her allies makes it too dangerous. I have a feeling she is nearby, though, in case she decides she is needed."

I nodded and was grateful my mother wasn't here. The thought of her fighting in the battle to come and drinking the blood of Konstantin and Johanna's minions made me ill.

Everyone was dressed for the assault, except me. I was still in the wrinkled blue travel dress I'd been wearing when we left Cairo. Even the empress and Grand Duchess Miechen wore the full dress uniforms of their patron guard regiments. The empress's white gown was trimmed in the silver and white braid of the Chevalier Guards regiment, of which she was colonel-in-chief.

The dark faerie was wearing the dress uniform of her Life Guard Dragoons, navy blue with gold-fringed epaulettes. The two women looked just as formidable as the men surrounding them. Like everyone else, they carried the sabers of their regiments, decorated with the imperial double-headed eagle and the Cyrillic cipher of Alexander the Third.

"Come forward, necromancer," the tsar said, his booming voice echoing across the enormous hall. I broke apart from Militza and the others, my boots clicking against the marble floor as I approached the imperial family.

Using the sword for balance, I went down on one knee. "Your Imperial Majesty."

"I see you have succeeded in finding the Morning Star and have kept it safe from Konstantin Pavlovich."

"Yes, Your Imperial Majesty," I said, "I have."

"Is Konstantin dead?" he asked.

"No, Your Imperial Majesty. But his wife, Princess Johanna Cantacuzene, is."

A murmur rippled through the court. Grand Duchess Miechen spoke up. "I believed the princess to have been dead for almost two years, Katerina Alexandrovna."

I nodded. "She was, but Konstantin performed a ritual whereby he killed a young girl and used her body to bring back the vampire princess. With the Morning Star and the help of an ancient Egyptian spell, I killed her once more in the Graylands. She will not be able to return."

There was utter silence across the Grand Hall. If few here knew my secret before, now all knew I was a necromancer. A monster.

"Konstantin must have been wild with grief," the tsar said. "He will seek vengeance, I am sure."

I took a deep breath as my tears threatened to return. "He

attacked George Alexandrovich in the Graylands, Your Imperial Majesty." I could feel my voice wavering. I could not, must not, cry in front of the tsar. I was strong even though my heart hurt. "Grief consumes me as well."

The tsarevitch came up behind me, touching me gently on the sleeve. "Georgi?"

I shook my head, too overwhelmed to say the words out loud. If I did not say that George was dead, then it hadn't really happened. Had it?

A silvery-white wolf nosed her way through the group of people clustered around the tsar. She nudged Nicholas's hand gently.

The empress turned pale and placed her hand in the tsar's own enormous one. I could not comfort them. My heart broke for them as much as it did for my own loss.

The doors opened and a messenger from the Order of St. John hurried in, bowing to the tsar as he approached. "Your Imperial Majesty, there is an army approaching from the north of the city. They will be here within the next half hour."

The tsar nodded. "Necromancer, you must prepare yourself."

I squeezed Nicholas's hand before stepping forward.

There was no time to lose. Miechen and Militza whisked me into the small parlor down the hall where they had a uniform waiting for me. Quickly, I changed into a military jacket and matching skirt in the same green and gold colors worn by the Order of St. Lazarus. Pinned to the jacket was the oval medal my soldiers wore, a green hand holding a sword. I was honored to wear the uniform of my creatures.

There was even a belt with a leather scabbard for the Morning Star. I slid the sword into its sheath, grateful I'd have both hands free for the bogatyr's ritual. Both Miechen and Militza nodded in satisfaction when I emerged in the uniform and hurried me back to the Grand Hall.

The tsar's face was sad, but he did not have time to grieve for his son. The Koldun stood beside him holding a golden box with the Maltese cross of the Order of St. John, and the priests were nearby with their incense and crosses.

Tsar Alexander stood in front of me. "Katerina Alexandrovna, you who bear the sword called the Morning Star are being called upon again to summon the bogatyr."

"Brother, you do not have to do this," the Koldun murmured. "She commands the Grigori. We will be able to defeat the lich tsar without putting you through this ritual."

"It is my duty to protect the people of Russia," the tsar replied, not bothering to look at the Koldun. Instead, his eyes bored into mine. "The bogatyr must be summoned. Are you ready, Duchess?"

I nodded, trying to ignore the lump in my throat. "I will do as you command, Your Imperial Majesty."

The prayers had already been said by the metropolitan of St. Petersburg. The Koldun chanted the words of the ritual. I placed one hand upon the Maltese cross and felt my cold light powers rising up. My cold light called to the ancient spirit of the bogatyr, the supernatural warrior bound to protect Russia in her darkest hour. I held out my right hand to grasp the tsar and help transfer the spirit into him. The bearlike tsar would be strong enough to crush me if he wanted. I loved our tsar, almost as much as I loved my own father, but I was very frightened of him as well.

The priest chanted more prayers as the Koldun finished reciting his part of the ceremony. The tsar had grown taller in front of us all. His eyes burned with cold light. I wished he could bear the Morning Star for me. I was sure he could wield a sword far better than I. But the cursed sword would kill even him if he held it.

A cloud of smoke poured forth from the golden candle held by the Koldun, and out of the smoke rose a large bird with long feathers the color of flames. It looked like the firebird of the fairy tales of old.

Everyone but the bogatyr and I stepped back and stared at the firebird as it flew toward the ceiling and swooped around in a graceful arch. We were all too stunned by the creature's beauty to move. It glided straight for me and I still did not step back. At the last minute, the bird dove and in a brilliant burst of flames transformed into the borrowed body of the crown prince. He grabbed the scabbard that held the Morning Star and shouted in triumph.

"Now the Grigori will follow me!" Konstantin Pavlovich exclaimed. He raised the sword in the air and used it to smash a window. "To arms!" he shouted to the crowds gathering outside. "Defend your true tsar!" With a wicked grin and a polite bow to me, he slipped out of the window and onto the palace grounds below.

CHAPTER THIRTY-FIVE

"Katerina, wasn't that the Montenegrin crown prince?" the empress asked amid the confusion of the shouting and scuffling as everyone hurried down the stairs. The sounds of swords clashing rang from the field outside. The battle had begun.

"The lich tsar has taken possession of the crown prince's body, Your Imperial Majesty," I said. And I had just let him steal the Morning Star from me. With the Grigori fighting on his side, he would be able to defeat the bogatyr, and it would be my fault. I had to steal the sword back from him. I pushed my way through the crowd and raced down the stairs and outside, searching for the lich tsar without another word to the empress.

Militza's vampires had joined the battle, but there were equal numbers of vampires still loyal to Konstantin. The latter wanted revenge against the vampire who had killed Princess Cantacuzene, and the field was quickly turning into a bloodbath.

The wolf pack I'd seen waiting near Grand Duchess Ella had formed a front on the far side of the lawn and were attacking the Grigori now under Konstantin's control. I hadn't seen the Grigori in battle before, and it was frightening to behold. Fiery wings stretched out from their shoulder blades and they attacked the wolves with flaming swords. I held my breath as one of the silvery-white wolves leapt out of a Grigori's reach just in time.

Members of the Order of St. John, led by my brother and his Preobrajensky Regiment, charged into the fray. I could not see Prince Kotchoubey, but I said a prayer for him, hoping he would return to Dariya safely. My undead soldiers, the members of the Order of St. Lazarus, did not seem to know what to do. They stood silently at attention, the normal blank stare on their faces. "Katerina!" my brother shouted. "They are waiting for your command!"

How stupid of me. Fumbling, I pulled the Talisman of Isis from around my neck and held it up. I pricked my thumb and let a drop touch the stone held by the goddess. "The blood of Isis, the soul of Isis, the power of Isis is mine," I said firmly.

A cold wind swept across the field as the undead soldiers seemed to become more animated. "Defend your true tsar, Alexander Alexandrovich! Protect the wolves!" I cried across the field. I hoped they would stand up to the flaming swords better than Alix and her sisters. Grim-faced, the Order of St. Lazarus clustered together and formed a long line of defense, then marched toward the Grigori.

The bogatyr was out on the battlefield now as well, circling Konstantin. The lich tsar might have had command of the supernatural Grigori, but the Morning Star did not give him the same supernatural strength that the bogatyr possessed. The bogatyr could still overpower him with sheer might. But Konstantin had black necromancy on his side as well. With a wave of his hand, the Morning Star began to glow with snakelike tendrils of cold light. The bogatyr had to take care not to get too close.

I used my talisman to focus my own cold light powers. I cast shadows around the Grigori, hoping to slow them down, but they were immune. And so were the undead Lazarus soldiers, who kept marching steadfastly, despite being ripped to shreds by the ruthless Grigori.

My shadows did help Militza and her vampires, though. I blanketed them with darkness that hid them from Konstantin's blood drinkers. They began to gain the edge, and the boost spurred them on in their bloodlust.

The empress still remained within the palace, but I could feel her fae magic raining down upon us. The same shimmering that I felt when she stared at me with her Sight wove its way across the battlefield. It was a cool, refreshing shimmer that lifted the soldiers' spirits and gave them courage. Their cold lights dimmed and their resolve to triumph dug in.

Miechen was creating glamours: images of frightening imps and sprites that flashed in front of the Grigori. Unable to tell which target was real and which was an illusion, they wasted a lot of their strength chasing the dark faerie's images. The Koldun stood close to his wife, keeping the protective wards around her in place.

Papus and the other mages from the Inner Circle concentrated on protecting the soldiers of the Order of St. John. Papus caught my eye and gave me a grim smile as he cast wards around the tsarevitch. Perhaps George had already spoken to him about his dying wish. I choked back tears. This was not the time to mourn.

I worried most for the bogatyr. Konstantin could not destroy his cold light as utterly as he had done with George's in the Graylands. This was the land of the living. But he could still manipulate cold light. Just as I could.

I had no idea if I was strong enough to affect the cold light of the lich tsar, who was really not a lich anymore but the flesh-and-blood false tsar in the crown prince's body. If only Danilo's cold light still existed, I might be able to unravel it from Konstantin's and surprise him in his weakened state. Perhaps that would be enough of a distraction to allow the bogatyr to get the upper hand.

I touched the talisman around my neck and felt my cold light growing more powerful. I pulled the light in tightly until I could feel it sizzling up and down my spine. Standing in the midst of the blood and bodies on the battlefield, I unleashed the cold light and sent it to Konstantin. It stunned him, but only momentarily. As I attacked the strands of his cold light, searching mentally for any that might still belong to Danilo, I focused on my bond with the crown prince. *"Danilo, are you still in there at all?"*

There was a mental tug in my mind. It was feeble, but I felt it all the same. *"You must fight Konstantin,"* I thought. *"I know you are strong enough."*

Several strands of cold light began to shift and separate from the rest of the light surrounding Konstantin. *"That's it, Danilo! Fight against him!"* My own strands snaked toward his, tentatively reaching out like helping hands. The cold light that belonged to the crown prince looped around with my own and held fast. I closed my eyes and concentrated on pulling as hard as I could.

Konstantin stumbled back, his balance upset by the disturbance. I sent another strand of cold light out like a whip, knocked the sword loose from his hand, and made a mad dash toward the fallen sword. Konstantin scowled and threw a blast of cold light that slammed into me and dropped me to the ground. I was too stunned to pick myself up.

From high above the palace, a large gray owl swooped down with an angry shriek. I held my breath as the creature dove at Konstantin. The striga. Angrily, he swatted at the bird, but she darted away, out of his reach. On her second pass, she drew blood from his arm. She was fast, and again and again she dove at him, striking with her talons and beak as many times as she could.

I realized she was trying to distract him, so I dragged myself toward the sword while I had the chance. Konstantin glanced at me and snarled. With another blast of cold light, he hit the striga, and she fell to the earth with a cry.

"Maman!" I shouted helplessly. I was so focused on her I did not see the bogatyr swing his sword down and cut off one of the lich tsar's hands. Konstantin roared in pain as he tried to grab the Morning Star before I could.

Blinded by angry tears, I had just enough time to scoop up the sword and roll out of the way before Konstantin sent another burst of his cold light hurtling toward me. It struck the dirt mere inches away, shaking the ground. I slowly picked myself up, clutching the sword tightly.

Every last one of the Grigori stopped fighting and looked

across the field toward me. "She holds the Morning Star!" someone shouted. "What is thy command, lady?" It was the elder Grigori who had accompanied me and Danilo and Mala in Egypt.

"Defend the true tsar!" I shouted the words so loudly I thought my throat would bleed. "All hail Alexander the Third!" Out of the corner of my eye, I saw the striga shake her feathers and fly off the field. I breathed a quick sigh of relief. She'd only been stunned by Konstantin's blow.

Only a few vampires loyal to Konstantin Pavlovich remained. They were soon surrounded by the forces loyal to the bogatyr. Militza descended upon them viciously. She was not about to let any of the traitors survive.

The bogatyr forgotten in his rage toward me, Konstantin had regained his footing and was storming across the field. "You have interfered with my plans for the last time, necromancer!" he roared. I was frightened, but I pulled in my cold light powers once more and prayed for strength.

Raising his remaining hand, Konstantin shot out a burst of cold energy that would have knocked me senseless if the empress's shimmering light had not intercepted it.

I did not have time to thank her. Konstantin raised his hand again and I took my chance. Reaching out with my cold light to meet him, I sank the Morning Star into his belly and then shouted the incantation from *A Necromancer's Companion* that would carry both of us into the Graylands, away from the bloody battlefield. "Open the path, thou doorkeepers of the dead!" I shouted, my voice almost completely gone. "Open the path for she who walks between both worlds!"

The battlefield fell away with a loud rushing sound, like the flapping of a million bird wings. The two of us were in the Graylands once again, surrounded by the familiar gray mist. I hated that I was getting used to the feeling of walking between the two worlds. I did not want this place to feel familiar at all.

Konstantin was temporarily bound by my cold light, but I knew it would not hold him for long. I had to recite the ritual of the second death to keep him from coming back.

"You . . . ," he gasped. "You have the blackest soul of any human I've ever met."

I did feel very black and very cold at that moment. He'd killed George. And I wanted him to pay for that. Every fiber of my being wanted him banished to oblivion. I wanted every last bloodthirsty Egyptian god of the dead to come and eat his heart.

But it wasn't the lich tsar I saw when I raised my sword. It was the crown prince, whose body the lich tsar possessed. I was angry on behalf of Danilo too. Angry at his mother and his sister and Princess Cantacuzene for damning him with their plots and schemes. For all of his own faults, he never deserved this.

But I had to protect the tsar from Konstantin Pavlovich. In order to make sure all of Russia was safe, the lich tsar had to die the second death. I raised the Morning Star above his head, ready to deliver the final blow.

And I knew it would not bring George back.

If I killed Konstantin, I would be no better than he. I would have a heart blacker than the crown prince's eyes, and my soul would be lost. I lowered the sword and wiped tears of frustration from my eyes.

I saw a spiral-shaped light wavering a little ways off from us.

It was the tendrils of the crown prince's cold light that I had dragged with me when I brought Konstantin back to the Graylands.

"Katerina, I am free. Protect the tsar and give Konstantin his second death. His heart will be judged much harsher than yours. Your heart has been judged and it is true."

It was Danilo's voice in my head.

"If I destroy Konstantin, will you be able to return?"

"While there is life, there is always hope," he replied.

"But where there is death," I thought painfully, "there is no hope." I did not want to destroy Danilo's chances of returning. But I had to believe I was doing the right thing.

Numbly, I raised the sword and recited the words of the ritual of the second death. "No sun shall rise over your grave. No birds will sing for you. Nothing but eternal rest waits for you, Konstantin Pavlovich." The talisman around my neck felt warm. An icy chill slid down my spine, my cold light giving me strength as I swung the blade at Konstantin's neck. His head tumbled to the floor, bloodless and eyes closed.

I saw Danilo's cold light slowly fade away. "No!" I whispered. I felt like a monster. I let the sword fall from my hands, and it clattered to the floor. I had held some hope that even if I couldn't save George, I would be able to save Militza's brother. But he had disappeared as well, and now I had more sorrowful news to bring back from the Graylands. It made me not want to return to the land of the living at all.

Both Konstantin's body and his head dissolved into bright cold light and then faded into the mist. There was nothing left of him or the crown prince. The lich tsar was gone; it was all over.

I picked up the Morning Star and stood slowly. What if I did not return to the land of the living? I did not belong with my family and friends anymore. George would not be there. And I could not stand the thought of facing his parents again. The look of grief on their faces had been too much for me to bear. I'd broken Nicholas's heart. I did not want to see that I'd broken Xenia's as well.

So I decided I would stay in the Graylands. The tsar did not need Katerina Alexandrovna anymore.

CHAPTER THIRTY-SIX

I wandered the halls of the Graylands for what seemed like hours, wary of the soft wisps of cold light that followed me down the dark corridors. I kept my own cold light reined in tightly and was careful not to touch the wisps. I did not want to interfere with any other beings anymore. The mist seemed to ebb and flow around me, but I never came across anyone else. None of the tsar's mages came looking for me, nor did Militza.

I still had my mortal body in an immortal land, and I was growing tired. I would have to find a room to settle in, much like Ankh-al-Sekhem the Egyptian had. I shuddered, hoping I would not run into him here. But if he had survived the attack of the resurrected mummies, then he was still in his pyramid in Giza. He would not wish to return to the Graylands any time soon.

I discovered a beautiful, cozy chamber with golden mosaic tiles embellishing the door and its frames. The room was full of bookcases loaded with heavy books. A table was set with a bronze tea service and plates of sweet cakes. I suddenly realized I was famished, but I was reluctant to eat anything here.

There had been spells in *A Necromancer's Companion* that requested nourishment for the dead. I'd seen hieroglyphics on the walls of the temple in Abydos that portrayed priests bearing gifts of food and drink and leaving it for the souls trapped in the afterlife. And the sweet cakes with their cardamom and vanilla did smell heavenly. It was as if they were waiting just for me.

A gold-embroidered satin cushion that was larger than the door itself stood up against one of the bookshelves. I placed it on the floor. Curling up with the Morning Star in my arms, I fell asleep for the first time in days. I slept a deep, dreamless sleep and felt at peace at last.

I awoke some time later. I had no idea how long I'd slept, but I felt much restored. I puttered around the chamber, looking at books and nibbling on some of the sweet cakes. I knew someone would be returning soon to these quarters, and whoever lived here was not likely to take kindly to a young girl invading their home in the land of the dead.

Reluctantly, I put the book of poetry that I'd found back on its shelf and tidied up. I was curious to know what kind of person this space belonged to. Male or female? Young or old? What had they done to earn this sort of cozy existence in the afterlife?

The heavy stone door began to slide open. I gripped my sword in alarm but hastily hid the Morning Star behind my back.

A brilliant glow of cold light preceded the person entering the chamber. I could barely make out the silhouette of a young man behind it. As the door shut, the glow dimmed, and I was able to see him more clearly. My heart stopped beating when he looked at me.

"Katiya?"

"George?"

No wonder I felt as if I'd come home.

CHAPTER THIRTY-SEVEN

George did not rush to take me into his arms. He actually looked unhappy to see me. "Katiya? What have you done?"

"What do you mean? You don't know how happy I am to find you! I hadn't even dared to look. I thought you were dead." I reached for him and was hurt when he flinched.

"Katiya, I am dead. And if you are here in this Hall of the Fallen, you must be dead too."

I shook my head. "I defeated Konstantin. I dragged him back to the Graylands and gave him the second death. And I realized I couldn't face your parents again. I did not want to return to St. Petersburg without you."

He reached up and touched my hair gently. "You are ridiculous. You chose to stay here? Alone?"

I nodded. "Can I stay here with you?"

He cupped my face in his hands and kissed me. My dead husband did not feel very dead at all. He felt very much alive. And his kisses lit my soul on fire.

Gently, George lowered me to the floor cushion. His lips never left mine as his fingers traced the curls in my hair and slid down my arms and around my waist. I stretched my arms around his neck, yearning for him.

"Katiya, are you sure you want to remain here?" His kisses trailed down my jaw and his hand played with my buttons.

"Where else would we go?" I asked. I did not want him to stop kissing me. My heart was pounding. My body shivered with fright and excitement.

He raised his head and looked at me. "You could take me home."

"What are you talking about?" I asked.

He searched my face uncertainly. "Katiya, you do realize that you have the ability to bring me back."

"But I saw your cold light disappear!" The thought that I might be able to bring him back to the land of the living filled me with hope. And a little fear. "I can't bring you back as one of the undead, George. That would not be any kind of life for you. And it would break your mother's heart."

He was trying not to laugh. "Love, why is it that I have learned more about your necromancer powers than you have?" His fingers were tracing the collar of my regimental jacket, making it extremely difficult for me to pay attention to what he was saying.

"I was too busy trying to study medicine," I said. "I didn't want to know how to be a necromancer." But I knew George had studied many schools of magic when he was in Paris. And he would have had a certain interest in learning about my powers.

"Katiya, if you want to go to medical school, I will still support you. We can live wherever we need to—Paris, Zurich, London. We'll go to America if that's what it takes."

I shook my head. "I want to continue learning from Dr. Badmaev. His Tibetan medicine has a better chance of finding a cure for your sickness." And since we were already married, what was the worst thing the tsar could do?

Exile. We could be sent away from Russia. Or the tsar might punish Dr. Badmaev for helping me and have him sent away. I'd have to convince the tsar that I was trying to save his son.

I looked at the grand duke more closely and realized his cold light had returned. It was still bright, betraying his delicate health, but it was there. That meant I could still save him.

I sat up straighter, pushing George back a little. "Your illness! Is it worse here in the Graylands?" Or had it disappeared? I didn't dare hope.

George shrugged. "It's no better, but I worry that the time spent here will affect it. I might be weaker if I return to the land of the living."

I started to protest, but he knew what I was about to say. He put his fingers to my lips. "No," he said. "I am willing to risk it. This is not a life, Katiya. What I'm doing here in the Graylands is just existing. I don't want to stay here trapped for centuries like your Egyptian friend. I want a life with you. A family."

I couldn't help blushing as I thought of having a family with him. Of carrying George's babies. I wondered, though, if our travels through the Graylands would alter our ability to have children. Princess Cantacuzene's greatest regret as a vampire had been her inability to give Konstantin an heir. I understood now how she must have felt, and I felt her sorrow as my own.

"You must think me stupid for not coming to look for you immediately," I said. "Will you ever forgive me?"

George shrugged as he smiled. "I was more worried for you, Katiya. I was safe here, away from Konstantin, and able to mend, while you had him engaged in battle. But I hated not knowing what was happening to you. And I hated not being at the battle with my parents."

"You'll hear the stories and legends for years, I'm sure." I sighed. "And your parents will think me very stupid for telling them that you were lost. I never even had a chance to tell them we were married." Which was probably for the best. And I'd had a reasonable excuse.

"Well then," George said as he stood up and held out his hand to me. "Shall we?"

I paused. I couldn't help thinking of Danilo and Mala. Perhaps they would be able to find each other somewhere beyond the Graylands.

I looked up at George and smiled. My beautiful boy. My husband. I gave him my hand. "Let's go home."

CHAPTER THIRTY-EIGHT

G eorge had to teach me the ritual that would bring him back. It was similar to the one I'd used when Grand Duke Vladimir had been in the Graylands, but this time there was no enchanted throne. Instead, George showed me how to use the large mirror hanging at the end of the hallway—the same one Militza and I had used. Only Militza and I had both been alive when we'd traveled through the mirror.

George's cold light had been almost completely severed from his body by Konstantin's spell. But he'd managed a spell that had kept him hidden, even if barely alive, while he healed. He was still too weak, however, to call upon the Grigori to make a portal of his own.

"I can tell you the words to say, but I have no control over the cold light," George said. "A necromancer can touch this light and manipulate it to overcome death. That is why you are able to walk between the two worlds so easily."

I waved my hand in front of the mirror, scattering the mist, and focused on the place we needed to go: Gatchina. His parents would still be there.

The trip back to the land of the living did not hurt quite so much this time. Maybe it was because I was too giddy to pay attention. I was worried about George, though, and focused my cold light energy on making sure he did not drag behind. The ritual took its toll on him anyway. Pale and coughing, George emerged with me in the cold snowy gardens outside the palace. I grabbed him by the arms to support him. He felt warm and solid, but I still couldn't believe he was back home with me.

"You're shaking!" I realized. "Let's get you inside."

The members of the Order of St. John who stood guard at the front of the palace could not believe their eyes when I shouted for them to open the gates quickly.

"Do as she says," George muttered.

I was not sure if they did not want to follow my orders or were just in shock at seeing him.

The doors opened, and one of the footmen sent for the tsar immediately. I helped them carry George inside and up to the bedroom he shared with Nicholas. The empress and the tsar arrived soon after, followed by Nicholas and Xenia.

"Georgi!" The empress rushed to his bedside and grabbed his hand. "Oh, my son!" she sobbed. "My prayers have been answered!"

The tsar took my hand. "I owe you everything, Katerina." He pulled me into his enormous arms and kissed me on the forehead. "I would be honored to call you daughter."

"That's a very good thing," George said happily from the bed.

He was already starting to get his color back. "Because we were married in Egypt."

"What is this?" The empress turned around sharply to look at me. I heard Xenia giggle from the doorway. Little Mikhail and Olga were peeking around from behind her skirts.

The tsar released me from his fatherly embrace, as if to distance himself from me. He did not wish to incur the empress's wrath, it seemed.

George tried to push himself up onto his elbow. "Maman, you know I've wanted to marry Katiya for a long time. I did not want to risk losing her again."

Everyone was staring at me. "It was an Orthodox ceremony," I said, as if that would make everything better.

The empress glared at me, her eyes flashing silvery white. I suddenly worried that I was about to feel the full force of her Light Court powers.

I turned back to the tsar, finally willing to say what he wanted to hear. "And I have decided not to attend medical school. There are other things more important to me right now."

The tsar beamed at me as the empress said, "Well, I should certainly hope so! When I think of those poor girls slaving away over textbooks in the European universities, I feel so sorry for them. And for the families who must miss them."

But I still had hopes that the tsar would change his mind one day and the universities of Russia would be open to all women who sought an education.

"No, Katiya," George said, struggling to sit up. "You are not giving up on your dream. We will move wherever we have to so you can become a doctor."

I did not want to agitate the empress any further. I did not want her keeping me away from George while he recuperated. We could decide where we were going to live much later.

Nicholas and Xenia came into the room to offer their congratulations and hug their brother. Nicholas winked at me, certain I would never betray his part in our wedding. I smiled back at him.

"Katiya, your family will probably like to know you are safe," the tsar said. It brought tears to my eyes when I realized he'd called me by my nickname. He had already accepted me. "Shall we send for them?"

"Of course, Your Imperial Majesty. I would be most happy to see my parents." I was glad they would be coming to Gatchina, for I feared if I were to leave, the empress might tell the palace guards not to let me back inside.

"Katerina, we must find you and George a suite of rooms while he is healing," the empress said. She was trying to maintain control over her son's life for as long as possible. "When he is healthier, we can discuss purchasing a suitable palace for the two of you."

George grinned. "Thank you, Maman. I am certain Katiya does not wish to spend the night here with me and Nicky."

Xenia and Nicholas laughed, but they knew the empress was not amused. She stood up and planted a kiss on George's forehead. Gathering her skirts, she looked at me, her faerie eyes still flashing silver with anger. "Come along, Katerina."

I moved first to George's bed to kiss him as well. I felt shy suddenly in front of all of his family, but I did not want to leave him for a moment. He smiled at me tiredly. "You need your rest as well, Katiya. I'll see you later."

The empress chose an elegant suite for George and me, far

from the children's rooms, furnished tastefully in the English style that she preferred. The rooms were cozy and full of trinkets and knickknacks she'd accumulated on her travels. "When I get a chance, we shall sit down and go through my jewelry to see if we can find a suitable wedding gift for you."

"I'd be honored, Your Imperial Majesty."

She sighed. "Thank you, Katerina, for saving my son's life. And thank you for saving us all from that odious vampire couple. Your marriage will take some getting used to, but"—she picked up my hand and patted it somewhat awkwardly—"I think you and Georgi will suit each other very well."

I finally let go of the breath I didn't realize I'd been holding. She wasn't banishing me. "Thank you, Your Imperial Majesty."

"Please, call me Mother Dear. It's what the children call me."

"Thank you, Mother Dear," I said. The term of affection felt strange on my tongue, but I was relieved that I was not going to be an enemy after all.

CHAPTER THIRTY-NINE

It did not take long for me to settle in. The only belongings I had with me were the sword and the Talisman of Isis. I kept both of them close. I was given a new scabbard to replace the one I'd lost on the battlefield. The sword remained at my side and the talisman remained around my neck. I was making a list of the dresses for Maman to send over when she and Papa arrived.

"Katiya!" Maman's face was covered in tears as she flung her arms around me. "We've been worried sick about you! Your father told me you were safe, but I know he was worried too!"

I put my arms around my father. "Everything will be fine now, Papa."

"Are you certain?" he said, his eyes twinkling. He seemed thinner than when I'd seen him last. And was there more gray in his hair? "Your mother just found out she's been denied a wedding." He was teasing me, but I could tell by the lines in his face I'd given them both a terrible fright by disappearing. Or perhaps it had just been the strain from the battle. It had taken its toll on all of us.

"I'm sorry, Maman. You will have to be satisfied with Petya's wedding one day."

"But that's not the same. My only daughter!" She pulled her handkerchief out and dabbed at her eyes. "We must plan a ball for you! As a belated wedding reception!" Her eyes took on a new animation.

I put my hands on hers. "Let's wait until George gets better, Maman. He is very ill right now."

Papa looked troubled. "Anything we can do for him at the Institute?"

I shook my head. "I don't think this is something modern medicine can cure."

"Does Dr. Badmaev know?" he asked.

"The empress will not let the Dark Court doctor attend him."

"It seems to me that the grand duke's wife may have something to say about that," Papa murmured.

I squeezed his hand. "If there's any way, you know I will send for him."

Maman touched my cheek gently, her eyes now brimming with tears. "Katiya, do you know how proud we are of you? You have fierce Romanov blood in your veins. You were so brave to stand up to Konstantin."

I had to blink back my own tears as I glanced from her to Papa. "As were both of you," I said. "I saw how each of you defended the tsar." I had not seen much of the battlefield upon my return with George, but the grounds around the palace looked

248

wrecked. It had only been a day since the fighting, and they were still removing bodies. "Is Petya safe?" I asked, suddenly ashamed that I hadn't asked sooner.

"He's fine," Papa said. "He and his friend Prince Kotchoubey are back at Vorontsov Palace guarding the wounded."

"Did we lose many on our side?" I asked. There had been so much blood.

My father shook his head. "Most of the casualties were the blood drinkers who followed Konstantin. Your little aunt is a vicious fighter."

He meant Militza. I was happy she had fought *with* us. But one day, I feared, she would come after my mother. "Maman was rather magnificent as well," I said, squeezing her hands.

Papa's face paled. "Your mother almost gave me a heart attack with her antics. Let's hope the striga's services are not required again anytime soon."

As I laughed, Maman made a face. "Oh, I hope not too. That boy's blood tasted horrible."

Before the night was over, I had more visitors at the palace: the two members of the Grigori who had accompanied me and Danilo to Egypt. "Your Imperial Highness," the elder one said, bowing. "The Grigori await your next orders."

I wanted to get rid of the Morning Star, and I wanted the Watchers to be free of its curse. But the Grigori were not permitted to carry the sword. "Your husband can pass beyond the seven gates," the elder Grigori said. "And he knows the names of the angels who rule the planets. Perhaps he can invoke one of our brothers from the highest realms. The sword should be returned to its original home."

"You mean heaven," I said, and the elder Grigori nodded.

It was true. The stars had always been George's favorite subject when he was in Paris studying with the mages. But he was not strong enough to complete such a ritual. I could not allow him to risk his health for this. "We'll have to find another way," I said, my hand going protectively to the sword at my side.

"Of course." The two Grigori bowed and took their leave. "We will speak again soon, Duchess. In the meantime, we will guard you and your family."

I wished I could simply turn the Morning Star over to the elder Grigori and be done with it. Miechen and Grand Duke Vladimir were both horrified that I should even consider letting such a valuable weapon go. But the tsar agreed with me; we both knew it did not belong in this world. The Grigori could not be freed from their curse, but I could ensure they would never again become the servants of a tyrant like Konstantin Pavlovich. For the present, the Morning Star would remain with me for safekeeping.

CHAPTER FORTY

In the end, George did not get better. The wedding ball did not happen. Winter melted into spring, and the empress finally allowed me to send for the Tibetan doctor. I'd been continuing my studies with him and was certain he would be able to discover the source of George's illness when I had not. Nor had any of the tsar's physicians. Or perhaps they had and were too frightened to tell the tsar and the empress the truth. Because none of their suggested cures seemed to work.

Dr. Badmaev smiled at us both kindly after he examined George. "I am afraid the air in St. Petersburg is too cold and damp for you, Your Imperial Highness. A drier, warmer climate would be much more suitable."

"Such as the Crimea?" I asked.

"Perhaps even farther south," the Tibetan said as he began to pack his instruments back into his black bag. "I would suggest the Caucasus or even northern Africa. Algiers is nice this time of year."

George took my hand in his. "Wherever you wish, Katiya," he said quietly.

"Can you tell us exactly what is wrong with him, Doctor?" I asked. All along I'd had my own suspicions, but I prayed I wasn't right.

"Oh, definitely. The wound the grand duke received from his duel with the crown prince of Montenegro continues to heal slowly. You yourself saw that his cold light seems to gather around his chest. But that should improve with time. The lung fever has me more concerned. I fear it may be consumption."

Dr. Badmaev could not have given a more depressing diagnosis. I knew doctors in Germany and France were studying the mycobacteria that caused tuberculosis and were rushing to find a cure. Papa had asked Dr. Pavlov at the Institute in St. Petersburg to consider the disease a priority as well. But there was still so much modern medicine did not understand. Dr. Badmaev had given my husband a death sentence. I pulled George's hand to my lips and kissed it.

"I suppose we should tell my parents," he said gloomily.

"I'll go and send for them," I said, getting up in a daze.

Dr. Badmaev patted me on the shoulder as I walked past him. "Do keep me informed of your arrangements, Your Imperial Highness. We will find a way of continuing your lessons. There are Tibetan herbs your husband can take that will ease his symptoms, but we cannot completely cure the disease."

The tsar and the empress refused to believe Dr. Badmaev's diagnosis, but they were willing to send us south to the Caucasus for the dry air. "There is a Romanov villa in the mountains where you can stay," the empress said. "It's very peaceful there. Perhaps you'll be able to return in a few months."

Each grand duke and duchess had an opinion on the best warm climate for George. The Mikhailovichi branch had grown up in Tbilisi, where Grand Duke Mikhail Nikolayevich had been viceroy for many years. Militza thought we should return to Cairo, of course. Miechen and Grand Duke Vladimir, who were fond of gambling, praised the merits of the French Riviera.

"There is a school of medicine in Nice," George said, his chin on my shoulder and his arms around my waist as we looked at the globe in his father's study.

"Dr. Bokova mentioned the university in Marseille as well," I said, turning around in his arms. One of the very first Russian women to become a doctor as well as a dear friend, she had agreed with the Tibetan's diagnosis and recommended that we travel to a city where we'd be close to the leading doctors and researchers. But I knew George needed someplace quiet.

Dr. Bokova also told me I should take care of my own health. "Tuberculosis is extremely contagious," she had warned me. "If you remain with your young husband, you will eventually contract the disease as well."

I said nothing to George of this conversation as we mulled over our choices. Together we would defeat the disease, or die.

CHAPTER FORTY-ONE

October 1891, Marseille, France

"Honestly, Katiya, must you argue with your professors every week?" George asked me. "This is the third time this month."

I sighed as I threw my books down onto my desk in our shared study. Our small but fashionable villa sat high on a rocky cliff outside of Marseille, looking down at the sapphire-blue waters of the Mediterranean. We were close enough to the city that the university was only a short carriage ride away and visitors could reach us easily. In the few short months since we'd moved to France, most of our family in Russia had come. My parents, George's parents, George's brother Nicholas, his aunt Miechen and uncle Vladimir. My step-aunt Zina and cousin Dariya. Even the expatriates of the family, my

Leuchtenberg uncles, had dropped in on us for dinner several times.

I still could not believe we were really here. I was officially a university student. My dreams of becoming a doctor were finally about to come true. My first day of attending lectures I'd sat in awe of the professor, too overwhelmed with emotion to even take notes. The sound of the renowned instructor's voice faded to the background as I inhaled the scents of the dusty books and chalk and felt the smooth aged wooden desk beneath my fingertips. I was in a large semicircular room, surrounded by mostly young men, all solemnly scribbling notes as the gray-haired man in front of us droned on about scientific theory. Only one other female joined me in this class; she was an older woman who I later discovered was a midwife and was auditing the lectures.

I quickly caught up to my fellow students over the next few weeks, saying a silent prayer of thanks to my father and his enormous medical library at home. I had been more than adequately prepared for my studies at the university. But the practical knowledge I'd learned from Dr. Badmaev, as well as some of the more spiritual aspects of Eastern medicine, seemed to be at odds with what the European scientists were teaching.

George was right; it seemed as if I were constantly antagonizing my professors with something Badmaev had taught me: a technique or a medical preparation that worked just as well as, if not better than, traditional Western medicine. And then there were the stubborn old men who still did not approve of higher education for women. Most of the younger professors were supportive; some were even married to female mathematicians and chemists. But members of the faculty who'd been there the longest shared the mind-set of my father-in-law: women belonged at home in the nursery and in the kitchen, not in a classroom.

George rubbed his forehead with a sigh, but he still managed a smile for me. He looked more tired this afternoon, I thought worriedly. "What was it this time?" he asked.

I made tea for both of us. The elegant silver samovar that sat in the corner of the sunshine-filled study had been a wedding present from my parents. This was our favorite room in the house. I would study my lecture notes from the university while George concentrated on his plans for an observatory. "My anatomy professor insists that I not be allowed to dissect the male cadavers," I said. "He thinks it would be most improper!"

My husband's eyes twinkled in amusement as he looked up from his star charts. "And did you tell him you were already well versed in dismemberment?"

I set a silver-handled glass of tea down on his desk and kissed him on the cheek before sinking into a chair nearby. "I do not think that would have helped my case."

"You will have other opportunities," George said, before succumbing to a fit of coughing.

Alarmed, I rushed to his side as he pulled his handkerchief out of his pocket. With relief, I noted there was no blood this time. We were doing everything we could for him. The open-air treatment, advocated by most European doctors, offered the most hope for restoring George's strength. He still had the occasional fever, and frequently I woke in the night to find him sweating and restless, with a rapid, weak pulse. But as the weeks went on, his appetite had been improving slowly, and the fresh sea air seemed to bring the color back to his cheeks.

He pushed back from his desk and got up, pulling away from me. "How do you stand this, Katiya? You are married to a corpse."

"You mustn't say that," I said, following him to the open window. I leaned my cheek against his back as he stared out at the sea. His breathing was ragged. "We will keep you strong until we can find the right medicine." Back in St. Petersburg, Dr. Badmaev had pored over his *Materia Medica,* and he'd mailed me packages of every healing herb or root that he thought might help.

George had been good-natured about it at first, agreeing to sample even the most foul-smelling of our infusions and tinctures. But he was growing despondent. Not even his study of the stars could pull him out of his gloom.

When Papa had first suggested he work on plans for an observatory, George's spirits had seemed to lighten. He had always preferred astronomy and astrology to any of the other subjects the mages taught him during his time in Paris. George began corresponding with a charming French scientist, Camille Flammarion, who wrote both thought-provoking articles for the *Journal of Astronomy* and fantastical novels about life on other worlds. He was interested in spiritism and reincarnation, and while Dr. Flammarion had not become initiated as one of the mages in the Order of the Black Lily, he was familiar with many of its members.

Our long-term plans were to build a palace in the mountains of Georgia after I finished my degree. George thought it would be an excellent place for an observatory, and I could build a small clinic where I would treat the villagers. We both had relatives there who were eager for us settle in the dry, mountainous country. I prayed the sea air of Marseille would keep George healthy long enough for me to finish school.

That night we were having dinner with Grand Duke and Grand Duchess Vladimir, who had come to the Riviera to gamble. Miechen looked regal, in a dark violet dress that matched her eyes. The Koldun looked younger and healthier than he had in months. He went straight to our small liquor cabinet and poured himself a tumbler of vodka, toasting our new home and new life.

Candelabras illuminated our dining table, perched atop a Persian rug laid out on the terrace. The table had come from Denmark and was set with the finest china from Russia. We dined among a lush jungle of potted ferns and palms. The breeze carried the scent of jasmine from a nearby garden.

We'd taken a very small staff with us to Marseille: only my Anya and George's valet, a cook, and a footman. The cook, who was thankfully not one of the fae, had been trained in France, and every night we enjoyed the most delicious food, even if George found some of it too rich for his stomach. He would have preferred to exist on the fresh seafood and fruits and vegetables that we could find in the city marketplace. But our cook insisted upon preparing roasts of beef and poultry, lamb and pork chops, duck breasts and veal cutlets, following the protein-rich diet the leading French doctors advocated. All appetizing, but we missed the simple brown bread and sour cream blini of home.

The conversation at dinner that night made us both homesick. Princess Aline, the wife of Grand Duke Pavel, had died during childbirth in September, leaving the grieving widower with a sickly premature son and a daughter who was not yet two. The whole imperial family was devastated. Pavel's brother Sergei and his wife, Grand Duchess Ella, were taking care of the children while the widower mourned. Under the table, George took my hand and squeezed it. I squeezed back.

"It's time for the two of you to think about having children soon, no?" Grand Duke Vladimir said, digging in to his lobster.

Miechen said nothing but looked from George to me with her shimmering gaze. I could feel my cheeks burning. George calmly said, "When Katiya is finished with school," and gave my fingers another affectionate squeeze.

The Koldun shrugged, but Miechen smiled. "I admire your ambition, my dear. But is the university degree absolutely necessary? Of course, there's no limit to what one can learn through tutors and books. The university climate can be dangerous these days. They say the classrooms are full of revolutionaries."

"I keep out of the politics, Your Imperial Highness," I said. Of course, I knew of the revolutionary ideas that were probably discussed in Miechen's own salon in St. Petersburg. She attracted the most elite of the Russian academia to her palace to share ideas and discuss the latest advancements in science and the arts. She and the grand duke were great art patrons but were always eager to host the latest scientific celebrity at the Vladimir Palace as well.

"Uncle Vladimir, have you had any luck with information on the sword?" George was trying to change the subject. But I knew discussing the Morning Star would cause just as much awkwardness as discussing our breeding plans. The Koldun's face turned red.

"No, and I don't expect to discover anything useful, Georgi. You and Katiya should forget all this nonsense about giving away the sword. It's safest right here with you."

"Think about what you'd be giving up anyway," Miechen added. "Right now the Grigori protect the tsar and his immediate family. You risk putting your father in danger again. And his heir."

Not that the Koldun nor his wife had any true concern for Nicholas. Now that Konstantin Pavlovich, the common threat to all, was gone, the Dark and Light Courts had returned to their subtle and petty bickering. Militza still chafed under Maman's gentle handling of the St. Petersburg blood drinkers. The wolf-folk had retreated to Moscow and everyone left the mages of the Inner Circle to do whatever it was they did to keep St. Petersburg safe. The members of the Order of St. Lazarus patrolled the palaces but waited for direct orders from me.

And the Grigori, I thought with a long sigh, still waited as well. Protecting both the Morning Star and the Talisman of Isis was a heavy burden. I kept the talisman around my neck at all times, refusing to take it off even to sleep. George had balked at this but understood. If there was a way I could destroy both talisman and sword, I would do it. I wanted to free all of the creatures under my control.

Taking my sigh for distress, George let his fork fall to his plate with a clang and tossed his napkin onto the table carelessly. Before he could say a word, Miechen put a hand on her husband's arm. "Vladimir, we should be leaving. Georgi is getting tired. And Katiya needs to see to her studies."

"My apologies, Aunt Miechen," George said. "You are always

welcome here with us. But certainly you are both anxious to visit the casinos in town?" His smile did not reach his eyes.

Grand Duke Vladimir seemed to be measuring his nephew up as he and Miechen both stood. Perhaps now he would no longer see George as a pawn in the Inner Circle for him to maneuver. I prayed he would not now see George as a threat either. "I will see what has been discovered about the sword," he said. "I will write to you as soon as we return to St. Petersburg."

"Thank you, Uncle," George said as we walked our guests to the door.

Miechen pulled George out onto the front steps to mention a book that she'd read by Dr. Flammarion, and the Koldun put his hand on my arm and motioned for me to speak with him in the hallway. "Katiya, I have a confession, my dear."

"Yes?" I kept my face as placid as I could.

"Papus and I may have already discovered the ritual you have been seeking."

"To return the Morning Star?" I asked. "Why did you not say so?"

His face was troubled. "In order to return the sword to heaven, one must travel beyond the seven gates and invoke the Angel of the Sword, Auriel. I don't know if George is strong enough to complete the ritual in the Graylands and return. But now that I've seen my nephew, perhaps it would be a kindness to send him back to the Graylands. Even if he does not survive."

"What are you saying?" My blood froze. I suddenly felt very cold.

The Koldun's eyes searched my face. "How much longer do you believe those idiot doctors can keep him alive? Do you want to see him waste away in front of your eyes? If you love him, you should let him go. Let the angel accept him along with the sword."

I stared at Grand Duke Vladimir Alexandrovich, too horrified to speak. In my heart, I worried that he was right. "There has to be another way," I murmured. "I can't lose him."

He shook his head and turned to go. I remained in the hallway, dazed, as I heard the grand duke and grand duchess say their goodbyes again to George and leave in their carriage. I did not wait for George to come back inside. I couldn't look at him right now.

Hastily, I retired to our bedroom. The Morning Star was safely hidden in a trunk at the foot of our bed. I would have to find another ritual to get rid of the sword without risk to George. Perhaps I could invoke the angel myself.

Although I pretended to be asleep when George joined me and kissed my cheek, I lay awake that night for hours, listening to his breathing. It started out shallow and uneven before settling into a steady rhythm once he was sleeping deeply. I rolled over to peek at his cold light, still a brilliant white glow with tendrils that fluttered carelessly around him. Did his light seem brighter than it had been? Or was it my imagination? I reached out to place my hand on his chest. His heartbeat tonight was slow and steady and perfectly regular. In his sleep, my husband stirred and wrapped his arm around me. I finally closed my eyes and willed myself to relax. The Koldun was wrong. He had to be.

CHAPTER FORTY-TWO

Exhausted, I returned home from classes the next afternoon, desiring nothing more than a cup of hot tea and my bed. The lecture on kidney diseases had been dull and long-winded. I'd already read the professor's article on nephritis in one of my father's medical journals years ago. He hadn't made any new discoveries since the article had been published, so the lecture consisted of nothing but old material. Anya took my books from me at the front door and curtsied. "A letter came for you today, Your Imperial Highness. It's on your desk."

"Thank you," I said. It still felt strange being addressed as a grand duchess. But I imagined it would seem even stranger when I would one day be addressed as a doctor. I smiled to myself, hoping that day would not be too far away. And I knew it would not take me as long to get used to such a title.

Our study was empty. George must have been napping, I

thought distractedly as I saw the envelope on my desk. The letter was postmarked from Cetinje.

Anya poured fresh water in the samovar and it soon started its comforting sounds of brewing. I sat down to read the letter. It was from Elena. I had not seen nor heard from her in over a year. Not since she'd been expelled from Smolni.

> Katerina Alexandrovna,
>
> How could you be so heartless? Militza told me everything that happened to our brother. She says you left him in the Graylands and will not bring him back. Did you truly believe your blood bond would be broken by Danilo's death? Could you really be that stupid? Mother has been patient, waiting for a sign of his return, but we have heard nothing, and it has been almost a year. You have read the Polish princess's spell book. You know what must be done!

I threw the letter down, too agitated to read on, even though her angry words went on for another page. I knew that Elena missed her brother terribly, but there was nothing more I could have done for him. Her handwriting was sharp and rushed; she had been in a great passion when she wrote the letter. I made a cup of tea and went searching for George. Studying could wait.

He was not sleeping. In the bedroom, I found the furniture pushed aside and a ritual circle drawn on the floor. Sigils were scrawled within the circle in what looked like chalk. The room smelled of burnt incense. A sliver of dragon's blood resin smoldered in a brass dish on the bedside table. What had he done?

"George?" I shouted, fear churning in my stomach. What if

he'd overheard the Koldun last night? Would he try to invoke the Angel of the Sword on his own? I searched the trunk, which had been pushed against the wall. The Morning Star was missing.

I shouted for Anya and she came immediately. "Where is the grand duke?" I asked.

She looked surprised. "He was out on the terrace with his visitors. I was going to bring them tea and cakes but he refused and said they were not staying long. In fact, the men left the villa a few minutes later."

"Who were his visitors?" I asked, my fear for George growing.

"I'm not sure. They were strange-looking men, Your Imperial Highness. They frightened me with their stony faces."

The Grigori. He had asked them to come to our villa to create a portal. Just that part of the ritual alone would sap his strength. I would have to follow them and pray I wasn't too late to stop him. "Anya, please cancel our dinner plans tonight with my aunt Zina. I don't care what you tell her—just make my apologies, please."

Anya's eyes grew wide. "Yes, Your Imperial Highness." With a curtsy and a bewildered look, she left.

I returned to the bedroom alone and stared at the magic circle on the floor. I'd have to use my cold light to open my own doorway to the Graylands. I prayed I'd be able to find the seven gates on my own.

I used the same word Militza had taught me, the Coptic word for "open," and suddenly found myself back in the Graylands. I focused on drawing my cold light as close to me as possible. The mist made it difficult to see, and I remembered dismally that George had carried coins for the ferryman the last time we'd journeyed here together. I had nothing on me save the Talisman of Isis.

Taking a deep breath, I pricked my finger and let a single drop of blood fall upon the black stone, the scarab in the middle of the talisman. I needed all the magic I could summon. "The blood of Isis, the strength of Isis, and the power of Isis is mine," I whispered. The mist swirled around me and I felt a tingling sensation up my spine. "Please help me find the seven gates." The talisman grew white-hot and I dropped it to the ground with a cry. The scarab fell out and shattered into tiny pieces. I'd broken the talisman.

Out of the mists stepped a figure. The crown prince.

CHAPTER FORTY-THREE

"Danilo?" My heart froze. What if it was the lich tsar?

He picked up the pieces of the talisman and handed them back to me. "Yes, Katerina."

"Your soul was in the scarab." No wonder Elena and Militza thought me stupid. Why hadn't they told me?

"Of course." He brushed a remaining sliver of the stone from his jacket.

"And you are safe from Konstantin now."

Danilo smiled. "You were magnificent. He can torment me no longer."

I felt an enormous sense of relief. At least I'd saved one soul in all of my blunders. But now I had to save George. "Can you lead me to the seven gates?" I asked. "I have to rescue George." I watched as his face showed no emotion. "My husband," I added.

"I see. I am bound by honor to assist you, if not bound by my affection."

"You never loved me, Danilo," I protested. "You needed a necromancer. You loved my powers."

"Perhaps. We are wasting time, Duchess. Or should I say, Your Imperial Highness?" He took off into the mists and would have left me behind if I had not hurried to follow him.

We did not come across the jackal-headed ferryman again. Instead, the route Danilo used took us through a cavern, lit by softly glowing lights. They looked like mushrooms. I expected the cave to be damp and smell of mold, but there was no scent. And no mist. The cavern descended into darkness, as the mushrooms grew more and more sparse. The path was smooth stone, but I still managed to trip a few times, much to Danilo's amusement.

After reaching the lowest point, we finally began to climb up the other side and at last emerged in a great hall. The floor and walls here were a brilliant gold. It hurt my eyes so badly that I had to close them and let Danilo lead me across the chamber. He took my arm in his and asked, "Do you know the ritual your grand duke is attempting? What are we in such a hurry to stop?"

"He is going to hand over the Morning Star to an angel. I wanted to free the Grigori, but not if it costs George his life."

"Ah, the angel Auriel," Danilo said. "You may open your eyes now. We have passed through the Golden Hall."

"Thank you," I said, pulling my arm out of his. "Is it much farther to the seven gates?"

But instead of answering, he waved his hand to indicate a door. "We are here, Your Imperial Highness. Go and save your grand duke."

"Thank you, Danilo." I stood on my tiptoes and kissed his cheek gently. His skin was cool. "Will you be able to leave the Graylands on your own?"

His expression was unreadable. "I will be fine, Katerina."

I turned away from him quickly and pushed open the door. Would my heart still be considered pure enough to pass through the seven gates? Obviously, Danilo did not think his would. I did not look back as I approached the first gate. The guardian lights still lined the hallway, but I could not see the chamber at the end.

My pulse quickened as I passed through the first gate. Nothing happened and I breathed a sigh of relief. As I took another step, however, there was an explosion of bright white light from the chamber beyond the seventh gate. Gasping, I began to run toward the chamber, not heeding the gates as I passed through.

In the Chamber of the Sword stood what looked like an enormous Grigori, with wings of blazing white flames. "Necromancer, you tread on holy ground." The voice was female.

I dropped to my knees immediately. George was kneeling to my right, holding a bundle of linen marked with protective sigils. That was how he'd managed to carry the Morning Star without harm. "Have you lost your mind?" I whispered. "What made you think you had to do this on your own?"

George had the sense to look sheepish. "I didn't want you to see this. I wanted it to be quick and painless."

"It is honorable that you wish to return the Morning Star to heaven," the angel Auriel said. "But there must be consequences. Whoever is chosen to carry the sword cannot return."

The angel's words sank in slowly. The Koldun had been right. One of us would not be going back to the land of the living. I stared at George, my heart numb. "You wanted to leave me?" I asked. "You knew you weren't coming back and you didn't even want to say goodbye?" I glared at him. "I'll take the sword," I said, rising to stand before the angel.

"Don't be ridiculous," George said, getting up as well. "I won't let you throw your life away, Katiya."

"And I can't live without you," I said. I could not believe we were arguing in front of an angel. I blinked back tears. Perhaps she would take both of us. Was my soul pure enough to earn eternity with George?

The white flames surrounding the angel grew into a raging inferno. And yet I felt no heat. The altar behind the angel where I'd originally found the Morning Star now looked like a pagan funeral pyre.

"Please go back," George said. "Finish your degree, Katiya. Do it for me."

I shook my head, furious at the tears running down my cheeks. "You can't make that decision for me!"

"Oh, for the love of the saints!" Danilo shouted as he pushed past me and snatched the sword from George. He took a step toward the pyre and turned around, looking at both of us. There was a flash of the old arrogance in his dark eyes. "You will name your firstborn son after me, of course." The holy fire burned around him like a halo.

I was too stunned to speak. George was silent as well but put an arm around me. Danilo looked sad, but only for a moment. Then the flames consumed him and the Morning Star. The angel Auriel vanished as well. George and I were left alone in the dark, silent chamber.

I could do nothing but stare at the space where Danilo had been standing only seconds before. Why would he perform such an unselfish act? That was not the crown prince I knew.

George's hand slid up and down my back. I sank to the floor in relief. The Morning Star was gone, safe from the world forever. And the Talisman of Isis had been destroyed. There would be no more Grigori armies. And no more undead soldiers. The members of the Order of St. Lazarus would have their rest at last.

George kissed the top of my head. "It's over, Katiya," he whispered into my hair. "We can go home."

I could not believe we'd just survived our first argument as a married couple. In front of an angel. But I was not ready to let go of all the emotions that had been stirred up. The more I thought about it, the angrier I became. Not just at George, but at myself as well. "You were willing to sacrifice yourself. You would have left me." I looked up at him. "Are you suffering that much? Am I being cruel to want to keep you alive with me? Do you think me selfish?"

He held out his hand to me, but when I ignored it, he sighed and sat down next to me. "You make my life worth living, Katiya. You give me the energy to keep going. To keep hoping. If you had left with the Morning Star, I wouldn't have been able to continue. Truthfully, I think I was being the selfish one."

Gently, he picked up my hand and laced his fingers with mine. "Not only did Danilo save you, but he saved me as well. And if you ask me, he did what he did out of love for you."

I sighed. "We'll never know, will we?"

This time, I took both of his hands when he offered and

stood up, blinking back tears for the crown prince before George could see. Summoning all my cold light, I forced open a doorway right there in the Chamber of the Sword that would take us back to our villa. I did not want to spend one second longer in the Graylands. I was eager for the two of us to get started living the rest of our lives.

HISTORICAL NOTES

Tsar Alexander III never did readmit women to the medical universities in Russia. But in 1895, his son Nicholas II approved the opening of the St. Petersburg Women's Medical Institute. His wife and eldest daughters became nurses during World War I and worked with Princess Vera Gedroits, a noblewoman from Kiev who had received her medical degree in Switzerland. Dr. Gedroits was a surgeon on a Red Cross hospital train that served on the front lines during the Russo-Japanese War. She later became a professor at the medical college in Kiev.

Tuberculosis claimed the life of the real Grand Duke George Alexandrovich in 1899. After falling sick during his voyage to Egypt in 1890, the grand duke followed his doctors' recommendations and relocated from the damp air of St. Petersburg to the hot and dry mountains of Georgia. During his exile from his family, he was responsible for the building of an astronomy observatory as well as the reconstruction of a local medieval church. To this day, there are rumors that he was secretly wed to a princess in Georgia, possibly related to one of the Dukes of Oldenburg by marriage.

Across Europe and America in the eighteenth and early nineteenth centuries, tuberculosis, or TB, was often assumed to be a case of vampirism. A family would find other members wasting away after the death of one person who had the disease, which was also known as consumption. Not understanding how the disease was transmitted, everyone assumed the deceased was returning from the grave every night to drain the blood of the rest of the family. The solution? Digging up the deceased, beheading him or her and/or cutting out the heart, and feeding it to the invalids. These measures, of course, seldom cured the patients.

Despite Dr. Robert Koch's discovery of the bacteria *Mycobacterium tuberculosis* in 1882, a cure for tuberculosis was not discovered until 1944, with the development of the drug streptomycin. The disease is now under control, but it has not been eradicated. Millions of people worldwide still become infected with TB every year. New drug-resistant strains continue to elude scientists and defy modern treatment. The search for a practical vaccine is ongoing.

ACKNOWLEDGMENTS

Once again, many, many thanks to my agent, Ethan Ellenberg, and his assistant, Evan Gregory, for all the amazing work they do for Katerina here and abroad. And to my Random House family: especially Françoise Bui, my favorite editor in the world, along with my copyediting team, and Nicole Banholzer, my superhero publicist, and Trish Parcell, who uses Michael Frost's gorgeous photography to design the most beautiful covers and bring Katerina to life.

Thanks to my hospital family, who have been so supportive of me, especially the ghouls who work with me at night and the former ghouls who now walk the halls on day shift. I love all of you ladies!

And thanks to my real family, who put up with the many, many weeks when I've forsaken you utterly to hang out with my imaginary friends.

And *spasibo* to my online groups: the Class of 2K12, the Apocalypsies, and the Elevensies. I would never have made it through these past few years without the support of such good friends, especially Annie Gaughen, who, late at night, helps me plot wicked things to do to my characters.

Hugs and cupcakes for all the librarians, booksellers, and book bloggers who have promoted the Katerina Trilogy to readers everywhere. Seeing my name on a book on a shelf sandwiched between Libba Bray and Meg Cabot was one of the greatest moments of my life. And much less messy than childbirth.

Finally, a Russian-sized thank-you to all the readers all over the world. Your continued enthusiasm and support for Katerina mean so much to me! *Spasibo!*

ABOUT THE AUTHOR

By day, Robin Bridges is a mild-mannered writer of fantasy and paranormal fiction for young adults. By night, she is a pediatric nurse. Robin lives on the Gulf Coast with her husband, one teenager, and two slobbery mastiffs. She likes playing video games and watching Jane Austen movies. The Katerina Trilogy began with *The Gathering Storm* and continues with *The Unfailing Light* and *The Morning Star*. You can visit Robin at robinbridges.com.